W9-BUF-887

THE FAMILY JENSEN:
HELLTOWN
MASSACRE

**Center Point
Large Print**

*Also by William W. Johnstone with
J. A. Johnstone and available from
Center Point Large Print:*

The Family Jensen
Mankiller, Colorado
Deadwood Gulch

**This Large Print Book carries the
Seal of Approval of N.A.V.H.**

THE FAMILY JENSEN:

HELLTOWN MASSACRE

William W. Johnstone
with J. A. Johnstone

CENTER POINT LARGE PRINT
THORNDIKE, MAINE

This Center Point Large Print edition is published
in the year 2012 by arrangement with
Kensington Publishing Corp.

PUBLISHER'S NOTE
Following the death of William W. Johnstone, the
Johnstone family is working with a carefully selected
writer to organize and complete Mr. Johnstone's outlines
and many unfinished manuscripts to create additional
novels in all of his series like The Last Gunfighter,
Mountain Man, and Eagles, among others. This novel was
inspired by Mr. Johnstone's superb storytelling.

The text of this Large Print edition is unabridged.
In other aspects, this book may
vary from the original edition.
Printed in the United States of America.
Set in 16-point Times New Roman type.

ISBN: 978-1-61173-272-6

Library of Congress Cataloging-in-Publication Data

Johnstone, William W.
[Family Jensen.]
Helltown massacre : the family Jensen / William W. Johnstone, with
J.A. Johnstone. — Center Point large print ed.
p. cm.
ISBN 978-1-61173-272-6 (library binding : alk. paper)
1. Jensen, Smoke (Fictitious character)—Fiction.
I. Johnstone, J. A. II. Title.
PS3560.O415F363 2012
813′.54—dc23
                                                    2011038263

PROLOGUE

Sounding something like gunfire, the sharp rapping of hammers driving nails deep into wood drifted past the iron bars in the jail cell's small single window. The man lying on the uncomfortable bunk underneath the window listened to the racket, and a grim smile tugged at the corners of his mouth.

"You think it's funny, Jensen?" The angry voice came from a man who sat on a three-legged stool in the aisle that ran between the iron-barred enclosures in the cell block. His hat was pushed back on a balding head, and a soup-strainer mustache drooped over his mouth. He had a lawman's star pinned to his vest and a double-barreled Greener shotgun across his lap. He was taking no chances with that prisoner.

The badge-toter went on, "Don't you know what that is? Mr. Longacre's men are buildin' a gallows for you, boy."

The prisoner nodded without looking over at the lawman. "I know, Sheriff."

"I wouldn't be grinnin' if I was you. I'd be tryin' to make my peace with the Lord, although I ain't sure He'd pay any mind to prayers offered up by a lowdown murderer like you."

The prisoner didn't respond. He'd had his say

5

in court already and declared his innocence. Of course, it hadn't done any good. How could it when the judge and the jury were bought and paid for by Cyrus Longacre's money, the same as the so-called lawman who was guarding him? The defense attorney had been a pitiful drunk, the witnesses had all lied, and the verdict was a foregone conclusion.

The young man on the bunk had always tried to stay on the right side of the law—well, most of the time, anyway—but what passed for law in that town wasn't the real thing. The place was like a medieval fiefdom, where the only real law was the word of Cyrus Longacre, its iron-handed king. Bloody-handed, too, when you got right down to it, because Longacre was responsible for the death of at least one person the prisoner knew of and probably more. For sure, Longacre planned to be responsible for more deaths, unless somebody came along to stop him.

Somebody was going to, the prisoner thought. Help was on the way.

If it got there in time.

The cell block door was ajar, so both the prisoner and the sheriff heard the door into the lawman's office when it opened. Heavy footsteps thudded on the plank flooring. The cell block door swung back even more. A large, powerful figure appeared in the opening, his bulky frame practically filling it.

"The boys and I thought we'd come give you break, Sheriff," the newcomer said.

The prisoner sat up and swung his legs off the bunk. He moved with a swift, easy efficiency that spoke of a man in peak physical condition. As he came to his feet, he looked past the man who had just entered the cell block and saw several more hardbitten hombres. They wore cold grins on their faces as they looked through the bars at him.

The sheriff stood up to greet the visitors. "I'm all right, Judd, I don't reckon I need any relief right now—"

"Sure you do, Sheriff," the man called Judd broke in. "It's getting on toward suppertime, and you must be hungry." He jerked a thumb over his shoulder. "Why don't you go down to the Swede's place and get yourself something to eat?"

"I-I dunno . . ."

"We'll watch the prisoner." Judd's voice hardened. "Don't you worry about a thing."

The sheriff lowered the shotgun to his side, holding it with one hand while he wiped the back of his other hand across his nose. "Well, I, uh, reckon it wouldn't hurt anything. I *am* feelin' a mite hungry."

Judd nodded. "That's what I thought. Go on now. Take your time. We'll be here when you get back."

The sheriff glanced at the prisoner, swallowed hard, and shuffled out of the cell block. One of he hardcases who had come in with Judd slammed the door closed behind the lawman.

Judd sauntered over to the door of the only occupied cell. He was tall, lean-hipped but broad-shouldered, with heavy slabs of muscle on his arms, back, and chest that bulged the shirt he wore. His hat was thumbed back on crisp, curly, black hair. As he grinned at the prisoner, he reached down to unbuckle the gunbelt strapped around his hips.

"How are you doing, Jensen? Starting to worry about what's going to happen come morning?"

The prisoner shook his head. "I'm innocent. They're not going to hang an innocent man."

Judd threw back his head and gave a booming laugh. "You're joking, right? Plenty of innocent men have wound up dancing at the end of a hang rope. But that doesn't matter, because you're guilty. You slaughtered that poor girl, and you know it."

"I never hurt her. *You* know *that*."

Judd touched his chest. "Me? How would I know?"

"Because if you didn't kill her yourself, you know who did . . . and why."

"You've got it all wrong, mister," Judd declared.

"Why are you here?" The prisoner had a hunch he knew the answer, but he asked the question anyway.

"The boys and I are just public-spirited citizens,

8

doing our civic duty. Helping out the sheriff guarding his prisoner while he gets some supper."

"He has deputies to handle that job," Jensen pointed out.

"Maybe so, but you don't see any of them around, do you?"

That was true enough. Nobody was there except Judd and his friends, and the man inside the cell.

Judd had coiled his shell belt around the holstered Colt. He handed it to one of his companions and said, "Hang on to that for me, would you?"

"Sure, Judd." The man practically chuckled with anticipation. "I'd be glad to."

Judd reached into his pocket. "Just so happens I've got a key here that'll unlock this cell door. You want me to unlock it, Jensen?"

"If you do, are you going to let me walk out of here and ride away?"

"You know better than that." The key rattled against iron as Judd thrust it into the lock. "But even if I said yes . . . even if we let you go . . . you wouldn't do that, would you? You wouldn't just ride away and never come back."

Judd didn't deserve an honest answer, but the prisoner gave him one anyway. "No. I wouldn't."

"Of course you wouldn't. You're too blasted stubborn for that. Step back."

Jensen didn't budge. Several of the men with

9

.d raised the guns they had drawn and
inted the revolvers at him.

"You're not going to shoot me," the prisoner
said in a cool, steady voice. "It's too important to
Longacre that I swing."

"Oh, you'll swing, all right," Judd said, "but
there's nothing saying you can't be carried to the
gallows with a couple of bullet-shattered knees.
It's up to you whether you're able to walk to
your death or not."

With his face hardening into bleak lines, Jensen
backed away from the iron-barred door.

Judd pushed it open and stepped into the cell.
"Might as well get this over with." He balled his
hands into massive fists. "You won't enjoy it, but
it won't kill you. That's for the hangman to do."
With that, he launched a punch at the prisoner's
head.

Judd was taller and heavier, and for a man of
his size, he was quick.

But the jailbird was quicker. He ducked under
the blow, causing Judd's fist to sail harmlessly
over his head. Missing threw Judd off-balance.
He stumbled forward a step, right into the hard
punch that slammed into his midsection.

With Judd's cronies right outside the cell,
Jensen had little chance of escaping a beating. He
was going to deal out as much damage in return
as he possibly could.

Judd gasped and turned pale as the blow drove

most of the air from his lungs. Twisting asid
assailant clubbed his hands together, and brou
them crashing down against the thick muscle
the side of Judd's neck, knocking him against th
bars on the cell's side wall. His hat fell off.

The prisoner lowered his head and drove his
shoulder into Judd's chest, causing Judd's head to
bounce hard off the bars. Almost too fast for the
eye to see, Jensen landed a left jab solidly on
Judd's nose. Blood spurted as cartilage crunched
under the impact. He howled in shock and pain.

One of the men outside the cell shouted, "Get
in there and get him!"

Judd swept out an arm like the trunk of a young
tree and bellowed, "No! He's mine!"

Like a maddened bull, he charged.

The cell was too small for him to work up much
momentum. Jensen's superior speed, quickness,
and agility once more came into play as his hands
shot out and grabbed the front of Judd's shirt.
Pivoting smoothly, he used the bigger man's
momentum against him and with a heave sent
Judd crashing face-first into the bars on the other
side of the cell.

Judd rebounded and went down hard, landing
on his back on the cell's stone floor. The prisoner
pounced on him, drove a knee into his belly, and
locked his hands around Judd's neck. Caught
without much air in his lungs, Judd's face
turned red as he struggled for breath. Jensen's

on his neck prevented him from getting any.

...dd bucked and writhed, but the prisoner ...ng on with grim determination, like a cowboy ...ding a wild bronc. He ducked his head and ...nunched his shoulders so Judd's flailing fists fell harmlessly on his back. He wasn't going to choke the life completely out of the big man, but wanted him to wake up sweating and crying out from nightmares when he dreamed about what happened in that cell.

With his pulse thundering so loudly inside his head Jensen barely heard the swift rush of feet behind him. He didn't have time to turn, and he probably wouldn't have let go of Judd's throat anyway. Something slammed into the back of his head and drove him forward. Probably a gun butt, he thought fleetingly. The men surrounded him, knocking him loose from Judd, kicking him, stomping him, pistol-whipping him. He still thought they wouldn't kill him unless it was by accident. Cyrus Longacre wanted the show that a hanging would provide.

So he could endure the beating, Matt Jensen told himself. He could endure, and soon Smoke and Preacher would be there and everything would be different. Longacre would realize the truth of that scripture about reaping the whirlwind.

But at that moment, as red-shot darkness descended on him, Matt couldn't help wish he had never ridden into Helltown.

BOOK ONE

CHAPTER 1

Ten days earlier

When the sign was first put up, it read HALLTOWN, probably because the town's founder had been named Hall, Matt Jensen mused as he brought his horse to a stop and smiled. Some wag had crossed out the *A* and above it painted a somewhat shaky *E*, so the sign now welcomed travelers to HELLTOWN.

Funny, Matt thought, the settlement didn't look very hellish. It looked like hundreds of other Western cowtowns. Tucked into a rugged region of Nevada, it was surrounded by rangeland that rolled up to the snow-capped mountains visible in the distance. It was pretty country in its way. Matt wondered how the hunting would be in those mountains. He was willing to bet the fishing would be good in the icy streams tumbling down from the heights.

A few weeks of hunting, fishing, and just taking it easy sounded pretty good to him. He would pick up some supplies in the settlement and move on. Might spend one night here, he told himself, sleep in a real bed with a roof over his head for a change.

15

Matt Jensen was young, but his face bore the permanent tan of a man who spent most of his time outdoors. The slight squint around his pale blue eyes spoke of the same thing. Those eyes had seen a lot. The frontier often grew an hombre up fast . . . either that or it killed him. The fact that Matt had survived revealed a lot about him.

So did the ease with which he carried the .44 double-action Colt on his right hip and the Bowie knife sheathed on his left. The stock of a Winchester .44-40 stuck up from a sheath strapped to his saddle. He rode a big sorrel and didn't have a pack horse. He was in the habit of traveling light. Everything he owned was in his saddlebags or rolled up in the bedroll tied on behind the saddle. That was the way of a wanderer.

And Lordy, Matt Jensen had done some wandering in his life, which he had begun with another name. Although he had never forgotten his murdered family, he considered his life to have really started on the day he met Smoke Jensen. Smoke had raised the youngster called Matt, becoming both adopted father and brother to him, teaching Matt everything he needed to know to survive on the frontier, but more important, teach-ing him to be a man. There was never any doubt in Matt's mind that when it came time for him to leave, he would take Smoke's last name.

Since striking out on his own, Matt had done a lot of things to make ends meet: cowboyed a little, ridden shotgun for various stage and freight lines, scouted for the army, cut trail for surveyors, guided wagon trains . . . anything to make a little money and at the same time keep him from being tied down. Anything legal and honorable, that is. Smoke wouldn't have had it any other way, and Matt was the same.

But always, always, the lure of the unknown was there, calling him on, tantalizing him with the prospect of what might be on the other side of the next hill or the next river.

Those mountains he could see were sirens singing to him. He would heed their summons as soon as he could, but they were mountains, he reminded himself, and would still be there tomorrow.

As he rode into town, he noticed a large building under construction at the eastern end of the settlement. The frame and the rafters were up, but it didn't have any walls or roof yet. Judging by its size, shape, and placement in the community, Matt thought it looked like a railroad station. But there were no railroad tracks running into Halltown.

Maybe some spur line was building in this direction, he thought. The folks in town could know about it and be getting a jump on the depot. Often the station would be built and ready before the steel rails ever reached a settlement.

Matt reined the sorrel to a stop in front of Gibson's Mercantile. He swung down from the saddle and looped the horse's reins around a hitch

17

rail. He had cast a thoughtful eye toward Temple's Saloon as he passed it, but told himself to deal with practical matters and buy supplies first. Once that was taken care of, he could wet his whistle. There might even be a pretty girl to flirt with.

He didn't have to go to the saloon for that, he realized as he walked into the general store, which seemed empty of customers. The tiny clinking sounds his spurs made were magnified by the high ceiling and echoed slightly as he went down a central aisle between rows of shelves filled with clothing, buckets, washboards, clothespins, pots and pans, chamber pots, bedding, lanterns, fancy lamps with shades, framed lithographs of famous paintings, rolled-up rugs, and scores of other odds and ends of daily life. Glass-fronted cases to the sides displayed candy and toys for the youngsters, and for the adults, knives, hatchets, axes, pistols, rifles, and shotguns. Barrels full of crackers and pickles sat in front of a counter that ran along the rear of the store. Beans, coffee, sugar, flour, and other staples were in barrels and bins behind the counter.

Also behind the counter was a young woman who smiled at Matt as he approached. She had red hair, a scattering of freckles across her face, and brilliant green eyes. "Can I help you, sir?"

Matt thumbed his hat back on his blond hair and returned the smile. "Ah, that lilt in your voice tells me you're from Ireland, and a prettier

Irish Maureen I've not laid eyes on in a long time."

"How did you know?"

"That you're from Ireland?" Matt asked, a little surprised by her question.

"No, that my name is Maureen. Maureen Ferguson, and 'tis only your eyes you'll be laying on me, good sir, and not even them if you don't stop being so bold about it. I have a good broom back here, and I don't mind using it to sweep trash out of my store."

She was smiling, but Matt had no doubt she meant what she said. Her eyes had turned fiery. He laughed. "I meant no disrespect, Miss Ferguson. It is Miss, isn't it?"

" 'Tis." She nodded and looked pointedly at his hat. "And to whom am I speaking?"

He reached up and took off the Stetson, holding it in front of his blue, bib-front shirt. "My name is Matt Jensen, and it's an honor and a pleasure to meet you, Miss Ferguson."

"Jensen. That's a Scandahoovian name, isn't it?"

"So they say," Matt replied, not bothering to tell her that in his case, it was also an adopted name. "But I've never been any closer to Norway or Sweden than Kansas. I was born there. I'm afraid I haven't seen as much of the world as you have."

"World travel is vastly overrated," Maureen said. "At least, it is when you have to travel in steerage. I much prefer Nevada." For the first time, her smile disappeared. "At least I did."

Matt wanted to ask her what she meant by that, but before he could do so, she brightened again and went on, "Now, what can I do for you?"

"I need some supplies."

She nodded. "I'm not surprised. You have the look of a man who's just passing through. Flour, sugar, salt, coffee, maybe some beans and bacon?"

"Yes, ma'am. Couple weeks' worth of each, I reckon."

"That I can do. I'll put the order together. Can you come back in about an hour?"

"I'll do better than that," Matt said. "I'm going to be spending the night here, so there's no rush. I'll just come by in the morning and pick the things up when I'm ready to ride out."

"That'll be fine, if you're sure it won't inconvenience you."

"Not at all." He gestured toward his clothes, which were coated with a fine layer of trail dust. "I think I'm going to get a hotel room, clean up a little, and try to act civilized for a night. Can you recommend a hotel?"

"Of course. The Ferguson Hotel."

Matt tilted his head slightly. "Same name as yours."

"My Uncle Colin owns it, as he does this mercantile."

"The sign says Gibson's."

" 'Twas Mr. Gibson who started the store. My uncle bought it from him several years ago and didn't see the need to change the name. The Fergusons are not vain people."

"Evidently not," Matt agreed. He put his hat on and gave the brim a tug. "I'm obliged to you for the help. If you want to figure up what the bill will be, I'd be glad to go ahead and pay you."

Maureen shook her head. "That won't be necessary. You can pay when you pick up the supplies in the morning."

"All right. Thanks." He gave her a friendly nod. He wanted to tell her that he had enjoyed the flirting, but decided she would probably think that was a mite too bold.

She might take that broom after him yet, and he didn't want that.

As Matt turned and walked up the aisle toward the double front doors of the mercantile a big shape filled the opening. Three men were coming into the store. The one in the lead was built like a mountain, tall and broad. He was sort of a dandy, wearing boots with fancy stitching on them, tight whipcord trousers tucked into those boots, an expensive shirt with mother-of-pearl snaps instead of buttons, and a cream-colored Stetson that looked like it had never seen much mud or sun. The only well-worn thing about the man was the butt of the revolver that stuck up from the holster on his hip.

Matt disliked the hombre on sight.

But he wasn't looking for trouble, so he moved easily to the side of the aisle as if he were look-

21

ing at the overalls stacked on the shelves. He gave the big gent and the man's hard-faced companions a curt nod as they passed.

The sneer on the big man's face showed he thought Matt had stepped aside out of fear, and the man took that as his due. Matt had a good mind to point out to him just how wrong he was, but . . . he wasn't looking for trouble and continued toward the door.

He stopped when he heard the fear in Maureen's voice as she asked, "What are you doing here, Mr. Talley? My uncle told you he didn't want your business."

"People don't tell me when they *want* my business, Maureen. I tell them when I'm going to *give* it to them. And I've asked you before to call me Judd."

"Are you here to give me some business, Mr. Talley?" Maureen still sounded afraid. Matt paused in the doorway to listen.

A burst of lewd laughter came from the two men with Judd Talley. He joined in with them. "I reckon you could call it that."

Matt's jaw tightened until a muscle jerked. He swung around, and his voice rang out clear and strong, echoing against the high ceiling. "By God, that's enough!"

CHAPTER 2

Like panthers, the two smaller gunmen whirled toward him. They reached for their guns, and Matt was ready to hook and draw. He figured he would have to kill them fast, to minimize the danger of Maureen getting hit by a stray bullet.

But before anybody could clear leather, Judd was between his friends and Matt, holding out his hands in a placating gesture. "Hold it, boys, hold it," he murmured. "No need for gunplay here."

Or maybe it was just a matter of if anybody was going to show off, it was going to be him.

Matt watched all three closely. If any of them made a move, he intended to burn powder.

"Did you have something you wanted to say, friend?" Judd asked in a mocking drawl. He hooked his thumbs behind his gunbelt.

"You heard me," Matt snapped. "I said that's enough. Miss Ferguson doesn't want you here, and where I come from, a man doesn't talk like that to a lady."

"Where you come from." Judd repeated. "Where's that?"

"Colorado." That was where Smoke's Sugarloaf Ranch was located, and the ranch was as close to a home as Matt had. Smoke and his wife Sally, and the old mountain man called Preacher, were the only people in the world Matt considered family.

"Well, you're not in Colorado anymore, and around here, I say and do as I please. You'd better remember that if you don't want to get hurt."

One of the other men spoke up, saying, "Yeah, you don't know who you're bracin', saddle tramp. This here is Judd Talley." He said the name like it ought to mean something.

Matt shook his head and smiled faintly. "Sorry, I can't keep track of every cheap, two-bit gunman west of the Mississippi."

Judd's contemptuous grin vanished. He lost his casual stance and squared up toward Matt as he snarled a bitter curse.

Matt knew he had pushed the confrontation right back into being a shooting matter. He didn't regret it. He had seen dozens of men like Judd Talley. They were a blight on the Western landscape.

Of course, he didn't know how fast that fella might be, he reminded himself. It might be the day Matt Jensen crossed the divide, but his instincts told him otherwise.

Before things could go any further, Maureen Ferguson came out from behind the counter and screamed, "Stop it! Stop it, you fools! I won't have anybody dying in here!"

Judd nodded toward the street and asked in a tight voice, "What say we take this outside, Colorado?"

"Fine by me." Matt backed toward the doorway.

He had just stepped onto the high porch in front of the mercantile when a pair of hard metal rings pressed against his back. Even through his shirt, he knew the twin muzzles of a shotgun when he felt them. He stiffened. If both barrels of that scattergun went off, they would blow him in two, literally. His bottom half might fall one way and his top half the other.

"Keep backin', mister," a man's voice told him. "Just keep backin', and keep your hand away from that gun."

Matt had no choice but to do as the shotgun-wielder commanded. The man sounded tense and nervous, even scared, and that was a mighty bad combination in a man who had a Greener against your back.

"Take it easy." Matt took a couple more steps backward. He kept his hands well away from his body.

"That's far enough."

Judd Talley and his friends came out of the store. "What are you doing, Sheriff?" Judd demanded. "This is none of your business. Just stay out of it."

"No, sir. Any blood spilled in my town *is* my business. When somebody told me there was fixin' to be a shootout in Gibson's store, I hustled right down here."

Judd sneered again. "It's just some blasted

saddle tramp. Nobody'll give a damn if I kill him."

"No killin'." The sheriff was trying to sound firm and in command, but Matt could tell it was hard for him. Even armed with a shotgun, the lawman was a little afraid of Judd and the other two hardcases. "You and your pards just go on now, Judd."

"What about that smart-mouth drifter?" Judd demanded as he gestured with his left hand toward Matt.

"I'll lock him up for disturbin' the peace. All right?"

Maureen had followed the men out of the store. Stepping forward on the porch she said, "That's not fair, Sheriff. Mr. Jensen didn't do anything except chastise these hooligans for being disrespectful to me."

A crowd was gathering on the boardwalks on both sides of the street. Any potentially violent fracas always brought gawkers out of the woodwork in frontier settlements. From the corner of his eye, Matt saw one man separate himself from the crowd and walk quickly across the street toward the general store. The man moved awkwardly with a limp and used a cane, but despite that he didn't waste any time.

"It sounds to me, Sheriff, like it's Talley and his bully boys you should be arresting," the man said. "They were harassing my niece, and I won't stand for it."

"Dadgummit, Mr. Ferguson, don't get mixed up in this," the sheriff muttered.

"I already am. That's my niece, and they were in my store."

"I'm not gonna arrest Judd and his pards. Wouldn't do no good. You know Mr. Longacre'd just bail 'em right out and pay any fine the judge levied against 'em."

"And I know that Judge Hiram Dunwoodie, venerable jurist that he is, would probably just dismiss the case with a stern warning, seeing as those men work for Cyrus Longacre." Ferguson sighed. "All right, then. Don't arrest anyone. Just order the combatants to disperse."

Judd threw his hands in the air in disgust. "God, this is stupid!" he burst out. "All you people do is talk, talk, talk. It makes my head hurt. Come on, boys. Let's get back out to camp."

He stalked to the end of the porch, stomped down the stairs to the street, and went to a hitch rack in front of the next building. His steely-eyed companions followed him.

"You're going to let them go when they're the ones who caused the trouble, Sheriff?" Matt asked in a low voice.

"Dang right I am," the lawman replied without hesitation. "That way nobody gets killed, includin' me."

The three men mounted up, Judd onto a silver-decorated saddle on a magnificent black big

27

enough to support his weight. He galloped out of town with the other two following him. As soon as they were gone, the crowd started to break up.

The man with the cane climbed to the porch. "You can take that shotgun out of the poor man's back now, Sheriff Sanger."

"All right," the sheriff said, lowering the twin muzzles, "but I don't want no more ruckuses around here."

"You should tell that to Cyrus Longacre and his gun-wolves," Ferguson said with a nod toward the east, the direction where Judd and the other two men had disappeared. The cloud of dust that had boiled up from the galloping horses had all but dispersed.

Matt sighed in relief, turned, and saw that the sheriff was a round-faced, middle-aged man with a drooping mustache. Sanger glared at him and asked, "What's your name, mister?"

"Matt Jensen."

"What brings you to Helltown . . . I mean, Halltown."

"Just passing through," Matt told him honestly. "I'm on my way to the mountains. When I saw there was a settlement here I thought I'd pick up some supplies."

"Well, get 'em and get gone. We don't need no saddle tramps in town stirrin' up trouble."

Matt could tell that Sanger knew good and well who had started the trouble. The lawman was just trying to hang on to a shred of self-respect by blaming Matt for it, since he had let the real culprits go.

"Mr. Jensen was planning to spend the night, Sheriff," Maureen said. "He was about to go over to Uncle Colin's hotel and rent a room."

"Well, he won't have to do that now." Ferguson stuck out his hand. "The best room in the house is yours, Mr. Jensen, at no charge. I'm Colin Ferguson."

"Matt Jensen," Matt introduced himself as he shook hands with the man. Ferguson was lean, with a look of sardonic humor on his face below a thatch of graying dark hair. "But I should warn you, by extending your hospitality to me, you risk offending that fella Longacre, whoever he is."

Ferguson snorted in contempt. "The day I worry about offending Cyrus Longacre is the day you can box up my remains and ship me back to County Cork. Come along, lad. I'll see that you're well taken care of. What would you say to a tub full of hot water to soak away the dust of those long trails you've obviously been riding?"

"I'd say that sounds like a little bit of heaven," Matt replied with a grin.

CHAPTER 3

He was right about that. Hot water and soap went a long way toward making Matt feel human again. After he dried off, he put on the one change of clothes he owned. Colin Ferguson had promised to have the dirty garments cleaned at the Chinese laundry down the street.

Still interested in having that drink he had thought about earlier, Matt went downstairs from his room on the second floor of the solidly built frame-and-stone hotel. Colin Ferguson was in the lobby, and it quickly became apparent that he'd been waiting for Matt.

"Come back to my office and have a drink with me, Mr. Jensen," he invited.

"I was just about to head over to the saloon—"

Ferguson scoffed. "My whiskey is better than any of that who-hit-John you'll get over there."

"That's a hard offer to turn down," Matt said with a smile.

"Then don't. Come along. As an added incentive, I'll tell you all about what sort of hornet's nest you've stepped into by making an enemy out of that brute Talley."

Matt nodded. "All right. Thanks. And call me Matt."

"All right, I will. I'm Colin."

They went through a door at the end of the registration desk and along a short hallway to Ferguson's simply furnished but comfortable office. Ferguson waved Matt into a red leather chair and moved to sit behind the desk. Taking a bottle and a couple glasses from one of the drawers, he poured drinks for both of them.

"*Slainte*," Ferguson toasted as he and Matt lifted their glasses.

"To your health," Matt said. He drank, enjoying the smooth fire of the liquor. Leaning back in his chair he went on, "I got the idea Talley works for this Cyrus Longacre you mentioned."

Ferguson took another sip of his whiskey and nodded. "That's right. He's Longacre's chief troubleshooter. And by that I mean—"

"Anything troubles Longacre, Talley shoots it," Matt finished for him.

Ferguson sighed and nodded. "That's exactly right, my boy. Talley's a hired gunman. And don't let the fact that he's such a hulking brute fool you. He's fast on the draw. He doesn't have to demonstrate that fact very often, though. He's so big that mostly he just pounds his opponents in submission, or cows them into going along with what he wants."

"I've seen men like him before. They can be whittled down to size."

Ferguson shook his head. "Not by the likes of

the men we've got around here. Halltown has always been a pretty peaceful place."

"I saw the sign outside town."

"Helltown, you mean? I suspect that was the work of Roscoe Goldsmith, one of our local attorneys. Roscoe thinks he's funny, you see, especially when he's in his cups, which he frequently is. Talley was angry when he saw the sign and was going to tear it down, but Longacre ordered him to leave it alone. I think it appeals to Longacre's twisted sense of humor. Either that, or he thinks it functions as a warning for people not to cross him."

"You still haven't told me who Longacre is," Matt pointed out.

"That's right, I haven't. He's become such a dominant figure around here in the past six months, it's difficult to grasp the concept that somebody doesn't know who he is." Ferguson leaned forward and clasped his hands together on the desk. "Longacre is the railroad, and the railroad is Longacre. He owns it, lock, stock, and barrel."

"The railroad that's coming to Halltown, you mean."

Ferguson nodded. "You know about that?"

"I saw the building going up at the edge of town and thought it looked like a depot," Matt explained. "I take it there's a spur line coming up this way from the Union Pacific, and Longacre owns it."

"That's right. The line is under construction now and is supposed to be here in another month or so. After that, Longacre plans to extend it even farther toward the mountains, into all the rich rangeland between here and there. He has a problem, though."

"What's that?"

"Paiutes," Ferguson said.

Matt shook his head in confusion. "I thought the Paiutes were pretty much friendly these days. I haven't heard anything about them being on the warpath."

"They're not. This particular bunch has signed a treaty, and they're trying to abide by it. The agreement gave them the land for several miles along either side of Big Bear Wash. It's not particularly good country, but the Paiutes seem satisfied with it."

Matt wasn't sure why Ferguson was telling him all this, but he gave in to curiosity and asked, "Why is that a problem for Cyrus Longacre?"

"Because Big Bear Wash lies between here and the big stretch of rangeland where the finest ranches in this part of the state are located. If Longacre could extend his railroad line that far, he'd stand to make a small fortune. But he'd have to build a bridge over the wash in order to do that, because it would cost too much to go around."

"And the Paiutes won't let him build it," Matt guessed.

Ferguson nodded. "That's exactly right. Long-acre sent surveyors and engineers to take a look at the ground and figure out the best way to handle the job, and some of the young Paiute warriors chased them off. A couple days later, some of the elders from the tribe rode into town and hired Roscoe Goldsmith to file a motion in court preventing Longacre's men from trespassing on their land to build his bridge. Judge Dunwoodie ruled against them right away, of course, since he didn't want to cross Longacre, but Roscoe managed to contact Carson City by wire and got a lawyer friend of his to file an appeal with the federal courts before the telegraph mysteriously went dead."

"Do you think Longacre had Talley pull down the wires to disable the telegraph?"

Ferguson shrugged. "I'd say it's highly possible, even probable. Longacre had to have had an idea what Roscoe would do. That's where things stand now. The railroad is still headed this way, but where it goes from here is up to the courts."

Matt downed the rest of the whiskey in his glass. "It's an interesting story," he said as he set the empty glass on the desk, "but what does it have to do with me?"

"I just wanted you to know what you're getting into by making an enemy out of Judd Talley, and by extension, Cyrus Longacre."

Matt shook his head. "Talley, maybe, because I

stood up to him when he was bothering your niece. But I don't have anything to do with Longacre. And unless Talley wants to follow me up to the mountains and interrupt my hunting and fishing, I'm done with him, too."

"Unfortunately, Talley's liable to do exactly that, and Longacre will back him. You see, Longacre doesn't want anybody standing up to his men and getting away with it. They've come in here, run roughshod over the town, done pretty much anything they wanted, and cowed Sheriff Sanger and Judge Dunwoodie into letting them get away with it. It's sheer arrogance, is what it is. They do those things because they can." Ferguson toyed with his glass. "Some of us here in Halltown would like to see a stop put to it. We're willing to do what it takes to make that happen."

Matt's eyes narrowed as he looked across the desk at the man. "Now I see what's going on," he said slowly. "You want me to be your hired gun, the same way Talley packs iron for Longacre."

Ferguson shook his head. "I didn't say that—"

"But it's what you were driving at," Matt insisted.

Again, Ferguson's shoulders rose and fell in a shrug. "It's clear that you can handle yourself, Matt, and you're not afraid of Talley and those other gunmen who work for Longacre. Nobody else around here can say that."

"I'm just one man," Matt pointed out. "Going

35

up against all of Longacre's men would be the same as suicide, wouldn't it?"

Ferguson's eyes narrowed in speculation. "I'm not so sure about that. I've got a hunch that if anybody could take on the whole lot of them and have a chance of coming out on top, it would be you."

"I'm flattered," Matt said, although his tone of voice made it clear that he didn't really mean it. "But I'm not a hired gun, Mr. Ferguson."

"Colin," the hotel owner reminded him.

Matt came to his feet. "I'm sorry, Mr. Ferguson. If you're making me an offer, the answer is no. I'm riding on in the morning. If you've changed your mind and want me to pay for my room tonight, I'll be glad to."

Ferguson waved away the offer. "No, no, you're welcome here for helping out my niece the way you did. Maureen and I are the only family we each have left, so she means a great deal to me. Actually, you're welcome to stay as long as you want. I'm in that much debt to you."

"Consider it square any time you want," Matt said with a shake of his head. He gestured toward the empty glass on the desk. "Thanks for the drink."

Ferguson nodded gloomily. He was obviously disappointed by Matt's reaction to the conversation.

Matt left the office and walked back to the

36

lobby. He slid his pocket watch out of his jeans and opened it to check the time. The hour was late enough to start thinking about supper. He gave the clerk behind the desk a polite nod and went to the front doors.

Halltown's main street was still busy. Cowboys from the large ranches in the area went in and out of the town's several saloons, restaurants, hash houses, gambling dens, and dance halls. Some of the houses at the edge of town were probably more unsavory establishments that also catered to the local ranch hands. Men came and went on horseback, and buckboards pulled up in front of Gibson's Mercantile and the other general stores in town. As afternoon wound down and evening came on, Halltown didn't look like a place that had been buffaloed by a bunch of hired guns.

Of course, Talley and his friends had ridden out earlier, so they weren't around to cause trouble. The townspeople and the punchers from the nearby spreads might be taking advantage of that fact. It might be different later, Matt reminded himself.

He wondered if the camp Talley had mentioned was the railroad construction camp. That seemed likely.

He didn't know which restaurant in town was the best, and he didn't particularly want to go back in the hotel and ask Ferguson for a recommendation. He would just have to make a choice and take his chances, he decided. He was about to do just that when a voice spoke behind him.

"Mr. Jensen?"

Matt swung around. The voice belonged to a woman.

And a mighty pretty one at that.

CHAPTER 4

The woman was a blonde, maybe twenty-five years old, Matt judged, and compactly built but with an intriguingly curved shape that was well displayed by the dark blue dress she wore. A hat of the same shade adorned with a feather perched atop the blond curls. Her eyes weren't quite as dark a blue as the dress and hat, but almost. Her lips curved in a smile as she looked at Matt. He had a feeling she was well aware of the way his eyes assessed her, and she didn't mind a bit.

"That's right. I'm Matt Jensen, Miss . . . ?"

"Barry. Virginia Barry. Why do you assume that I'm unmarried, Mr. Jensen?"

Matt gestured toward the hand that held an elegant bag. "No wedding ring."

"I'm wearing gloves."

"They're tight enough that I think I'd see a ring through them."

Actually, Matt was guessing. It was pure

instinct on his part that told him Virginia Barry didn't have a husband. That, and a vibrant boldness to her gaze that he thought would be uncommon in a married woman.

"Well, how about it?" he said. "Am I right?"

Smiling, Virginia tucked the bag under her arm and used her right hand to pull the glove off her left hand. When her fingers were uncovered, she held them up where Matt could see them. Just as he had suspected, there was no wedding band on her ring finger. In fact, no jewelry of any kind decorated the slim, supple fingers.

"You're a perceptive man, Mr. Jensen."

"I try to be. Now that we've settled your marital status, Miss Barry . . . what can I do for you?"

"I'd heard that you were probably staying at Mr. Ferguson's hotel. I looked you up so I could extend an invitation to you."

That took Matt a little by surprise. He didn't know Virginia Barry, or hadn't until a moment ago. He didn't know anyone in Halltown except Colin Ferguson and Ferguson's niece Maureen. Who else could be inviting him anywhere?

"What sort of invitation?" he asked.

"For dinner," Virginia replied.

"With you?" If that turned out to be the case, it wouldn't be the first time an attractive woman had decided to pursue him. Matt was far from vain, but he was pragmatic enough to know that women often thought he was good-looking.

"I'll be there"—Virginia continued to smile—"but actually I'm delivering the invitation on behalf of my friend, Mr. Cyrus Longacre."

That really took Matt by surprise. So far he hadn't heard anything good about Longacre, and the fact that an arrogant varmint like Judd Talley worked for Longacre was another mark against the man. But Matt had to admit he hadn't heard both sides of the story.

"I'm not acquainted with Mr. Longacre," he said. "I'm not sure why he'd invite me to dinner."

"Well, you weren't acquainted with me just a few minutes ago, were you? Mr. Longacre has heard about you, and he wants to meet you." Virginia paused. "And Cyrus is the sort of man who usually gets what he wants."

Her casual use of Longacre's first name told Matt quite a bit. He was curious. "Where's this dinner going to take place?"

"In Mr. Longacre's suite at the hotel."

Matt turned his head to glance at the building he had just left.

"No, not this hotel," Virginia said. "The Sierra House. It's two blocks down, on the other side of the street. You can't miss it."

Matt wasn't the sort to spend a lot of time brooding or fussing over a decision. He made up his mind quickly. "What time should I be there?"

Virginia's smile brightened. "You're accepting?"

"I am."

"Then we'll be expecting you at seven o'clock. Good evening, Mr. Jensen."

Matt touched a finger to the brim of his hat. "Good evening, Miss Barry."

She turned and moved off along the boardwalk. Matt watched her go, and he would have been lying if he'd said that he didn't enjoy the view.

He hadn't accepted the invitation just because Virginia Barry was a beautiful young woman. He was genuinely curious what Cyrus Longacre thought he stood to gain by wining and dining an hombre who was just passing through Halltown. From what Matt had heard about Longacre, the man struck him as the sort who wouldn't do anything if he didn't think he might somehow profit from it.

Maybe Longacre was afraid Matt would stay around town and cause trouble for him because of the little ruckus with Judd Talley. Maybe he worried some of the town's citizens might try to recruit Matt to stand up to Longacre's rule. After all, that was what the conversation with Colin Ferguson had amounted to. Longacre might be trying to get to him first.

He wasn't going to be bought off by either side, Matt told himself. His gun wasn't for hire unless you counted things like riding shotgun on a stagecoach, which was an honest job. But it wouldn't hurt anything to let Longacre buy him a meal, he thought.

Besides, he would get to see Virginia Barry again, and there was no denying he was looking forward to that.

Since there was a little more than an hour until he was supposed to show up at the Sierra House for his dinner engagement, Matt walked down the street to the livery stable where he had left his sorrel earlier. The old-timer who ran the place greeted him with a friendly nod.

"I'm takin' good care of your horse, son," the hostler said. "You don't have to worry."

"I'm not worried," Matt assured him. "I just thought I'd stop by for a minute." He reached over the stall gate and patted the sorrel's shoulder. "I've heard a lot of talk around town about this fella Cyrus Longacre. What do you think about him?"

Matt knew that fellas who ran livery stables were often good sources of information about what went on in a town. They dealt with many of the citizens, and they saw most of the strangers who came and went, as well. And when they were old-timers, like that one, he knew they could be counted on to have a hankering to talk.

The short, wiry, grizzled hostler grimaced, twisting up his weathered face in a look of distaste, like he had just bitten into a rotten apple. "Longacre," he repeated. "Well, he's got a lot of money, I reckon. But that's just about the best thing I can say about him."

42

"To some people, that's all that would matter." Matt picked up a curry comb and began running it over the sorrel's sleek hide.

The liveryman shook his head. "Not to me. Oh, I don't mind money. I wish I had more of it. But that ain't all that counts in the world. There's such a thing as bein' honorable, too."

"You wouldn't describe Longacre as honorable?"

The old-timer took a deep breath. "You had your own run-in with that hombre Talley who works for him. You reckon an honorable man would hire a skunk like that?"

"You can't always condemn a man just because of what his employees do."

"I know that. But the first thing Longacre done when he come to town was to sic Talley on poor ol' Joe Dunaway."

"Who's that?" Matt asked.

"He owned the freight line that ran betwixt here and Reno. Longacre tried to buy him out."

"Why would he do that? Because Dunaway was competition?"

The old-timer nodded emphatically. "That's right. The way I see it, Longacre thought he could buy the freight line and shut it down, so there wouldn't be no way to get goods up here for a while, until the railroad rolls in. By that time, folks'd be so desperate for regular freight service again, they'd pay whatever Longacre wants to charge for shippin' things on his trains."

Matt frowned. "But he could've just waited until the tracks get here, undercut Dunaway's prices, and run him out of business that way."

"Would've cost more, at least startin' out, and would've taken longer," the liveryman explained. "One thing about Longacre, son, and it didn't take folks long to learn it . . . he wants what he wants *when* he wants it and *how* he wants it. He don't take kindly to anybody gettin' in the way of that."

Matt nodded slowly. That agreed with what Ferguson had told him about Cyrus Longacre. It was starting to sound familiar. Matt had run into men like that before.

"What happened with Dunaway and his freight company?"

"Joe told Longacre to go to hell. I reckon he knew he couldn't compete with the blasted railroad over the long run, but he was bound and determined to hang on as long as he could." The old-timer shrugged. "Somebody jumped him one night, beat the hell outta him, and busted him up so bad he didn't have no choice but to go back east and live with his daughter and her family, so they could take care of him. Longacre wound up buyin' the freight outfit after all, but he only give Joe pennies on the dollar for what it was worth."

"I suppose everybody thinks Judd Talley is the one who attacked Dunaway."

"Joe said it was like a mountain fell on him. Ain't nobody else around here who's that big."

"But the sheriff didn't do anything about it," Matt guessed.

The liveryman snorted in disgust. "By that time Walt Sanger had figured out it was in his best interests to go along with whatever Longacre wants, even if it ain't best for the town. Walt never was what you'd call real strict on the law, but he was always pretty honest . . . until Longacre and Talley scoured it outta him."

"Aren't you a little worried, talking about them like this? What if it got back to them?"

"Shoot, son, you was ready to shoot it out with Talley, I was told. I don't figure you're pards with him and his boss."

"No," Matt admitted, "I'm not. I was just curious, and you've confirmed what I suspected."

"If your suspicions were that Cyrus Longacre and Judd Talley and the rest of that bunch are lowdown polecats, you're sure as shootin' right about that!"

"Longacre has a friend, a Miss Barry . . ."

"Friend would be a polite word for what that gal is, and Lord forgive me for sayin' such an ungentlemanly thing."

"She's a looker, though."

"That she is," the old-timer agreed. "But looks don't count for as much when you associate with the likes of Longacre."

Matt patted his horse's shoulder again. "Well, I've got to be going . . ." Something stirred in his brain and made him pause. "What about Long-acre's trouble with the Paiutes?"

The liveryman shook his head in dismay. "The dang fool's gonna wind up causin' an Indian war if he keeps tryin' to push 'em off that land of theirs. It's theirs by rights. They signed a treaty and they've abided by it. If Longacre had tried to strike a deal with 'em, he might've been able to. But he figured since they was redskins, he'd just take what he wanted."

"Do you happen to know the chief?"

"I sure do. Fine old fella name of Walkin' Hawk. Pretty fierce warrior in his time, I suspect, but now he just wants peace for his people. I don't know if Longacre's gonna let him have it."

Matt nodded. Everything he had heard about Cyrus Longacre was starting to remind him of something else. He wanted to learn more, though, before he sent a couple wires.

He couldn't do that anyway, he reminded himself. The telegraph lines were down.

Maybe they wouldn't stay that way. Western Union probably had a crew on their way to repair the line. As soon as the wires were humming again, Matt might have to get in touch with Smoke and Preacher. A while back, the three of them had run up against a problem big enough that it took all their guns to settle it. The situation in Halltown was shaping up to look like it might be connected.

If that turned out to be true, Helltown really was a better name for the place.

Matt said good-bye to the old-timer and left the livery stable. He had killed enough time that it was late enough for him to stroll toward the Sierra House. Earlier he had told himself to be fair and give Longacre the benefit of the doubt. After everything he had heard, he wasn't sure if he could still do that.

The Sierra House was as nice as the Ferguson Hotel, maybe even a little nicer. That didn't surprise Matt. A rich man like Longacre wouldn't want to stay in a construction camp when there was a town nearby, and he would stay in the best place in that town. When Matt told the desk clerk he had an engagement with Cyrus Longacre, the man nodded instantly and said, "You're Mr. Jensen?"

"That's right."

"Miss Barry instructed me to tell you that you should go right up. Mr. Longacre's suite is at the end of the hall, the biggest door up there. You'll see it."

Matt nodded. "Obliged." He went up the stairs.

The door to Longacre's suite was indeed bigger and fancier than any of the others on the second floor. Matt knocked on it, then took off his hat and held it in his left hand.

He kept his right hand free, and it didn't stray far from the butt of the .44 holstered on his hip. Habits like that helped keep a man alive.

When the door opened, Virginia Barry stood there, a smile of welcome on her lovely face. Her hair was down, in two shining blond wings, and she had traded the more sedate dark blue gown with its long sleeves and high neck for a pale pink dress that left her arms bare except for short, puffy white sleeves. Her shoulders were uncovered, and the dress's neckline dipped low enough to reveal the twin swells of creamy breasts.

"Right on time, Mr. Jensen," she said. "Won't you come in?"

It was an invitation most men wouldn't be able to resist. Matt could have, if it were necessary, but after hearing so much about Cyrus Longacre —all of it bad—he wanted to meet the man for himself.

That introduction was imminent. As Matt stepped into the room, a man strode toward him, thrust out a hand, and said in a hearty voice, "Mr. Jensen! It's good to meet you. I'm Cyrus Longacre."

CHAPTER 5

The railroad man was a solid six-footer, with shoulders broad enough to indicate he had done some physical labor in his life. His strong grip as he shook Matt's hand was more evidence of that. His face was broad and beefy, with a large nose and a slab of a jaw. Graying sandy hair topped his features. He wore a brown tweed suit, a snowy white shirt, and a silk cravat with a diamond stick-pin in it. The pin was probably worth ten times what Matt's belongings were worth, including his horse and his guns.

Matt gave him a polite nod. "Hello, Mr. Long-acre."

"Come in and have a seat. Virginia, if you'd be kind enough to pour us some brandy . . . ?"

"Of course," she murmured. "Mr. Jensen, won't you give me your hat?"

Matt handed over the Stetson. He was glad she didn't ask him for his gunbelt. He wouldn't have given it to her.

Longacre waved him into a thickly upholstered armchair. Matt looked around as he sat down. They were in a spacious sitting room furnished with several comfortable chairs, a divan, and a dining table covered with a white linen cloth and already set for dinner with crystal, silver, and fine china. A mahogany sideboard sat against one wall. The floor had a thick rug on it, and dark red velvet drapes with gold-tasseled pull cords hung over the windows. Like most fancy hotel rooms, the place had an air of elegance about it, which was the main thing separating it from a sitting room in a high-class whorehouse.

Longacre sat in a similar armchair on the other side of a spindly-legged table. He reached for a box made of some gleaming dark wood. "Cigar?" He grinned. "I'm told they're rolled on the thighs of Cuban virgins."

"No thanks," Matt told him. "I'm not much of a smoker."

"Your loss." Longacre took one of the fat cheroots from the box, clipped its end, and struck a match to set it on fire. He blew out a cloud of smoke. "Ah, thank you, my dear," he said as Virginia brought over a tray with two snifters of brandy on it. She handed one of them to Matt, and as she did so, he thought her fingers pressed warmly against his for a moment longer than they had to.

"To your health, Mr. Jensen," Longacre said as he raised his glass. Matt raised his in return and nodded, but he didn't say anything.

Longacre took a sip of the brandy and sighed in satisfaction. "Excellent. Much better than what you'd think you could get in a town like this, wouldn't you say?"

"I'm sure you had it brought in special for you," Matt said.

Longacre chuckled. "That's true. I knew the creature comforts to which a man such as myself is accustomed probably would be sorely lacking here, so I brought my own brandy, my own cigars"—he glanced at Virginia, who stood nearby with a smile on her face—"and other things I would need."

"I'll go down and see about dinner while you gentlemen talk," she murmured. She set the tray back on the sideboard and left the room.

Cradling the snifter in his left hand, Longacre leaned back in his chair and crossed his legs. "Shall we speak frankly, Mr. Jensen?"

"I'd rather you did," Matt replied honestly.

"I know you had a run-in with my man Talley earlier today."

"That's true."

"And it almost came to gunplay."

"Seemed like it might," Matt allowed.

"I'm very glad it didn't. I don't like it when my employees are forced to kill people."

"You're assuming he would have beaten me to the draw."

Longacre smiled. "Judd's fast with a gun. Very fast."

Matt returned the smile and asked, "Fast enough? We can't really say, can we?"

Longacre stared coldly at him for a few seconds, then laughed abruptly. "By God, I like you, Jensen! You've got the sort of confidence that reminds me of myself when I was a younger man. You wouldn't happen to be looking for a job, would you?"

"I don't think Talley would appreciate it too much if you were to hire me," Matt pointed out.

Longacre's rugged face hardened again. "Judd appreciates what I pay him to appreciate. Trust

51

me, if you sign on with me, there won't be any trouble with him."

"What sort of work are we talking about?" Matt asked, even though he knew exactly what Longacre meant.

Longacre swallowed the rest of his brandy and set the empty snifter on the table next to the cigar box. "You've probably heard that I'm bringing the railroad to Halltown. I plan to extend it farther north and west, all the way to the mountains. That's prime land up there, Jensen . . . cattle, timber, mining. There are fortunes waiting to be made, fortunes, I tell you!"

Matt nodded. "I believe it."

"But whether it's cattle or lumber or gold and silver ore, it'll all need to be shipped, and that's where my railroad comes in."

"I don't know anything about building a railroad," Matt said. "I can swing a sledge-hammer, but that's about it."

"I thought we were going to speak frankly," Longacre shot back with a frown. "You know good and well what I need. I can get hundreds, thousands, of men to swing sledgehammers and carry rails. I need men to cut through all the problems that rise up and get in my way."

"That's what you have Talley and those other men for."

Longacre shrugged. "There are always losses in any campaign, and that's what building a railroad is like, a military campaign. The railroad advances, and the enemy tries to stop it. You can never have too many good men when you're going into battle."

Longacre put the cigar in his mouth, puffed on it, and leaned back in his chair again, clearly satisfied that he'd had his say.

There was no chance in hell Matt would ever work for a man like Longacre. He was debating whether or not to tell that to the railroad baron when Virginia Barry came back into the suite, followed by a couple waiters carrying big silver trays.

"Dinner is served, gentlemen," Virginia announced, allowing Matt to postpone his next move.

In fact, Longacre grinned and said, "We can finish our talk later, Jensen. Never allow business to interfere with a good meal, eh?"

"Sounds like words to live by," Matt agreed with a nod.

The waiters set the food on the table, filled the glasses with wine, and then withdrew. Longacre held one of the chairs for Virginia, then took the one at the head of the table so she was seated to his right. Matt was at the other end of the table.

The food was fairly simple, thick steaks, potatoes, greens, but very good and excellently prepared. "Not the sort of meal you'd get in New Orleans or San Francisco," Longacre commented, "but probably the best you can expect in a place like this."

"Better than beans, bacon, and biscuits out on the trail," Matt said. "That's what I've been eating."

To tell the truth, he would have preferred one of those rough meals to sharing a table with Cyrus Longacre. Virginia Barry was a mighty pretty dinner companion, though, so he supposed he could put up with Longacre for a while.

The wine was good, too, but Matt just sipped it. He'd already had that drink with Colin Ferguson and the brandy before the meal. He didn't want his brain to get muddled. He didn't trust Longacre and knew he needed to remain alert for some sort of trick.

Longacre appeared to have been sincere with that offer of a job, Matt mused as he ate. It was one way men like Longacre operated. Figure out who might provide some opposition and get those men on your side to start with. Longacre had probably pulled that off plenty of times in the past.

He hadn't been dealing with Matt Jensen then. Matt wasn't going to be fooled, and he wasn't going to be bought off.

But it wouldn't hurt to pretend to play along, until he was sure just how much of a threat Longacre really represented.

When they were finished with the meal, Longacre leaned back in his chair and fired up another cigar. "Now that you've had some time to think about it, what do you say, Matt? How would you like to throw in with me? You won't regret it, I promise you."

Matt knew better. If he ever allied himself with a man like Longacre, he would never know another peaceful night's sleep. His dreams would be haunted by the way he had sullied himself.

But he put a smile on his face and said, "I'd like to ponder it a little more, if that's all right with you, Mr. Longacre."

Matt saw the quick flash of anger in the railroad baron's eyes, but Longacre controlled the reaction almost instantly and managed to smile in return. "Of course," he said with an expansive wave of his hand. "I don't want to rush you"—his voice hardened slightly—"but don't take too long to make up your mind. You know how opportunities are . . . they present themselves, and then they move on."

Matt nodded. "I'll let you know by tomorrow evening."

"That's fine." Longacre got to his feet. He clamped the cigar between his teeth and said around it, "Now if you'll excuse me, I have some work I really need to tend to. I have one of the rooms in this suite set up as an office. Building a railroad is a complicated business, you know."

"Sure, I understand." Matt started to get up, too.

Longacre motioned him back into his chair.

"No, no, there's still some wine in the bottle. Why don't you and Virginia finish it off at your leisure?"

"Yes, Mr. Jensen," Virginia put in with a smile. "Once Cyrus starts working, he's not very good company for the rest of the evening."

Curious as to what they were trying to do, Matt settled back in his chair. "All right. If you're sure."

"I'm positive." Longacre went over and stood behind Virginia's chair, leaning down to plant a kiss on her cheek. "Good night, my dear."

"Good night, Cyrus," she said, but her blue eyes were still on Matt.

Longacre turned to Matt and held out his hand again. "It was a pleasure to meet you, Matt."

"Likewise," Matt lied as he shook with the man.

Longacre went through one of the doors that opened off the sitting room and closed it firmly behind him, leaving Matt and Virginia alone.

She reached for the bottle of wine. "Let me refill your glass."

Matt nodded his thanks, but took only a small sip.

Cradling her own glass in her hands, Virginia said, "So Cyrus offered you a job."

Matt nodded. "That's right."

"I thought he might. He was impressed when he heard about the way you stood up to Judd Talley."

"I'd think that would make him mad, since Talley works for him."

"That's because you don't know Cyrus. He appreciates daring and resolve. When he looks at a man who's determined, it reminds him of himself."

"He said pretty much the same thing to me," Matt told her. "I'm not sure it would work out. I reckon Talley wouldn't be happy about it."

"Judd Talley is an uncultured brute," Virginia said without hesitation. "He's a blunt instrument, nothing more. You don't have to worry about him."

"And I'm just a drifter, what most folks would call a saddle tramp." Matt smiled. "I'm not all that cultured myself."

"Don't sell yourself short. I find you quite intriguing." Virginia looked directly at him. "I hope you take that job."

"Why?"

She looked down at the table when Matt asked her that blunt question, and a faint rosy tinge crept over her face and neck. "Because it would mean that I'd have a chance to see a lot more of you," she said in a quiet voice.

Matt stood up and came around the table toward her. She stood up to meet him, and when she raised her eyes to his, they had that bold fire in them again. He reached up and rested his hands on her shoulders, feeling the smooth warmth of her bare flesh under his fingers.

She didn't resist at all when he drew her toward him, leaned down, and kissed her.

All the passionate urgency he could have asked for was there as she sagged against him and her hands clutched at his broad chest. Her lips were warm and alive and compelled him to continue kissing her. She was so pliant he had no doubt that he could have done anything he wanted with her.

And it was all a lie. He knew that as well as he knew his own name.

Virginia was just one more payoff from Cyrus Longacre, one more incentive not to take the opposing side in any trouble. If Longacre was that desperate, Matt thought, he must have plans looming that he believed might cause open warfare to break out across that part of Nevada. Matt was more convinced than ever that Longacre needed to be stopped.

He broke the kiss. "I really ought to go."

"You don't have to," Virginia replied in a voice husky with passion.

Maybe it wasn't completely feigned after all, Matt told himself . . . but it didn't really matter either way. "I'll be seeing you again," he promised as he slipped out of her embrace. "After all, I promised Mr. Longacre I'd give him a decision by tomorrow night."

"I hope it's the right one."

It would be, Matt thought . . . but it wouldn't be the one she and Longacre wanted.

Leaving the rest of the wine where it was, he got his hat from the little table where she had placed it earlier. Virginia stood beside the table, the fingertips of her left hand resting on the snowy cloth and her right hand pressed lightly to the valley between her breasts. Matt had to admit that she made a lovely picture. Most men wouldn't be able to walk away from her.

It wasn't easy for him, but he managed to smile. "Good night. Please pass along my thanks to Mr. Longacre for his hospitality."

"Of course," she said. "Good night, Matt."

He got out of there while he could, easing the door closed behind him. He paused in the corridor and took a deep breath that he blew back out in a long sigh. He could still taste the hot sweetness of Virginia's lips on his.

By the time he reached the street, the more pragmatic side of his nature had taken over. He chuckled. Longacre had wined and dined him, then played a trump card by practically throwing Virginia at him. It wasn't going to work, but you had to give the man credit for trying, Matt thought. He grunted and started walking toward the Ferguson Hotel.

He had reached the hotel porch when he paused to look across the street toward the mercantile, which was closed for the night. The building was dark and locked up.

Matt immediately tensed and thought something

was wrong when he saw a brief, sudden flare of light through the window in one of the doors.

Someone had struck a match inside the mercantile.

CHAPTER 6

Matt didn't hesitate. His instincts told him something was wrong, and he had learned—Smoke had taught him—to trust his instincts. He loped quickly across the street toward the darkened mercantile.

He didn't head for the front door, which he was sure would be locked. If somebody was in there who wasn't supposed to be, as seemed likely, that person had probably gone in through the back. Matt hurried toward the alley that ran alongside the building.

As he ran, he saw a flare of light from the corner of his eye and paused for a second. He watched as a tongue of flame suddenly licked upward in the darkened store. That was all the evidence he needed to know what was going on. He palmed his Colt from its holster as he bellowed, "Fire! Fire!"

Then, gun in hand, he plunged into the shadow-choked passage beside the mercantile.

He was lucky he didn't run into anything or

trip on some trash as he dashed toward the rear of the building. He reached the corner just as several dark figures spilled from an open back door. One of them looked big enough to be Judd Talley, but there wasn't enough light for Matt to be sure. He brought up the .44 and shouted, "Hold it!"

A couple of the figures twisted toward him. Colt flame bloomed in the darkness, and Matt felt the wind-rip of a bullet's passage close beside his ear. His own revolver roared and bucked in his hand as he triggered a pair of swift shots. One of the men yelled and crumpled, but the other stayed on his feet and fired again. A bullet tugged at the side of Matt's shirt.

Matt squeezed off another shot and saw the second gunman go over backward like he'd been slapped down by a giant hand. That left the biggest of the trio, but he wasn't putting up a fight. He was running away. Matt was about to squeeze off a shot when the man abruptly disappeared around the far corner of the building. Matt grimaced and held his fire. No point in wasting a bullet.

He had a more pressing problem. Those men had set a fire inside the mercantile, and it had already had a minute or so to catch hold. He ran to the door, hurdling the body of one of the men he had shot, and raced inside.

The smell of smoke was already thick in the

air. Garish, flickering light from the flames spilled through an open doorway, revealing that he was in some sort of storeroom. He hurried through the door and found himself behind the counter. The floor in front of the counter was on fire. The reek of coal oil mingled with the choking, eye-stinging smoke. Without slowing down, Matt pouched his iron, put a hand on the counter, and vaulted over it to land beside the flames, which jumped at him hungrily and assaulted him with heat.

A stack of blankets sat on a shelf nearby. Matt grabbed one of them, shook it out, and started slapping at the burning floor with it. The men must have poured a pool of coal oil in front of the counter, so fiercely was it burning, and they had scattered more of the stuff around the store, but the flames hadn't reached the rest of the oil yet. If Matt could put out the fire, the mercantile might be saved.

He didn't think about the heat or the danger of his own clothes catching on fire as he slapped at the flames with the blanket. The fire kept trying to spread, and he kept beating it back. Vaguely, he was aware of men shouting somewhere nearby. Then someone yelled, "Get back!"

Matt paused in his efforts, and a man appeared beside him holding a bucket with water sloshing out of it. The man threw the water onto the flames, then handed the empty bucket to another man and took another one filled with water. Matt stepped back, blinking his smoke-irritated eyes, and watched as the quickly-formed bucket brigade put out the blaze. Fire was one of the deadliest and most-feared enemies in all frontier towns, and most communities reacted swiftly and efficiently when it threatened. Halltown was no different.

Matt spotted Colin Ferguson in the line of men passing the water buckets back and forth. Ferguson's narrow face was set in grim lines, but when he saw Matt looking at him, he managed a quick smile.

"Was it you who discovered this fire?" he called out.

Matt nodded. "A couple of the men who started it are in the alley behind the store."

Ferguson's eyes widened in surprise. "You killed them?"

"I don't know. I got lead in them."

Matt went around the counter and through the door into the storeroom, drawing his gun as he did so. He heard footsteps behind him and looked around to see that Ferguson had dropped out of the line and was hurrying after him.

Matt paused. "I don't know if you ought to go back there, Mr. Ferguson. Those varmints might still be alive."

The third man, who Matt suspected had been Judd Talley, might have returned and be lurking around behind the store, but he didn't take the time to explain that.

"I'm coming with you," Ferguson insisted. "Nobody can set fire to my store and get away with it!"

Matt shrugged. He had warned Ferguson it might be dangerous. He couldn't make the decision for him.

Making sure he stayed in front Matt approached the rear door, which still stood open. He went through it in a crouch, sweeping his gun from side to side, ready to squeeze the trigger if anybody opened fire on him.

"Are they still there?" Ferguson asked from just inside the doorway.

Matt sighed and bit back a curse. The two huddled shapes he had left on the ground were gone. Either the men had only been wounded and had been able to get up and stumble away, or someone else had carried off the bodies while the battle against the fire was going on.

"They're gone." Matt lowered his gun. With his other hand, he fished a lucifer out of his pocket and snapped it to life with his thumbnail. As the match flared up, it cast a flickering glow over the area behind the store. In its light, he saw two dark, irregular patches on the ground he knew had to be blood.

"You hit them, no doubt about that," Ferguson said as he stepped out of the building and came to stand beside Matt.

Preacher and Smoke had taught Matt quite a

bit about tracking, and experience had taught him even more. He holstered his gun and hunkered on his heels as he studied the marks left in the dirt by several pairs of high-heeled boots. "Looks to me like one man picked up both of them and carried them off. They probably had horses hidden somewhere nearby."

"It would take a strong man to do that," Ferguson pointed out.

"I saw a third man, and he was plenty big."

"Talley." Ferguson made the name sound like a curse.

Matt felt the same way about the big man. "It had to be him," he agreed. "But I never got a good look at him, so I can't prove it."

"Can't prove what?" a new voice asked from the back door of the mercantile. As Matt looked up, Sheriff Walt Sanger stepped out of the store.

The match had burned down almost to Matt's fingers. He dropped it and crushed it out with the toe of his boot. "Three men started that fire in the store, Sheriff. I shot a couple of them, but the third man got away. He came back and retrieved the bodies of his partners while I was inside, trying to put out the fire. I'm convinced the third man was Judd Talley."

"But you didn't really see him. You said so yourself. I heard you."

"I saw him well enough to tell how big he was. Nobody else but Talley fits that description."

"I dunno," Sanger said dubiously. "There are lots of pretty big hombres in Nevada."

"Is there anybody that big around here?"

Sanger snorted. "Shoot, I don't know who might've ridden into these parts. You only showed up yourself today, mister . . . and already you've got mixed up in a heap of trouble. For all I know, you started that fire yourself, and now you're just makin' up some story about three other men 'cause you almost got caught."

Ferguson stared at the lawman in flabbergasted amazement for a moment before he was able to say, "Sheriff, you can't be serious! Look at the blood on the ground. That proves Mr. Jensen wounded two of the men."

Stubbornly, Sanger shook his head. "I see some dark spots on the ground. That don't prove nothin'. Might not even be blood."

"But . . . but . . ." Ferguson began to sputter.

"Let it go," Matt told him. "I don't think the sheriff is going to believe anything that might cast some of Longacre's men in a bad light."

Sanger glared at Matt. "Are you implyin' that I'm dishonest, Jensen?"

"No, Sheriff, I'm not," Matt said, and as far as he was concerned, it was an honest answer. He was saying flat-out that Sanger was a crook, or at least, in the pocket of a crook. There was no "implying" about it.

But forcing a confrontation with the lawman

wasn't going to do any good, Matt knew. He wanted to look into a few more things, and once he had, then he would decide what steps to take next.

One of the townies who had been fighting the blaze in the store appeared in the doorway. "The fire's out, Colin. Doesn't look like the damage is *too* bad. You're gonna have to replace some floor and maybe part of your counter."

Ferguson nodded. "Thanks, Roy. I'll come take a look."

Matt followed Ferguson inside, ignoring the baleful look Sanger gave him as he stepped past the lawman. In the mercantile's main room, a man was in the process of lighting a lantern, and Matt said, "Better be careful. Those varmints splashed around quite a bit of coal oil before they started the fire."

Ferguson sniffed the air. "Yes, I can smell it. If you hadn't kept the flames contained, Matt, the whole place would have gone up like a pile of tender. I'll probably lose some merchandise due to the damage from the oil, but it could have been a lot worse."

They examined the hole in the floor created by the fire, and Halltown's local carpenter discussed the necessary repairs with Ferguson. While that was going on, Maureen Ferguson emerged from the crowd of volunteers and bystanders and approached Matt.

"From what I hear, you saved the store," she told him. "I can't thank you enough."

Matt shrugged. "I just happened to see something going on in here that shouldn't have been. Anybody would have done the same."

"No, they wouldn't have. It takes a lot of courage to run *into* a burning building."

"The fire was still pretty small when I got to it," Matt pointed out.

Ferguson turned from his conversation to say to his niece, "Which was after he'd gotten in a shoot-out with the skunks who started the blaze, I might add."

Maureen's green eyes widened. "Is that true?"

"Well, the sheriff doesn't seem to believe it . . . but it happened," Matt said.

"Dear Lord, you could have been killed!"

"That's true every time a man gets out of bed in the morning."

Maureen took hold of his arm. "Have you had supper? If not, I'm going to make sure you have the best meal you've had in months!"

"Sorry, I've already eaten," Matt told her with a regretful shake of his head.

"Well, then . . . breakfast tomorrow morning! In the hotel dining room. I'll see to it."

Matt smiled. "That sounds mighty nice."

Maureen turned to Ferguson. "Uncle Colin, you're putting him up in the best room in the house, aren't you?"

"Of course, my dear. After what he did for you earlier, I felt like he deserved it, and that goes double now."

The crowd began to disperse. Sheriff Sanger clumped out of the store, still casting unfriendly glances over his shoulder toward Matt. It wasn't long before Matt, Ferguson, and Maureen were the only ones left.

Ferguson explained to his niece, "Matt thinks it was Judd Talley and a couple of Longacre's men who started the fire."

"Probably the two who were with Talley earlier," Matt said.

"But why?" Maureen asked. "Simply because of the trouble here?"

"That's enough reason for no-good rapscallions like them," Ferguson said. "You know how Talley gets when anybody tries to stand up to him. He can't stand anybody defying him."

Maureen nodded. "That's true. And you say they shot at you, Mr. Jensen?"

"Don't worry, I shot back at them," Matt said with a dry chuckle. "I winged the other two, but not Talley. He carried them off while I was in here trying to keep the fire from spreading."

"Do you think they'll come back?"

Matt had thought about the same thing. "After what happened, it's not likely they'd make another try, especially tonight. But it might be a good idea for somebody to stay here and keep an eye on things, just in case. I can do that—"

"You've already done more than enough," Ferguson said. "I'll stay myself."

"I'm not sure that's a good idea, Uncle Colin," Maureen said.

"I plan to have a loaded shotgun in my lap, and plenty of shells close at hand! Anybody who comes messing around here bent on mischief will soon regret it, that I can promise you!"

Matt said, "The hotel's right across the street. I can spell you later on."

"Won't be necessary."

"Are you used to staying up all night and standing guard?"

"Well . . . no."

"Then it won't hurt to switch off. I'll get some sleep and be back later."

"All right. I won't argue with you. But sing out before you come in, just to be sure I don't get nervous while I'm holding that shotgun."

"Count on it," Matt said with a smile.

CHAPTER 7

The rest of the night passed quietly. Several hours after midnight, Matt took over guard duty in the store, as he had promised. Ferguson stumbled off to the hotel, yawning. Matt sat on a crate with the shotgun across his knees and tried not to let the smell of ashes and the charred wood in the floor bother him too much.

Maureen kept her promise as well. When Matt returned to the hotel the next morning, she was waiting for him. She led him into the dining room, where a table was already set for him with platters of flapjacks, bacon, and eggs, along with a pot of strong black coffee. The table was actually set for two, so Matt wasn't surprised when Maureen joined him for breakfast.

The food and coffee revitalized him, and the company put a smile on his face. He told her that nothing else had happened at the store during the night.

"I guess we'll have to be closed for a few days while Uncle Colin has all that damage repaired," she said.

"Does that mean you won't have to work during that time?" Matt asked.

"Oh, I'm sure I'll need to help my uncle go through the stock and weed out the goods that were damaged by smoke or coal oil." Maureen looked curiously across the table at him. "Why do you ask, Matt? What did you have in mind?"

"I thought I might do some riding in the country around here. I wouldn't mind having a pretty girl show me around." He smiled.

She returned the smile and blushed. "That sounds very enjoyable. When would you like to start?"

"Whenever would be convenient for you."

"Let me talk to Uncle Colin. I'm sure he'll be agreeable, considering all you've done for us so far."

After breakfast, Maureen went over to the general store, leaving Matt to stroll around Halltown. Quite a few people recognized him and spoke to him. Between his near shoot-out with Judd Talley the day before and then saving the mercantile, he had gained a certain amount of notoriety in the settlement.

Matt was glad to meet the townspeople. It gave him the opportunity to listen to what they had to say. The subject of Cyrus Longacre usually came up, and it quickly became obvious to Matt that most of Halltown's citizens didn't like the railroad baron and were afraid of Judd Talley and the rest of Longacre's hardcase crew. In most towns, the settlers were thrilled to have the railroad arrive, and that might have been the case if Longacre's men hadn't caused so much trouble.

When Matt dropped by the mercantile in the middle of the day, he found Ferguson and Maureen hard at work sorting through the stock. The carpenter and his helper were there, too, tearing out the fire-damaged wood from the floor and getting ready to replace it. Maureen managed to get a moment alone with Matt on the front porch and told him, "We're just too busy today for me to take off. Would it be all right if we went riding tomorrow?"

"Sure," Matt told her. "I'll be looking forward to it."

A few minutes later, after leaving Maureen at the mercantile, he saw Virginia Barry coming toward him. She wore a fashionable green dress and hat and carried a matching parasol. She smiled as she and Matt met on the boardwalk.

"I saw you talking to the Ferguson girl," Virginia said. "You looked a bit disappointed."

Matt shrugged. "We'd talked about going for a ride, but she has to help her uncle in the store today."

"That's a shame. But if you're still in the mood for female company . . ." Virginia didn't finish the sentence, but Matt thought the invitation was obvious.

"How would Longacre feel about that?" Matt knew from what had happened the night before that Longacre didn't care what Virginia did, as long as he got what he wanted, but he was curious to hear what she would say.

"Cyrus isn't even in town today," Virginia replied. "He took the buggy and drove out to the construction camp at the railhead. He probably won't be back until dark, or maybe even later."

"And you're at a loss for something to do while he's gone, is that it?"

Virginia's tone was cooler as she said, "I'm never at a loss for something to do, Mr. Jensen. I have a very inventive mind."

"I'm sure you do."

"If you'd like to come down to the Sierra House with me, I could demonstrate it for you."

Matt was tempted, as any man would have been, but not for very long. He shook his head. "I'm sorry, Miss Barry. I don't reckon that would be a good idea."

Anger flashed in her eyes. "If you'd just accept Cyrus's job offer, we could both have what we want."

"I doubt that."

Her chin lifted defiantly. "Fine. But Cyrus has a lot of friends in high places, and he's accustomed to getting what he wants. I think you'll discover that you're making a mistake."

"Wouldn't be the first one," Matt drawled.

Virginia flounced off, obviously furious and not trying very hard to conceal it. Several people along the boardwalk noticed her reaction and cast curious glances at Matt, clearly wondering what had happened between the two of them.

Matt ignored the puzzled looks. As far as he was concerned, Virginia had made her play and lost. He was willing to wait for Maureen.

They had breakfast again the next morning, and Matt noticed Maureen was dressed for riding in boots, a split skirt, and a white blouse with a brown leather vest over it. A flat-crowned brown hat sat on the table next to her food.

"I see by your outfit that you're ready to show me around the countryside," he commented as he poured coffee in his cup.

"That's right. Uncle Colin said he could spare me today. We got the damaged stock sorted out yesterday, so today there won't be anything going on except carpentry work. I can't be any help with that."

"Do you have your own horse?"

"I do. A sweet little mare named Daisy. I've been riding ever since I was a little girl. You don't have to worry about me falling off."

"I wasn't worried," Matt assured her.

After breakfast, with Maureen carrying a pair of saddlebags slung over her shoulder, they went to the livery stable. Maureen's horse was there, as well as Matt's sorrel. Matt saddled the animals and led them out of their stalls. He and Maureen mounted up.

"Where would you like to go?" she asked.

"Let's take a look at that railroad," Matt suggested.

Maureen frowned. "Why would you want to go there? We're liable to run into some of Longacre's men."

"We'll keep our distance," Matt promised. "I just want to see how far out from town they are."

That wasn't strictly true. He was actually much more interested in the telegraph wires than he was in the railroad. He had already spotted the poles leading into town, carrying the Western Union lines, and knew the railroad would roughly parallel the route of the telegraph. In many cases, the rails arrived in a settlement first, to be followed by the telegraph, but that wasn't the case with Halltown.

Maureen shrugged. "All right. Just don't blame me if we run into trouble."

"Don't worry, I won't."

They rode out, heading southeast from town. The terrain was a mixture of grassland, rocky ridges, and wide, semi-arid flats. They talked as they rode, Maureen telling Matt about her childhood in Ireland and asking him about his background. He glossed over some of the bloodier parts of his history, like the murder of his family when he was a boy, and concentrated on what it was like being raised by Smoke and Preacher.

"Smoke Jensen the gunfighter?" Maureen asked. "I've heard of him. They say he's killed more men than Wild Bill Hickok!"

"I wouldn't doubt it," Matt said. "But the thing you've got to remember is that Smoke never killed anybody who didn't need killing. He's actually a peaceable sort of hombre as long as nobody pushes him. He doesn't go looking for trouble."

"When I heard your last name is Jensen, I never thought you might be related to Smoke Jensen."

Matt explained there was no blood relation

between him and Smoke, or between him and Preacher, for that matter. Though they didn't share blood, the bonds between them were just as strong as if they did, maybe even stronger. That was how Matt knew he could always count on Smoke and Preacher for help if he needed it.

"What about that fellow Preacher?" Maureen asked. "What's he like?"

Matt grinned. "He's one of a kind, that's for sure. I don't know how old he is, exactly, but he's got to be at least eighty. He's as spry as a man half his age, and as feisty as a bag full of polecats. Smells about as bad sometimes, too, although he'll deny it up one way and down the other. He taught Smoke how to get along out here on the frontier, and Smoke taught me."

"So Preacher is like your grandfather, and Smoke is like your father."

"Well, Smoke's only about eight years older than me, so he's not really old enough to be my pa. More like an older brother, maybe. He's packed a lot of living into those years, though. He and his wife have a ranch in Colorado called Sugarloaf, and he keeps making noises about how he wants to settle down and just be a rancher, but trouble seems to have a way of finding him."

Maureen laughed. "I'd wager you have more than a passing familiarity with trouble yourself, Matt Jensen."

"You could say that," Matt agreed with a grin.

77

After a couple hours of riding, Matt spotted what he was looking for. The telegraph wire dangled loosely from one of the poles, the end trailing on the ground. He could see the next pole, and more broken wire hung from it. He had seen wires downed like that before. Someone had tossed a rope over the wire, dallied the rope around his saddlehorn, and used his horse to pull until the wire snapped, cutting off Halltown from speedy communication with the rest of the world.

If the saboteur had broken the wire in only one place a connection still existed at the last pole before the break. Matt had a telegraph key in his saddlebags, and knew how to shinny up a pole, tie into the wire, and tap out his own messages. But before he did that he wanted to find out more about the situation in those parts.

"I think we've gone far enough this way," he said as he reined in.

Maureen brought her mare to a halt and gave him a puzzled look. "I thought you wanted to see the railroad."

"Women aren't the only ones who can change their minds." He smiled at her, then asked, "Are you in a hurry to get back to town?"

"Actually, no. In fact, I brought some lunch with me. I thought we might stop and eat somewhere."

"That sounds like a fine idea to me. Let's head northwest for a while."

Maureen was still confused. "Back toward town?"

Matt shook his head. "Nope. I thought we'd circle around the settlement. I've got a hankering to take a look at Big Bear Wash."

CHAPTER 8

As they rode, Maureen kept casting thoughtful glances toward Matt, as if she were trying to figure something out. Finally she said, "I know what you're doing."

"Looks to me like I'm riding with a pretty girl," Matt replied with a grin.

"No, I'm serious," Maureen insisted. "You wanted to find the place where the telegraph lines are down. Now you're going to look at Big Bear Wash, where Cyrus Longacre is trying to force the Paiutes off the land they were given by the treaty they signed. What I can't figure out is why you're doing it." She paused, then asked bluntly, "Are you a United States marshal, Matt?"

He let out a laugh. "Me, a federal lawman? Not hardly."

"Then some other sort of government agent, maybe?"

Matt shook his head. "I give you my word,

Maureen, I'm not any kind of a lawman. I didn't come to Halltown to investigate anything. I was just passing through on my way to the mountains so I could get in some hunting and fishing."

"Then why didn't you leave yesterday morning? You could have, you know. There's nothing keeping you here."

"I wouldn't say that."

Maureen blushed under the fine layer of trail dust that covered her face. "If you're staying because of me—"

"That's not exactly it," Matt broke in, "and I swear, I mean no offense by that. Getting to spend more time with you is a mighty good reason for me to hang around this part of the country."

"But it's not the real reason, is it?"

Matt reined in, his expression growing solemn as he did so. Maureen brought her mount to a halt as well.

"No, not really," Matt admitted. He thought Maureen deserved to hear the whole story. "Have you ever heard of something called the Indian Ring?"

Maureen frowned in thought for a moment before saying, "Just vaguely. I recall seeing something about it in one of Uncle Colin's newspapers, I think. He has them sent out here from Boston, where we used to live. The news is weeks or months old before we get the papers, of course." She paused. "The Indian Ring was a group of crooked politicians in Washington, or something like that, wasn't it?"

"Crooked politicians, crooked bureaucrats, crooked businessmen," Matt explained. "They joined forces to rake off hundreds of thousands of dollars worth of graft from the Bureau of Indian Affairs. Most of what they did was actually petty crime, but at such a big scope they wound up stealing a lot of money and causing a lot of misery among the tribes."

"But they're gone now, isn't that right?"

Matt shrugged. "Their chicanery was exposed, that's true. Some of them went to jail, but most of the ringleaders found ways to get around that. A lot of bribes changed hands when that scandal broke. Since then, they've been lying low for a few years, but a while back Smoke, Preacher, and I found out a new Indian Ring is back at work again. We helped put a stop to a land grab they tried to pull off."

"Wait a minute!" Maureen said as understanding dawned on her face. "Are you saying that Cyrus Longacre is part of this new Indian Ring?"

"I don't know," Matt replied honestly, "but I suspect that might be the case. I started wondering about it when I found out Longacre is trying to push the Paiutes off their land so he can build a bridge over Big Bear Wash. He needs that bridge so he can expand his rail line all the way to the big ranches—between Halltown and the mountains."

Maureen nodded. "I know. Chief Walking Hawk probably would have sold him a right-of-way so he could build the bridge, but Longacre wouldn't have that. He just wanted the Paiutes to clear out. That's when Roscoe Goldsmith got involved. He and Uncle Colin are friends."

"He's the lawyer who stood up for the Paiutes?"

"That's right. He sent a wire to Carson City about it . . . and it was only a few hours later that the telegraph went out," Maureen went on in a voice that said she was really beginning to understand what Matt was getting at. "Longacre was afraid Roscoe might do something like that, so he sent his men to pull down those wires!"

"Yeah, I reckon that's what happened. He just wasn't quick enough about it. He probably didn't have any of his gunmen in town at the time, so he had to send word out to the construction camp to bring down the wires. That took a while. I'm just guessing about that, but I'd bet a hat that's what happened."

"And I think you'd win that bet," Maureen agreed. "But how do you know Longacre's part of the Indian Ring, instead of just some greedy, arrogant scoundrel?"

Matt chuckled. "Oh, he's those things, too. But I've been told he has friends in high places, and that smacks of Washington to me. Anyway, whether Longacre is actually part of the Ring or not, he needs to be taken down a peg. Don't get me wrong, it's important to bring in the railroad, but he can't get away with running over innocent people in the process."

"How can you stop him? You're just one man."

"One honest man can make a difference," Matt said. "Three can make an even bigger difference."

"You're talking about Smoke and Preacher?"

Matt nodded. "I figure they'll want to know what's going on here. After that last little dustup, we agreed that we'd let each other know if we ran into the Indian Ring again. As soon as I've talked to Chief Walking Hawk, I plan to get in touch with them."

"How? The telegraph doesn't work."

"It doesn't work in town. Those poles we were looking at earlier are a different story."

"You can get a message out?"

"I think so. If not"— Matt shrugged—"we'll just have to see how much damage one man can do to Longacre's plans, I guess."

Maureen looked at him intently. "Not just one man. You can get help in town. Nobody likes Longacre and his henchmen, especially that Judd Talley." A little shiver went through her as she spoke the big man's name. "What a vicious brute he is."

"I don't want to get any innocent folks hurt."

"You'd risk your own life to help us, but deny us the chance to stand up for ourselves?"

"Let's just see what Chief Walking Hawk has to say before we make any decisions."

They rode on, swinging to the north to circle around Halltown and then heading west again. A couple miles later, they came to Big Bear Wash.

Matt had no idea how the place had gotten its name. Probably something as simple as somebody seeing a big bear wandering along beside the wash or even in it one day. That was usually all it took. The wash itself wasn't anything spectacular. It was about thirty feet deep, maybe sixty wide, with sheer walls and a flat, sandy bottom. Building a trestle to span it wouldn't require any great feats of engineering.

Matt and Maureen sat their horses on the wash's southeastern bank. He asked, "How do the ranchers on the other side get their herds across now?"

"There are places where the banks have caved in and created paths down into the wash," Maureen explained. "It's an obstacle when you're driving cattle, no doubt about that, but not an unsurmountable one. I've heard plenty of cowboys in the store talking about it. They have to be careful of flash floods, but otherwise it doesn't seem to be too difficult."

"The Paiutes don't bother them?"

"There are half a dozen ranches between here and the mountains. The men who own them have made arrangements with Chief Walking

Hawk. His people are allowed to cut out some of the cattle for beef, and other than that they don't bother the herds. From what I've heard, it wasn't like that ten or fifteen years ago, when the ranchers first started to establish themselves in these parts. Back then, there were a lot of fights with the Indians. It's been peaceful for quite a while, though, or at least it was until Cyrus Longacre showed up. He's going to start another Indian war if he keeps trying to push them off their land."

Matt's eyes narrowed as he thought about what Maureen had just said. The old liveryman back in Halltown had made a similar comment about an Indian war breaking out.

Matt realized that might be exactly what Longacre was trying to accomplish. If he could prod the Paiutes into resuming hostilities, Longacre would have a perfect excuse to appeal to the government for help. Then his political cronies in Washington could make some fiery speeches about how the savages were threatening the country's westward expansion, and public sentiment would force the War Department to send in the army to wipe out the Paiutes, leaving Longacre free and clear to do whatever he wanted.

Matt was no starry-eyed idealist. He knew in the continuing conflict between the whites and the Indians, there were good and bad hombres on both sides. He had helped the army fight Indians who lived for nothing more than to torture, mutilate, and kill innocent settlers who were trying to make a new life for themselves in the west. He had watched as promises and treaties were broken, also on both sides. He had heard soldiers bitterly refer to those red warriors as Mister Lo, because of the bleeding-heart newspaper writers back east who proclaimed, "Lo, the poor Indian!" They scribbled their stories about how the noble tribes who wanted only peace were being mistreated, without having even the faintest notion of how bloodthirstily those same tribes had wiped out their enemies in the past.

And behind it all, taking advantage of the situation, spinning webs of greed and deceit like fat spiders, were the politicians, the financiers, the robber barons. Men like Cyrus Longacre, who would stop at nothing to get what they wanted and who would gleefully crush anyone who got in their way.

"Matt . . ."

Maureen's voice broke into his reverie. She sounded worried—a grim cast had settled over his face. He looked at her and smiled.

"It's all right—" he started to tell her.

"I'm not so sure of that," she broke in. "Look."

He saw the way her eyes were slanting behind them, and he hipped around in the saddle. A number of riders had appeared and arranged themselves in a loose half circle pinning Matt and Maureen against the wash. The newcomers had brought their ponies to a halt and sat there watchfully, some of them holding rifles while others gripped long lances that tapered to sharp, deadly points.

They were Paiutes, and they didn't look the least bit friendly.

CHAPTER 9

Matt kept his hands in plain sight as he lifted the reins and turned his horse so he faced the Indians. "Stay behind me," he told Maureen in a quiet, steady voice.

"I'm not afraid of them." Her words were a little shaky despite that declaration. "I've seen Chief Walking Hawk in town. He's an honorable man."

"Is he part of this bunch?"

"Yes, that's him in the middle."

As if the chief had heard them, the rider Maureen indicated moved his horse forward in a slow walk. The buckskin-clad man was big, with a bronzed, hatchet-like face and strands of silver in his thick dark hair. He carried a Winchester in front of him, across his pony's back. He brought the horse to a stop when he was about twenty feet from Matt and Maureen.

Matt lifted his left hand with the open palm out in the universal symbol of peace. "Chief," he said in a clear, calm voice. "My name is Matt Jensen."

Maureen edged her mare to the side so the Indians could see her, even though Matt had told her to stay behind him. They knew she was there anyway. It wasn't like there was any place to hide on the edge of that barren wash.

"Chief Walking Hawk," Maureen said. "I'm Maureen Ferguson from Halltown. My uncle is Colin Ferguson, who owns the hotel and the general store."

The Paiute chief's face was still stony and unreadable. He ignored Maureen and looked at Matt as he asked in more than passable English, "Are you another of Cyrus Longacre's hired killers?"

"Longacre is my enemy," Matt replied with a shake of his head. He pointed to Walking Hawk and then to himself. "That makes us friends, I think. And I'm friends with the man known as White Wolf and Ghost Killer."

Walking Hawk didn't control his reaction soon enough to prevent Matt from seeing the flicker of recognition in his eyes. The Paiutes had heard of Preacher. There probably wasn't a tribe west of the Mississippi that hadn't been visited by the legendary mountain man at one time or another. He was more than a legend to some. To the Blackfeet, Preacher's sworn enemies, the old-timer was considered a supernatural being, a demon who could slip into their camps unseen and unheard, cut the throats of their bravest warriors, and disappear like a phantom, a spectral wind of death blowing in the darkness.

"Ghost Killer is a friend to the Paiutes," Walking Hawk confirmed. "Why are you here, Matt Jensen?"

"Why are you and your men armed for war?" Matt asked in return. They weren't painted for war, but that would be the next step, he suspected.

"Longacre has sent his men to drive us from our land, or to kill us if they fail in that." Walking Hawk's jaw thrust out belligerently. "We will not be driven from our land . . . and they will find that the Paiutes are not so easy to kill."

Matt shook his head. "We don't want Longacre to get away with that, Chief. I'm going to try to stop him."

"We will stop him," Walking Hawk declared. "We will kill any white man who comes on our land, just as they have murdered us!"

Matt rested both hands on the saddlehorn and leaned forward a little as he frowned. "What do you mean by that? I didn't know anybody had been killed out here."

"Twice, hunting parties from our village have been attacked. Men opened fire on them from ridges. The last time, two of our young men were killed."

Matt glanced over at Maureen, who had turned

more pale than normal under the scattering of freckles. He swung his attention back to Walking Hawk. "I'm sorry, Chief. I didn't know that. I don't think anybody in Halltown did."

"This is the first I've heard about it," Maureen added. "I think it's terrible."

"If Longacre wants war, we will give him war," Walking Hawk went on. "Tell the people in the settlement not to come out here anymore. They risk their lives if they do." The sharply-hewn face softened slightly. "The two of you can leave. No one will harm you. But do not come back."

"Chief, I understand how upset you and your people are, but this is the wrong thing to do," Matt insisted. "If you start attacking anybody who comes onto your land, you'll be playing right into Longacre's hands. What about the white cowboys who ride across here? If you kill any of them, the ranchers will turn against you. If you kill Longacre's men, he'll ask the government to send in the army, and the ranchers will back him. All the trust you've built up with the settlers will vanish. Then you really will have a war on your hands . . . and you know it's a war you can't win."

Walking Hawk lifted his rifle in his right hand and shook it. "We can fight! Better to die defending our home than to be shot down like dogs from ambush!"

Matt couldn't argue with that sentiment, but he knew Longacre intended to take advantage of the way the Paiutes felt. He tried another tack. "If you can convince your warriors to wait, I'll send word to Preacher and to another man you may have heard of, Smoke Jensen. Smoke and I are like brothers. He and Preacher will come and help me stop Longacre."

"Can you promise that no more of our young men will die?" Walking Hawk demanded.

Matt's mouth tightened into a grim line. "I can't do that," he admitted. "I don't know how long it'll take Smoke and Preacher to get here. But I'll send word to them today. If Longacre's really trying to provoke an Indian war, there's no time to waste."

"What will you do? Kill Longacre and his men?"

"We'll do whatever it takes," Matt said.

For a long moment, Walking Hawk regarded Matt intently. Then he jerked his head in an abrupt nod. "We will wait . . . for now. But if you are lying to me about Ghost Killer—"

"It's no lie. He'll come, and he'll help you."

Matt hoped that was true. Even though Preacher had seemed to be in splendid health the last time Matt had seen him, the mountain man was getting on in years. There was no telling what might have happened in the months since. The same was true of Smoke, who had never shied away from danger in his life.

"Go now," Walking Hawk commanded. "My warriors will not harm you."

Matt nodded. He turned to Maureen and asked,

91

"Can you get back to town from here by yourself?"

"Of course," she said. "It's not that far. What are you going to do?"

"Remember those telegrams we were talking about earlier? I reckon it's time to send them."

"So you're headed for the telegraph line?"

"That's right."

"Be careful, Matt," she urged him. "Longacre could have men watching the line, just to make sure nobody gets a message out."

Matt smiled. "I'll keep my eyes open, don't worry about that. I'm sort of in the habit of it."

Walking Hawk moved his pony aside and gestured to his men. Matt and Maureen rode past him, away from Big Bear Wash and toward Halltown. The half circle of Paiute warriors broke apart to let them through. Matt felt a stirring of unease as he saw the angry looks on those bronzed faces. He didn't blame them for hating anybody with white skin, but they had to understand that he was on their side.

He urged the sorrel into a trot. Maureen kept the mare even with him. The wash and the Paiutes fell behind. A short time later, the buildings of Halltown came into view in the distance.

Matt lifted a hand and waved Maureen toward the settlement. "I'll see you later!"

"Be careful, Matt!" she told him again.

He smiled and waved as he heeled the sorrel into a gallop.

Smoke would know where Preacher was and how to get word to the old mountain man. Matt could send one wire to Smoke, in care of Sheriff Monte Carson in Big Rock, the town near Smoke's Sugarloaf Ranch. Carson would see to it that Smoke got the message, and Smoke would get in touch with Preacher. Both of them would head for Halltown—or Helltown, a name that would certainly be more fitting if Cyrus Longacre got his way and provoked a bloody Indian war—and they would come a-runnin'.

All Matt had to do was keep the lid on the boiling pot until then.

As Maureen sent the mare Daisy loping toward the settlement, she turned her head to watch Matt Jensen galloping away. She knew there had been plenty of violence between the red men and the white settlers as civilization expanded westward across the continent, but she was horrified by what Chief Walking Hawk had told them about two young men from his tribe being murdered. It was one instance where killing could have been avoided and peace maintained.

It was also about Cyrus Longacre's greed and, perhaps to an even greater extent, his arrogance. He believed Paiute land was his to use any way he wanted, simply because he was rich and powerful and had hired gunmen working for him. That was uncomfortably reminiscent of some of the things Maureen had seen in Ireland, as the English landholders kept their boots on the throats of the Irish peasants.

If anybody could put a stop to Longacre's plans, it was Matt Jensen, she thought. Matt had the confidence, the courage, and the ability, and if his friends Smoke and Preacher were anything like he was, Longacre would have a real fight on his hands. But that depended on Matt being able to get a message to the other two.

The trail Maureen followed took her past a low ridge topped with rugged boulders, dipping into a depression where she could no longer see the settlement. Suddenly a couple horsemen spurred out from behind those boulders and headed down the slope. Daisy shied instinctively as she saw the horses coming toward her. Maureen gasped as she recognized the hard-planed, beard-stubbled faces of the men. They worked for Longacre, and from the looks of it, they were trying to cut her off from town.

She hauled back on the reins as she quickly tried to turn Daisy around.

The men were too close, and were on her before she could wheel the mare and get away. One of them reached out and grabbed the reins, ripping them out of her hand. "Hold on there, girl. Where are you goin' in such an all-fired hurry?"

"Let go of my horse!" Maureen cried. "I have to get back to town."

"No, you have to come with us." The second

man said with an ugly grin. "I reckon the boss is gonna be mighty interested in findin' out why you and that Jensen fella have been gallivantin' around all over the country today."

"You've been following us!" Maureen exclaimed.

"That's right. And I don't figure Mr. Longacre's gonna be too happy when he hears that Jensen's been talkin' to those redskins. That's not a very friendly thing to do after the boss fed him dinner and offered him a job and all."

The hardcase holding Maureen's arms snickered. "From what I hear, that ain't all the boss offered Jensen. Or rather, it was that Barry gal doin' the offerin'."

Maureen felt her face grow warm. She didn't know what had happened between Matt and that blond trollop of Longacre's— probably nothing, she told herself—but she didn't really care at the moment. She just wanted to get away from those men.

"You'd better let me go," she warned. "You'll be in a lot of trouble if you don't."

"Is that so? Who's gonna give us trouble? That tame sheriff?"

"When Matt Jensen finds out about this—"

Maureen stopped short as harsh laughs came from the men. Obviously, they weren't afraid of Matt, and Maureen's eyes widened in fear and shock as she realized why.

They didn't expect Matt Jensen to live through the day.

CHAPTER 10

As Matt pushed the sorrel at a hard run toward the spot southeast of the settlement where the telegraph wires were down, his belly reminded him that he hadn't eaten since breakfast, and it was past midday. That picnic lunch he and Maureen had planned on sharing was still in her saddlebags on Daisy.

It certainly wasn't the first time in his life he'd gone hungry, and it probably wouldn't be the last. A growling stomach in a good cause was nothing to worry about.

As he rode, he thought about the message he would send to Smoke. If he couldn't tie in to the telegraph wire where it was down and get a signal through there, it would mean Longacre's men had sabotaged the wire somewhere else. He would just have to follow the line until he found the last break.

There was no doubt in his mind that Longacre was part of the reborn Indian Ring. If the railroad baron was willing to have his men attack the Paiutes so blatantly in hopes of starting a war that would ultimately involve the army, he had to have the utmost confidence in his Washington connections. That meant the Indian Ring.

Matt saw the telegraph poles ahead of him. Halltown was behind him. Even though a sense of urgency hammered in his brain, he pulled the sorrel back to a walk. The horse was a loyal, valiant companion and would run until its heart gave out if Matt asked it to. But he didn't think it was necessary to ride his horse into the ground. He knew how to put the miles behind him in a hurry by alternating a gallop and a walk, so the sorrel would have a chance to rest a little along the way. Matt swung down from the saddle and walked, too, holding the reins and leading the horse.

Sunlight winked off metal on a knoll a couple hundred yards ahead of him. That split-second reflection was enough to make Matt jerk to his left. At the same time, a puff of smoke jetted from the rocks on top of the knoll. The sharp crack of a rifle shot whipped through the air, and the reins in Matt's right hand gave a violent jerk. He stumbled to his left, thrown off balance by the sudden move, and saw that he still gripped a few inches of the bunched reins.

The bullet that had slashed through the reins would have gone through his body if he hadn't moved so fast.

A second shot blasted out from the knoll. The sorrel whinnied in pain and leaped away, a long, bloody furrow on it's flank. Momentarily maddened by the pain of the wound, the horse stampeded away from Matt.

The rifleman on the knoll had been trying to kill the horse with that second shot, so he could finish off his true quarry at leisure. The sorrel wasn't dead, but the shot had accomplished its purpose anyway. Matt was on foot, armed only with his .44 and Bowie knife, and the closest cover was at least a hundred yards away, a distance he could never cover before the rifleman riddled him with lead.

Or *was* the closest cover a hundred yards away? Matt asked himself that question as he broke into a run. Another slug screamed past his head. High-heeled boots were made for riding, not running, but he managed to work up some pretty good speed as he zigzagged back and forth across the open ground. The threat of imminent death gave wings to the man's feet.

He had spotted a dark, twisting line on the ground, maybe twenty yards away. The possibility existed that it was a narrow gully. As he drew closer, a fourth bullet kicked up dust at his feet. A fifth whipped past his ear.

It *was* a gully, a seam cut in the ground by runoff from one of the region's rare but fierce thunderstorms. No more than three feet deep and about that wide, it was barely big enough for him. But the way it was angled would make it a lot harder for the bushwhacker's lead to find him.

Matt left his feet in a rolling dive. His hat flew off his head, and dust swirled around him. The ground dropped out from under him and he thudded into the gully, coming to a sudden, bone-jarring stop. He stretched out and flattened himself against the hot, sandy dirt.

Shots sprayed out from the top of the knoll, bullets chewing at the top of the gully, bare inches from his head. Matt could tell from the way the rifleman was cranking off the rounds as fast as a Winchester's lever could be worked that the man was angry at his quarry for eluding him, even if it was only for the moment. Closing his eyes to protect them from the flying grit, Matt lay there waiting for the fusillade to run its course.

When the shooting stopped, he fought the impulse to get up and run while the bush-whacker was reloading. The man might have more than one rifle, might just be waiting for Matt to make a break for it.

He looked around, but he couldn't see how far his sorrel had bolted before the animal's panic subsided. If he could get his hands on his own Winchester, it would go a long way toward evening the odds. As far as he could tell from the sound of the shots, there was only one man on the knoll.

He knew that lifting his head would be a good way to get a .44-40 slug drilled through it, so he twisted his neck to look along the gully. He couldn't tell how far it ran, but maybe he could inch his way along until he reached better cover. It was worth a try.

There wasn't much else he could do. He certainly wasn't going to lie there and wait for somebody to come along and kill him.

Using his toes to push himself along and staying as low as possible, Matt worked his way along the shallow slash in the earth. After a moment the rifle on the knoll began to crack again. He could tell from the way the dust flew in a wide swath along the gully that the bushwhacker didn't know where he was anymore. The man was firing blindly. A grim smile tugged at Matt's mouth.

The gully began to curve. Matt's heart leaped as he realized the gully was angling toward the knoll. If it ran far enough in that direction, he might be able to get behind the bushwhacker and turn the tables on the would-be killer.

The shooting continued, but the bullets were landing well behind him. He risked moving a little faster, working hard to keep himself low so the bushwhacker didn't catch a glimpse of him. Matt thought it was a chance worth taking since the man seemed to be looking at other parts of the gully.

Like a snake twisting back and forth, the trench cut its way across the ground. Suddenly, Matt bit back a curse as he saw it was about to peter out. It had curved through an almost ninety-degree angle before it came to an end. The question was whether it had brought him close enough to the knoll to make a dash for it.

The rifle shots stopped again. Matt risked lifting his head and saw that he was about twenty yards away from some boulders clustered at the base of the slope. He wasn't the sort of hombre who endlessly pondered a decision. He thought he could make it, so he quickly got his hands and feet under him, levered himself up and out of the dwindling gully, and launched into a run.

He had covered more than a fourth of the distance to the rocks before the bushwhacker spotted him. Shots roared, coming so close together they sounded almost like a single peal of thunder. Dust and dirt spurted from the ground, and more slugs whipcracked past Matt's head. A few long heartbeats later, he threw himself behind the rocks and knew he was safe. As if to prove that, a slug ricocheted from one of the boulders with a high-pitched scream.

Matt drew his Colt and risked a look. The range was still pretty far for a handgun, but when he saw a flicker of movement on top of the knoll, he triggered two swift shots. The bushwhacker returned the fire as Matt ducked behind the rock.

The rifle fell silent, and the silence stretched into several long minutes. Maybe the bushwhacker was trying to work his way around to a place where he would have a better angle, Matt mused.

Or maybe he lit a shuck out of there rather than taking on his intended victim in a more even fight, Matt thought when he suddenly heard hoofbeats drumming across the rugged terrain. He waited a minute or so, in case it was a trick, then darted from the slab of rock where he had taken cover to another boulder where he could see the flats on the other side of the knoll.

A lone rider was galloping east, pushing his mount hard. He was already several hundred yards away. At that distance it was difficult to be sure, but Matt thought the hombre was pretty big.

Judd Talley. Matt's eyes narrowed as the name went through his brain. It made sense. Despite his noncommittal stance the night before, Longacre must have figured out there was no way on God's green earth Matt was going to work for him. Sensing a threat, Longacre must have told Talley to follow him and dispose of him if possible.

Did that mean Talley had been following him and Maureen earlier in the day? Had Talley been alone, or did he have more of Longacre's men with him? Men he could have sent after Maureen . . .

A cold finger of fear for the lovely young woman trailed along Matt's spine. He wanted to rush back to Halltown and make sure she was all right.

But now that Longacre had tried to have him killed, the gloves were off, and it was more important than ever that he get word of the brewing trouble to Smoke and Preacher. Matt was enough of a realist to know he might not survive open warfare with Talley and the rest of Longacre's gun crew. If he wound up dead, Smoke and Preacher would have to take up the fight.

With his lips a tight, bleak line, Matt punched out the two empties from his .44 and thumbed in fresh cartridges to replace them. Then he holstered the gun and looked around for his sorrel. He spotted the horse grazing contentedly about two hundred yards away and trudged in that direction, picking up his hat along the way.

The sorrel had calmed down and didn't shy away. Matt patted the horse on the shoulder and frowned at the bullet graze in the sleek hide. "We'll get that tended to as soon as we can. I'm sorry, but right now I've got to get that message through."

He swung up into the saddle and sent the horse running southeast again along the line of telegraph poles. After what seemed like longer than it probably was, he reached the place where the line was down.

"Should've sent the wire when I was here this morning," he muttered disgustedly to himself as he dismounted and reached into his saddlebags for his telegraph key. He had gotten the key and learned how to tie in to the singing wires while he was scouting for the army. He stowed the apparatus inside his shirt, took off his hat and boots, and walked over to the pole. He hoped that junction box at the top was live.

Shinnying up one of these rough wooden poles without climbing gear took a lot of strength and effort and usually left a man with splinters in his hands and feet. Matt ignored the stinging pain and worked his way up. About halfway to the top, the thought occurred to him that he'd make a heck of a target up there. Since he couldn't do anything about that, he continued up the pole, trying not to think about it.

Sweat coated his face and soaked his shirt by the time he reached the top. Wrapping his legs around the pole and his left arm around the crosspiece he used his right hand to get the key out of his shirt. He twisted the wires from the key around the terminals on the junction box, braced the key against the crosspiece, and tapped out a signal. He paused to wait for a response, experiencing a few agonizing moments before the key began to clatter. Matt translated the code in his head, then asked the sender to identify himself. *C-a-r-s-o-n—C-i-t-y* came back to him.

He began pounding out his message in a rough but serviceable hand, addressing it to Smoke Jensen, care of Sheriff Carson, Big Rock, Colorado. The gist of it was that Smoke should find Preacher and get to Halltown, Nevada, as fast as he could. Trouble was brewing. Matt didn't say anything about the Indian Ring, but he figured Smoke would realize that crooked bunch had to be involved somehow, otherwise Matt wouldn't be asking for help. He signed the message *M-a-t-t*, then asked the key-pounder on the other end for confirmation. After a moment, the operator acknowledged and sent the series of dots and dashes that meant the message had been passed on to its destination. Matt heaved a sigh of relief.

He unhooked the key from the junction box and stowed it in his shirt again. Climbing down the pole was almost as arduous a task as climbing up it. But a few minutes later his feet were on the ground again.

He didn't waste any time as he pulled on his boots, put the telegraph key back in his saddlebags, and settled his hat on his head. "Sorry I have to keep asking you to do more," he said to the sorrel as he put his foot in the stirrup and reached up to grasp the saddlehorn. "But I've got to get back to town as fast as I can and make sure Maureen's all right."

If she wasn't, a whole heap of powder was about to be burned, he vowed. And he wasn't going to wait for Smoke and Preacher.

About five miles away, at the railroad construction camp, a man sat at a scarred desk in the caboose of the work train and laboriously printed words on a piece of paper with a stub of a pencil. On the desk in front of him was a telegraph key, and the wires leading from it ran out the window and up to a junction box on top of a nearby pole. The man had been surprised when the key suddenly chattered to life a few minutes earlier. He hadn't tried to cut into the exchange, but had listened to the messages passing back and forth. Years of experience as a telegrapher meant he had memorized them without even thinking about it. Maybe not verbatim, but pretty blasted close, and he was writing out the words before he forgot them.

When he finished, he stood up and went to the rear of the caboose, taking the paper with him as he stepped onto the car's platform. He called out to one of the workmen passing by the train, "Hey! Go find Mr. Longacre, Benjy. I got something here I think he's gonna want to see!"

CHAPTER 11

Maureen tried not to let her fear get the best of her as she sat on an unsteady three-legged stool in an old abandoned cabin not far outside Halltown. One of the early settlers had lived there. She didn't know whether something had happened to the man or if he had just moved on for some reason, but the one-room shack was empty and had been ever since she and her uncle had come to the settlement. It was slowly falling into ruin.

It was a good place for her captors to hold her prisoner, far enough from town that nobody really paid any attention to it. If she screamed, someone in the settlement *might* hear her, but the two hard-cases had warned her it would go badly for her if she did.

She told herself they wouldn't really hurt her. This was the West, after all. Anyone who harmed a decent woman would be hunted down relentlessly and dealt with ruthlessly. Even the most hardened outlaw was usually respectful to women.

She wasn't sure those two had ever figured that out, though. They had leered at her constantly during the ride, and the one who stood on the other side of the room watched her with undisguised lust in his eyes.

But so far neither of them had touched her.

Maureen knew the man's partner had ridden to town, checking to see if Cyrus Longacre had returned yet from the railroad construction camp.

Longacre must be getting desperate if he'd go so far as to have his men kidnap her, she thought. Of course, it was possible he hadn't given that order. The two men could have made that decision on their own.

Desperate . . . or confident? Her spirits sank even lower when she asked herself that question. With the sheriff and the judge under his thumb, Longacre might feel that he could get away with whatever he wanted. So far there wasn't a lot of evidence to dispute that.

If something had happened to Matt . . . if more of Longacre's men had followed him and killed him . . . then there wasn't much hope. Cyrus Longacre's word, backed by the guns of his hired killers, truly would be the only law in that part of Nevada.

Fear and pain twinged inside Maureen as she thought about Matt. She wished she knew where he was and whether he was all right.

A rataplan of hoofbeats sounded outside the shack. Maureen's head lifted as a few feeble stirrings of hope went through her. Maybe Matt had found her—

It wasn't Matt who pulled the sagging door open and stepped into the shack. "Longacre's not back yet, and neither's Judd," the hardcase announced.

The guard nodded toward Maureen. "Then what do we do with her?"

"Looks like we'll have to hang on to her a while longer."

"Reckon we can do anything to help pass the time?" An ugly grin accompanied the suggestive words.

The hardcase shook his head. "Nix that. The boss can fix a lot of things, but I reckon molestin' a woman's still a quick way to meet the hangman." The man crossed his arms over his chest and gave Maureen a baleful stare. "No, we'll wait. Once we know for sure that Jensen's dead . . . well, we'll see."

So Matt might still be alive, Maureen thought. She was going to cling to that hope as long as she possibly could.

Because she knew if breath remained in Matt Jensen's body, he would come to help her.

From the top of a hill about a quarter mile away, Matt watched the shack through a pair of field glasses he had taken from his saddlebags. He had seen the man ride up and enter the dilapidated old building a few minutes earlier, and had gotten a good enough look at the hombre's unshaven face to recognize the type. The low-slung revolver on the man's hip was further evidence that Matt was looking at one of Cyrus Longacre's gun-wolves.

He had a distinctly uneasy feeling Maureen was inside that shack with at least two of Longacre's hired killers.

Matt had been on his way back to Halltown when it had occurred to him to cut across to the spot where he had parted company with Maureen. If she had made it back to town safely, then everything was fine. But if she hadn't . . . if some of Longacre's men had grabbed her, which was possible since it appeared the hired guns might have been trailing them all day . . . it would be easier to pick up her trail there.

Hope for the best but prepare for the worst.

That was another lesson Smoke and Preacher had taught him.

Matt hadn't had any trouble finding the spot he was looking for, and had followed the tracks left by Maureen's horse. For a while it had looked like everything was fine and she had headed back to the settlement without any trouble.

But he noticed the tracks of two other horses coming from the direction of a rocky ridge nearby. He could tell from the muddle of tracks and the horse droppings that Maureen had stopped, and all three horses had milled around some.

Then all three riders had gone on toward Halltown, with the distinctive hoofprints of the mare Daisy between the tracks left by the other two horses.

Matt had a hunch Maureen was a prisoner of the two men who had stopped her on the trail.

With anger and worry growing inside him, he followed the tracks, pushing the sorrel as hard as he dared considering the horse's played-out condition. When they were still about a mile from the settlement, the three riders had veered off the trail and headed north. Matt pressed on, and after a few minutes he'd spotted the isolated cabin.

Charging full-blast into that old shack without knowing exactly what the situation was inside might get Maureen killed. As soon as he was certain the tracks led to the cabin, he had circled around to come at the cabin from a different direction. Leaving the sorrel on the other side of the hill where it couldn't be seen from the shack, he'd taken the field glasses and climbed to the top. A few minutes later, the hardcase arrived from the direction of town.

Matt figured he was outnumbered. It was just a matter of by how much.

He focused the field glasses on the broken window and strained to see inside the cabin through the sections where the grimy glass no longer existed. At first all he could make out was an occasional movement. He continued watching, convinced Maureen was in there, and after several minutes he was rewarded by a brief flash of red hair. His heart slugged hard in his chest. She was in the shack, all right, with at least two of Longacre's men.

Matt lowered the glasses and looked down the hill at his sorrel, ground-hitched, with its head down in exhaustion. He would leave the mount there, he decided, and approach the old cabin on foot.

There wasn't much cover around the place, but the rear wall didn't have any windows in it. If he went in from that direction, the men inside the ramshackle building couldn't see him unless they happened to catch a glimpse through a knothole or a crack between two boards. It was his best chance. He went back down the hill, stowed away the field glasses, and paused for a second

111

to look at the butt of his Winchester sticking up from the saddle boot.

He decided to leave the rifle where it was. It was going to be close work, and the .44 was best for that. Any closer and he had the Bowie knife sheathed on his left hip.

Matt trotted around the hill, slowing down and being careful as the shack came into view again. He drew his gun as he moved quickly but quietly toward the shack. When he reached the old building, he saw two horses were picketed on the far side, where he hadn't been able to see them before. Daisy was one of them, further confirmation that Maureen was inside.

He stopped, took off his hat, and leaned close to the wall. Time and weather had warped and swollen the planks. He put his eye to one of the cracks and peered into the shack.

His jaw tightened as he saw Maureen sitting on a rickety old stool. Rays of sunlight slanted down around her through holes in the rotten roof. One of the men was to her left, perched on the edge of a table the owner had left when he abandoned the cabin. The other man was off to the right, bent over rummaging around in what appeared to be an old grub box.

"You don't really think you're gonna find anything fit to eat in there, do you?" the man sitting on the table asked.

"You never can tell," the other man said.

"Might be a can of peaches or tomatoes, and they'd be all right as long as they were still sealed up, I reckon. I'm hungry. We didn't get any lunch, you know, because we were followin' Jensen and this red-headed gal."

"Yeah, I know. I was there, remember?"

"How long do you think it'll take for the boss to get back?"

"I don't have any idea. By nightfall, I expect."

The hardcase continued pawing through the debris left in the grub box. "I'll have to wait until then to eat—"

His complaint stopped short as he let out an ear-splitting screech.

Leaping down from the table, his partner yelled, "What in blazes!" His hand went to the gun on his hip.

The hardcase reared up and stumbled back from the grub box. "It got me!" he howled as he gave his right hand a frenzied shaking. "Biggest damn scorpion I ever saw! It got me!"

The man's partner lowered his gun and said disgustedly, "You blamed fool! Is that all?"

"Is that all?" the stung man repeated in a wounded tone. "It hurts like a son of a—"

His companion had turned his back on Maureen, and before either of them knew what was happening, she leaped to her feet, snatched up the stool she had been sitting on, and brought it crashing down on the man's head.

CHAPTER 12

Matt moved before the blow even fell. Gripping his Colt tightly, he raced around the shack and reached the front in time to see the door burst open. Maureen ran out with lines of fear etched on her face. In her terror, she wasn't thinking straight, and dashed blindly away from the shack. She didn't try to reach the horses.

Yelling curses, the man she hit raced out of the shack and ran after her. Matt lifted his gun to shoot him, but remembered the other hardcase was still inside. Drawing back, he concealed himself at the corner of the building.

It took the man only a few strides to catch up to Maureen. He reached out and grabbed her arm, jerking her to a stop. "You blasted little hellcat!" he bellowed.

The hardcase came out of the cabin, shaking his injured hand. "Did you get her? Did you—"

"Hold it!" Matt stepped into the open and leveled his Colt.

Both men twisted toward him. The one holding Maureen's arm let go and reached for his gun. The other man clawed at the butt of his revolver, handicapped by his swollen finger.

"Maureen, get down!" Matt shouted. He took

out the man closest to her first, slamming a couple slugs into the hombre's chest just as the man cleared leather. The .44 bucked in Matt's hand as he pivoted toward Scorpion Man and squeezed off a shot. He would have liked to take one of them alive, but Scorpion Man's gun came up fast, sting or no sting. His gun roared but he was already twisting around from the impact of Matt's slug driving into his body. His shot went wild, screaming off harmlessly into the air. He buckled to his knees and pawed at his chest for a second before blood bubbled from his mouth and he pitched forward on his face.

"Stay there!" Matt shouted to Maureen, who had thrown herself to the ground and rolled several yards away, out of the line of fire. He hurried forward and kicked the fallen guns out of reach of the men he had shot. Keeping his gun ready, he checked both men. They were dead, each man drilled through the breast pocket of his shirt.

As he reloaded his Colt, he asked Maureen, "Are you all right? Did they hurt you?"

She pushed herself up on one arm and shook her head. "No, I'm fine, Matt. They didn't do anything except threaten me. At least, not until that one grabbed me just now. I may have a few bruises from that."

He holstered his gun and went over to her to help her up. When she was on her feet again, she went on, "What about you? They seemed convinced you were dead."

"I almost was. Somebody ambushed me while I was on my way to the telegraph line. I think it was Judd Talley."

"You didn't kill him?"

Matt glanced at the bodies of the two men and shook his head. "No, I'm afraid not. He got away."

"But he tried to kill you. Longacre told him to murder you and sent these men to kidnap me. We can get the law on him now!"

Matt hated to dash her hopes, but he knew how such things worked. Sure, it would be obvious to any reasonable person that Longacre was behind the violence that had happened, but there were no witnesses to prove it. No one who would be willing to testify in a court of law could say that Longacre had given the orders, and Longacre would claim that his men had acted on their own and been overzealous in kidnapping Maureen. As for the attempt on Matt's life, well, who was to say that such a thing had actually happened? A smart lawyer—and Longacre wouldn't have any other kind working for him—would blow any case against the railroad baron right out of the water.

The eager smile disappeared from Maureen's face as she looked at him. "What is it, Matt? Isn't this a good thing?"

"It's good that you and I are still alive," he told her, "but this isn't going to help us put a stop to Longacre's plans. We'll have to flush him out into the open even more before we can get the law on our side. Right now it's still backing him."

"But . . . but that's not right!" Maureen paused and then let out a bitter laugh. "I'm being foolish, aren't I, thinking the world should be fair and that right should prevail."

"It usually does. Sometimes it just takes a little longer. In the meantime, the fact that those men grabbed you will at least make Longacre look bad. It might help some folks who hadn't made up their minds about him yet decide that he's really a polecat. That can't hurt anything."

Some movement in the direction of Halltown caught Matt's eye. He saw a man striding toward the cabin and recognized the bulky figure of Sheriff Walt Sanger. Several citizens followed him. The sound of the shots had reached the settlement, and they were coming to see what all the commotion was around the old shack that should have been empty and deserted.

"Are you going to get in trouble for shooting those men?" Maureen asked worriedly.

Matt shook his head. "No, it was self-defense. Besides, they kidnapped a woman. Not even Longacre will raise too much of a stink about them getting killed."

As it turned out, Longacre didn't raise any stink at all. He disavowed any knowledge of what the two men had done and in fact claimed he had fired them several days earlier.

"If they stayed around these parts, they must have been planning on causing trouble," Longacre declared as he stood in the sheriff's office, "but I didn't have anything to do with it."

Judd Talley stood behind Longacre, thumbs hooked in his gunbelt and a smug grin on his face. Sanger sat behind the desk, and Matt was off to one side with Maureen and her uncle. Colin Ferguson had a protective arm around Maureen's shoulders.

"That's a lie," Ferguson said. "Maureen heard those scalawags talking about their boss. That's you, Longacre."

Calmly, Longacre shook his head. "They may have had some far-fetched notion that kidnapping your niece would somehow get them back in my good graces and cause me to rehire them, Ferguson, but I can hardly be held responsible for such madness."

"What Mr. Longacre is sayin' makes sense." Sheriff Sanger rested his hands palms down on the desk. "I don't reckon there's any need to bother him anymore. The varmints are dead, and all that's left is for the undertaker to plant 'em."

"As a goodwill gesture, I'll pay for the burials," Longacre said. "That'll save the town the expense."

Sanger pushed himself to his feet. "That's mighty generous of you, Mr. Longacre."

Ferguson shook his head and made a disgusted noise in his throat.

Maureen said, "But what about—"

Matt closed his hand lightly on her arm to silence her. He knew she was about to bring up the ambush. Nothing had been said about that so far, and he thought they might as well leave it that way. It would be his word against Talley's, and he knew who Sanger would believe.

"Sorry to bother you with all this," Sanger went on to Longacre. "You can go on about your business now."

"No bother." Longacre smiled, then nodded to Matt, Maureen, and Ferguson. He put on his hat and jerked his head at Talley. "Come on, Judd."

When the two of them were gone, Ferguson said to Sanger, "Is that all you're going to do, Sheriff? You're just going to take Longacre's word for it? Really?"

Sanger thrust out his jaw defiantly. "I got no reason to doubt Mr. Longacre. He's a mighty successful businessman."

"That doesn't mean he's not a blasted liar!"

"You better not go around town talkin' like that," Sanger said. "That's liable to get you in trouble. There's laws against such things, you know."

Ferguson's face flushed so darkly with rage

119

that he looked like he was about to pop a blood vessel. He started toward the desk, but Matt got between him and the sheriff.

"Maureen, you'd better take your uncle back over to the hotel," he said. "Everybody needs to calm down."

Maureen looked almost as angry as Ferguson, but she nodded and took hold of his arm. "Come on, Uncle Colin." Ferguson continued to mutter under his breath, but he allowed her to steer him out of the sheriff's office.

Sanger said, "Do you plan on movin' on any time soon, Jensen?"

Matt turned toward him and asked coolly, "Why do you want to know, Sheriff?"

"Because ever since you showed up in Halltown, trouble's been poppin' right and left! I got a feelin' that as long as you're here, it's gonna be Helltown, all right."

"Maybe you'd better ask yourself where the trouble's really coming from, Sheriff," Matt advised as he put his hat on. "But then, I think you already know, don't you?"

He strode out of the office before Sanger could do anything else except sputter.

Matt paused on the boardwalk outside. Night was settling over the town. He moved so he wasn't silhouetted against the light from the window. He wouldn't put it past Talley or another of Longacre's men to take a potshot at him.

One thing was certain, Matt thought. It wasn't over. He had killed two of Longacre's men and had frustrated the man's attempt to get rid of him. Not only that, but Longacre was aware by now that he had been talking to the Paiutes. Longacre was smart enough to know Matt would keep causing him trouble unless he was put out of the way. So it was just a matter of time until Longacre made another try for him.

Something else was certain, Matt corrected himself. If his wire reached Smoke, and Smoke knew where to find Preacher, they would be heading for "Helltown" hellbent-for-leather.

Matt smiled faintly. And Sheriff Sanger thought he'd already seen trouble.

"Let me bring every man we can spare from the camp," Judd Talley suggested. "Jensen can't kill all of them."

They were in Longacre's suite at the Sierra House. The railroad baron paced angrily back and forth across the sitting room rug, a cigar clamped between his teeth. He swung around toward Talley, who was sprawled in one of the armchairs.

"What would you have them do?" Longacre asked around the cigar. "Drag Jensen into the street and beat him to death with sledge-hammers?"

"That would get rid of him," Talley said.

"Yes, in full view of the town, you idiot,"

Longacre snapped. "My associates back in Washington insist we maintain at least an appearance of legality. They were lucky not to be sent to prison when their arrangement was broken up a few years ago. They don't want to risk being exposed again."

"Then we've got to get rid of Jensen," Talley argued. "He's the only one who's got the guts to do anything. As soon as he's dead, everybody else around here will fall right back into line, the way they were before."

Longacre puffed on the cigar for a moment, then stabbed it out viciously in a silver ashtray. "Don't forget about that wire he sent to those friends of his. They caused all sorts of trouble for one of our partners in Wyoming a while back. Reese Bannerman's dead, in fact."

"We don't know they're coming here," Talley pointed out. "All we know for sure is that Jensen got that telegram out."

"Yes, thanks to the fact that you failed to kill him," Longacre said scathingly.

Talley's face flushed, and for a second Longacre thought he might have pushed the giant gunman too far. Talley got control of himself and said, "What we need to do is make sure Smoke Jensen and Preacher never get here if they start in this direction. I could ride back out to the camp and send some wires of my own to a few friends of mine who are good at things like that."

Longacre started to make a comment about hoping Talley's friends were better than he was at killing the men they set out to kill, but thought better of it. He nodded and said in a conciliatory tone, "That's a good idea, Judd. Why don't you go ahead and take care of that?"

"All right." Talley reached for his hat on the table next to his chair and stood up. "But what about Matt Jensen?"

At that moment, the door to the bedroom opened and Virginia Barry strolled out. Her blond hair was loose around her shoulders, and she wore a thin silk wrapper that didn't conceal much of the bare flesh underneath it when she moved. She gave Talley a casual smile and didn't seem bothered to be so scantily clad in front of him.

A smile slowly stretched across Longacre's face. He slid another cigar from his vest pocket and told Talley, "Leave Jensen to me. I've got an idea. . . ."

CHAPTER 13

Matt expected to have to fight a holding action against Longacre's schemes until Smoke and Preacher arrived, but to his surprise, Halltown was so peaceful nobody had any reason to call it Helltown. The day after the shoot-out at the old shack, Cyrus Longacre made a show of driving out of town in his buggy, taking Judd Talley with him. Longacre told several people he was going out to the construction camp and intended to stay there for a while as workers continued building the railroad toward the settlement. Matt suspected some sort of trick, but neither Longacre nor Talley showed their face in town, nor did any of Long-acre's other hired guns.

Virginia Barry was still staying in the suite at the Sierra House, so Matt knew Longacre would be back sooner or later.

Knowing he was running a risk Matt rode out to Big Bear Wash. The watchful Paiutes saw him coming, and he found himself surrounded by grim-faced warriors. He coolly asked to be taken to Chief Walking Hawk, and was soon in the Paiute village, several miles up the wash from the spot where Longacre wanted to cross it with a trestle.

Walking Hawk confirmed there had been no more trouble from Longacre's men. The cowboys from the ranches were steering clear of Paiute land for the time being, probably on orders from their bosses to stay out of harm's way until the trouble was ironed out. Walking Hawk didn't believe for a second that Longacre had given up on his plans, and neither did Matt. But there was nothing to be done except wait to see what happened.

And wait for Smoke and Preacher to come riding in, armed for war and ready to burn some powder.

Matt spent quite a bit of time with Maureen and her uncle, and enjoyed getting to know them better. He learned that Ferguson's leg injury had happened when he was a boy in Ireland. He had fallen off a wagon, and one of the wheels had rolled over his leg, snapping the bone. The injury had healed, but Ferguson had been left with the bad limp he'd had ever since.

It hadn't stopped him from immigrating to America with his brother's family, including Maureen, who had been just a little girl at the time. A couple years later, a fever that swept through Boston had killed her parents and her brothers and sisters, leaving her alone. Ferguson had taken over raising her, and as far as Matt could see, the man had done a good job of it. Maureen was as fine a young woman as anybody could ever want to meet. Most men would have started thinking about marriage if they got to know her.

But not Matt. The urge to drift was still too strong in him. Someday he might put down roots, the way Smoke had done with Sally on Sugarloaf, but that day was still far in the future.

Despite that, Matt enjoyed Maureen's company and even helped her some in the store once the repairs had been made and the mercantile was open for business again. Preacher would have gotten a big kick out of seeing him in a clerk's apron, Matt thought, and that was the only reason he was glad Smoke and Preacher hadn't shown up yet. The salty old codger never would have let him hear the end of it.

An atmosphere of peace might have descended on the settlement, but Matt knew better than to let his guard down. He remained alert, and was ready for trouble when he heard footsteps on the boardwalk close behind him a week after Longacre and Talley had left town. He stopped and turned quickly, his hand moving to his gun in a blur of speed.

He stopped short with the .44 half drawn as Virginia Barry gasped in surprise and fell back a step. "Mr. Jensen . . . Matt! It's me! Don't shoot."

The tension that gripped Matt's muscles eased, but not completely. Virginia was mixed up with Cyrus Longacre, and for that reason he couldn't completely trust her, even though he didn't regard her as much of a threat.

"Sneaking up on a fella like that is a good way to get shot." He let his gun slide back into leather.

"I didn't sneak up on you. I was just coming out of the milliner's when I saw you going by."

Matt glanced at the window of the building. It was indeed the milliner's shop, the only one in Halltown. He hadn't paid any attention to it as he went past, since he wasn't likely to be needing a lady's hat any time in the foreseeable future.

His natural politeness made him reach up and take off his Stetson. He held it in his left hand as he said, "Sorry. I didn't mean to startle you, Miss Barry."

"You can call me Virginia," she said with a smile.

"I don't know how your friend Longacre would feel about that."

The smile vanished as her lips pressed together in anger. "I don't think I care very much how Cyrus feels about anything anymore."

"Trouble?" Matt asked dryly.

"He went off and *abandoned* me here! I'm sure this is a perfectly nice little town, but there's nothing to do here. I'm used to going to the theater, and to elegant restaurants, and . . . and all the sorts of places they don't have in a frontier hamlet like this!"

"Sorry," Matt said again, although he really didn't care. "I'm sure Longacre will be back soon."

"I wouldn't be so sure of that. I wouldn't be surprised if he's gone back to Reno and just deserted me here."

"Why would he do that?"

"Well, you have to admit, the people around here have been pretty hostile to him. I don't understand it. You'd think they would be grateful. He's bringing in the railroad, after all."

"They're grateful for the railroad," Matt said, "just not for all the trouble Talley and the rest of those gunslingers have caused."

"Those were just misunderstandings," Virginia insisted.

"And they don't want Longacre getting the Paiutes so stirred up that another Indian war breaks out," Matt went on.

"I wouldn't think people would care so much about a bunch of savages."

"Chief Walking Hawk and the rest of the Paiutes just want to be left alone."

Virginia shook her head. "I don't want to argue about this, Matt. When I saw you passing by, I thought it would be nice to have dinner with you."

"Why me?" Matt asked with a frown.

"Because I can tell that you've seen more of the world than the yokels who live here. Despite your rugged exterior, you're a man of culture and breeding, Matt."

He couldn't keep himself from laughing. "No offense, Miss Barry—"

"Virginia," she insisted.

"All right. No offense, Virginia, but you couldn't be any more wrong about me. Yeah, I've been around some and seen the elephant, I guess, but my whole life has been pretty hardscrabble. I haven't had time to worry about things like culture and breeding."

"Then you won't have dinner with me?"

Matt thought about Maureen and shook his head. "Sorry, but no."

She stepped closer to him and brought her hand

up, moving quickly enough that she took him by surprise. Her palm slapped him across the face with a loud crack that caused several people walking past in the street to look around.

"How dare you talk to me like that!" she shouted.

Taken aback, Matt stood there blinking like an idiot. He didn't know what he had done to make Virginia so mad. It didn't seem likely that a woman such as her would be so offended by the simple refusal of a dinner invitation, but maybe she really was scared that Longacre had left her and wasn't coming back for her.

With his jaw set tight, Matt clapped his hat back on his head. "I'd better be going."

"You'll be sorry, Matt Jensen," Virginia said hotly. "Mark my words, you'll be sorry."

"I already am," he muttered as he turned away.

It was tempting to think women were just loco, he thought. But that wasn't fair. One of these days he'd ask Preacher about it, he told himself. The old mountain man would claim to have the answer, whether he really did or not!

Matt had supper as usual that evening with Maureen and her uncle in the hotel dining room. He didn't say anything about Virginia Barry approaching him earlier. That might upset Maureen when there was no good reason for it.

After the meal, Colin Ferguson asked Matt to

come up to their living quarters for a drink, but Matt shook his head and declined. "I'm a little tired tonight. I think I might just turn in early. Sorry."

"No need to apologize, lad," Ferguson said. "That's certainly your prerogative."

Matt said his good nights and headed upstairs. As he approached the door of his room, a warning instinct stirred inside him. He looked closely at the door, lowering his gaze to a spot a few inches above the floor.

Whenever he stayed in a hotel, he was in the habit of sticking a small, broken piece of a match between the door and the jamb when he left the room. It was unlikely anybody would notice the match, and if the door was opened by someone other than him, it dropped to the floor and warned him that somebody had been in his room . . . and might still be in there.

The match was where it was supposed to be. Nobody was waiting inside to ambush him.

Then why were those alarm bells going off in his brain?

Matt sniffed the air, thinking he might catch a whiff of tobacco smoke or other telltale odor drifting under the door. There was no balcony outside the single window in his room, but somebody could have gotten in that way, he supposed. It would be difficult but not impossible.

He didn't smell anything unusual. "You're

getting touchy in your old age," he muttered to himself under his breath. Despite that, he used his left hand to unlock the door and open it, keeping his right hand on the butt of the .44.

Light from the hallway spilled into the room. Matt stiffened as he saw a folded piece of paper lying on the floor. He stepped inside, leaving the paper where it was for the moment, and lit the lamp on the bedside table before he closed the door. He took a look around just to make sure the place was empty.

He was the only one there. The gap between the floor and the bottom of the door was big enough that somebody could have slid the paper through it. Finally he picked up the note and sat down on the edge of the bed. The paper was sealed with a small blob of wax. As he broke the seal and unfolded the paper, he smelled a faint scent of perfume.

Virginia, he thought. Had to be.

He thumbed his hat to the back of his head and started reading the words written on the paper in a precise hand with a definite feminine slant.

Matt,

I'm sincerely sorry for that scene earlier. I don't know what got into me. I'm very frightened, but not that Cyrus won't come back. I'm afraid that he *will* come back, because I know what he has planned, and it's terrible. He's going to recruit enough gunmen to wipe out the Indians once and for all. Before he left, I told him I wouldn't have any part of it, and he threatened me. Please, Matt, if you'll promise to protect me, I'll tell the sheriff and the judge everything. I know some of the other things Cyrus and that brute Talley have done. Please come to the Sierra House and I'll tell you everything. Come tonight, and bring this letter with you because I don't want it falling into the hands of any of Cyrus's spies. You didn't know he has spies here in town, did you? I'll tell you who they are, and everything else, if you'll just come to see me as soon as you get this. I'm begging you.

Virginia

Matt stared at the note for several more seconds, then grunted and shook his head. Did she really expect him to believe any of that hogwash?

It was a trap, pure and simple, and Virginia was the bait. Talley had probably slipped back into town and was waiting in Longacre's suite at the Sierra House for Matt to show up. Virginia would let him in, and then Talley would step up behind him, gun or knife in hand . . .

But what if it *wasn't* a trap, a persistent part of his mind asked? What Virginia had written about Longacre coming back with enough gunmen to wipe out the Paiutes sounded like it could be true.

Would Sheriff Sanger believe that if Virginia told him about it? Even if he did, what could the sheriff do against a small army of gunslingers?

He could deputize all the able-bodied men in town, Matt thought, himself included. Such a posse could give Longacre a lot hotter reception than he was expecting. Maybe it was worth talking to Virginia, just to be sure.

But he wasn't going to forget his hunch about a trap. He wasn't going to waltz in blindly.

He folded the paper and stuck it in his shirt pocket. The notion that Longacre had people in town who were working secretly for him was an intriguing one. Matt wanted to find out if that was true.

After putting the match back between door and jamb, he went downstairs, luckily not encountering Ferguson or Maureen on the way. He didn't want to have to explain to them why he was going back out after he had told them he was turning in for the night.

Some people were still out and about, but Halltown was settling down for the night. Matt walked to the Sierra House and entered the hotel with a nod for the sleepy clerk behind the desk. As he started up the stairs, he thought maybe he should have come in the back way. Then he discarded the idea. He didn't have any reason to be skulking around.

The second-floor corridor was deserted. His

hand rested lightly on the butt of his .44 as he walked toward the big door at the end of the hall. When he got there, he used his left hand to knock.

"Virginia?" he called quietly. "It's Matt Jensen."

It was going to be awkward if Longacre had shown up again, he thought. Virginia might not have expected that.

No one came to the door. Matt leaned closer and listened but didn't hear a sound from inside the suite. He knocked harder, thinking that Virginia might be in one of the other rooms.

Still no response.

It couldn't be an ambush if no one let him into the room, he told himself. Maybe he'd been wrong about it being a trap. He was about to knock again when he paused and sniffed the air, like he had outside the door of his own room in the Ferguson Hotel.

He smelled something that made the hair on the back of his neck stand up.

It was a coppery tang that he had smelled before. As soon as he realized what it was, he reached down with his left hand, grasped the doorknob, and twisted. The knob turned. He threw the door open and stepped into the room with the Colt in his right hand.

The odor thickened and made his stomach clench in horror. His gaze dropped to the floor, and he saw Virginia Barry lying there on the thick rug without a stitch of clothing on, but there was nothing erotic about the sight. A dark red puddle was soaking into the rug around her head, and blood still welled slowly from the gaping wound in her throat, adding to the puddle.

Matt took an instinctive step toward her even though he knew it was too late to help her. Her blue eyes were wide open, staring lifelessly at him, and they seemed to draw him on. At the same time, his brain screamed a warning and he started to twist around.

Too late. What felt like the whole world fell on his head, crashing down with such stunning force he had no chance to resist. He started to crumple, but before he passed out and hit the floor a few feet away from Virginia Barry's gruesome corpse, he knew he was wrong. It wasn't the whole world that had come crashing down on him. More like a mountain.

A man-mountain named Judd Talley.

CHAPTER 14

The pain seeping into Matt's brain told him he was still alive, and that was better than the alternative. Not by much, though. It felt like a bunch of lunatic blacksmiths had set up a giant forge inside his skull and were pounding out enough horseshoes for the whole blasted U.S. Cavalry.

Something hard prodded his shoulder, setting off a fresh clamor of agony in his head. A voice, distorted by the pain but still recognizable, ordered, "Wake up, Jensen."

Matt pried his eyes open and found himself staring down the twin barrels of a shotgun.

"Don't you try nothin'," Sheriff Walt Sanger said. "Right now I'd like nothin' better than to blow your head off, mister." The lawman's voice trembled a little with outrage. "Anybody who'd do somethin' like that to a woman deserves whatever happens to him."

Despite the pain in Matt's head, his brain was functioning well enough for him to realize what was going on. He tried to speak, but his lips and tongue were so dry that they wouldn't work. Finally, he was able to husk, "Sheriff, I . . . I didn't . . ."

"Don't waste your time lyin', boy." Sanger glanced at somebody Matt couldn't see. "Get him on his feet."

A couple men stepped up, grasped Matt's arms, and hauled him upright. The room spun crazily around him for a moment, as if the world had started turning the wrong way. When it settled down and he could see straight again, he saw that he was still in the sitting room of Cyrus Longacre's suite in the Sierra House. Virginia Barry's body still lay there a few feet away. The puddle of blood had soaked into the rug and darkened, until it was almost black.

The men continued to hold on to Matt's arms, gripping them painfully tight so he couldn't get away. He recognized them as hombres he had seen around town. They glared at him with loathing and seemed to be making an effort not to look at the grisly sight on the floor.

Matt licked his lips and said in a stronger voice, "Sheriff, I didn't do this. Miss Barry was dead when I got here."

Sanger stepped closer and poked Matt hard in the belly with the shotgun. "Damn you, I said not to lie about it," he grated. "I see it with my own eyes. That's your knife on the floor beside her, ain't it?"

With his spirits sinking, Matt looked down and saw his Bowie laying just outside the puddle of blood. The broad, heavy blade was smeared with crimson. "Yes, but whoever knocked me out took my knife and wiped Miss Barry's blood on it."

Sanger gave a contemptuous snort. "Yeah, that's a likely story."

"It's the truth," Matt said as a feeling of desperation grew stronger inside him. "Think about it. You came in here and found me lying unconscious on the floor, right?"

"Yeah, right next to that poor dead woman. You know good and well that's what I found, Jensen."

"Well, then, what do you think happened? Do

137

you really believe I cut her throat and then knocked myself out?"

"No, I think she tried to fight back when you came at her with that knife," Sanger said. "She grabbed that pitcher off the table and busted it over your head, probably with her dyin' breath."

Matt's gaze shifted. He saw the broken shards of a heavy ceramic pitcher lying scattered on the floor at Virginia's feet.

"That pitcher wasn't broken when I came in," he said. "Whoever knocked me out broke it to make it look like Virginia hit me with it. Can't you see that, Sheriff?"

Sanger shook his head. "All I see is a no-good, lyin' polecat who killed a young woman. Maybe she wasn't quite what you'd call a respectable woman, but that don't matter."

For the first time, Matt agreed with something Sanger said. No matter what Virginia had been, she didn't deserve the gruesome fate that had claimed her.

He tried again to get through to the lawman. "Someone's trying to make it look like I killed her, Sheriff, but I swear I didn't."

He knew who was behind it. Judd Talley had knocked him out, and Talley was probably the one who had killed Virginia. And he'd done it on Cyrus Longacre's orders. It was hard to believe Longacre could be so ruthless as to have his own mistress murdered just to frame Matt for the

138

killing, but that was obviously what had happened.

It was obvious to him, anyway, Matt thought, but he seemed to be the only one.

Sanger said, "Take him over to the jail, fellas. I'm puttin' this lobo behind bars where he belongs."

"Wait a minute, Sheriff," Matt said, trying one final time to make the man see reason. "Why did you come up here?"

Sanger frowned. "What do you mean, why'd I come up here?"

"You didn't just wander down the hall and find us."

"Well, of course not! The clerk downstairs come runnin' into my office and said somebody was screamin' up here. Said it sounded like a woman bein' killed. That was right after you came up here." Sanger grunted. "Turned out he was right."

Matt took a deep breath. "He was lying. Like I told you, Virginia Barry was dead when I got here. She couldn't have screamed."

"I got your word for that, nothin' else," Sanger said. "And I don't believe a word that comes outta your mouth, mister."

"Why not?" Matt knew he ought to keep his anger under control, but he couldn't. "Because you're scared of Judd Talley? Or because Cyrus Longacre has paid you off? Or is it both of those things, Sheriff?"

The shotgun shook a little in Sanger's hands. The men holding on to Matt looked nervous. They knew at that range, if Sanger pulled the triggers the double load of buckshot would cut them down, too.

After a moment, Sanger lowered the Greener. Holding it at his side in his left hand, he used his right to draw the revolver on his hip. He pointed the gun at Matt and said hoarsely, "Take him to jail. And if you want to make a break for it, Jensen, you go right ahead. I'd plumb enjoy puttin' a bullet in your brain."

As a matter of fact, Matt had already thought about trying to get away. He knew he could break loose from the grip of the two men holding him, but didn't want them to get hurt. They were innocent citizens trying to help the sheriff. They weren't part of Longacre's scheme.

He also didn't want to be considered a fugitive. If he escaped, it would be the same thing as admitting he was guilty. Then every lawman in the West would be against him. As much as it went against the grain for him, it might be best to put his faith in the legal system and prove his innocence. Obviously the hotel clerk was lying about what had happened. If there was some way to make him tell the truth . . .

"I want a lawyer," Matt said as the two men hustled him out of the room.

"You'll get one," Sanger said as he followed

closely with his gun barrel pressed against Matt's back. The sheriff laughed. "You'll get one, sure enough."

It was morning before Matt found out why Sanger had found that so amusing. They had marched him to the jail with Sanger's gun in his back, shoved him into a cell, and slammed the door with an iron clang that rang of finality in Matt's ears. As soon as he was locked in, Matt told himself he should have tried to escape, even though that meant becoming a fugitive from the law—or getting killed.

Sanger refused to send word to Colin Ferguson about the arrest. Ferguson and Maureen were Matt's only real friends in Halltown, and he knew they would try to help him. They would see to it that he had a lawyer.

When morning came, the door between the cell block and the sheriff's office opened and Sanger came in with a grin on his walrus-face. "Your lawyer's here, Jensen. You said you wanted one."

Matt had been stretched out on the uncomfortable bunk. He sat up and got to his feet.

Sanger beckoned through the open door to someone in the office. "In here, Roscoe."

Matt remembered the name. Ferguson and Maureen had both talked about Roscoe Goldsmith, the attorney who had tried to help the Paiutes stand up to Cyrus Longacre. The short, stocky figure who came shuffling into the cell block didn't appear very heroic. In fact, despite the early hour, he was unsteady enough on his feet that he looked like he was on the verge of falling down.

Sanger pointed into Matt's cell. "There's your client, right there. That's the dirty murderer."

Goldsmith turned toward the cell and reached out with trembling hands to grasp the iron bars and support himself. He blinked bleary, red-rimmed eyes at Matt. "Doesn't . . . doesn't look like a mad dog," he managed to say.

Sanger laughed again. "Reckon I ought to leave you two alone to talk. That'd be the legal way of doin' things."

Matt started to make some bitter comment about Sanger caring only about Longacre's way of doing things, not the legal way. But he figured he would be wasting his breath, so he kept quiet.

Goldsmith made a visible effort to pull himself together. He gripped the bars and straightened up, planting his thick legs far enough apart to brace himself. He was in his fifties, Matt guessed, although drinking often made a man look older than he really was. His face was broad and flushed. His hair under a tipped back derby was brown and thinning. His tweed suit looked like it had been slept in every night for a week. The odor of rotgut whiskey came off him in waves, mixed with the reek of unwashed flesh.

"My name"—the visitor began, then paused to belch before he resumed—"my name is Roscoe Goldsmith. I'm going to . . . be your attorney, young man."

"I didn't hire you," Matt snapped.

"Maybe not, but if you want . . . want a lawyer, you're sort of stuck with . . . with me. I'm the only one in Helltown except for . . . the prosecutor." Goldsmith stopped, looked around wildly, and exclaimed, "The prosecutor! What . . . Wait a minute. I said that, didn't I?"

Matt kept a tight rein on his temper, but it wasn't easy. "You're drunk as a skunk."

"Having never seen . . . an inebriated polecat . . . I assure you, young man . . . I am drunker than a skunk!" Goldsmith waved an arm, swayed as that gesture threw him off-balance, and grabbed the bars again to steady himself. "But drunk or sober, I am also . . . the only *honest* lawyer in Helltown."

Something glittered in his eyes as he said that, a fleeting flash of anger, and Matt wondered how much of it was directed at Cyrus Longacre and his henchmen, and how much was turned inward, at the sort of man Goldsmith had become versus the sort of man he might have been.

Matt shoved that thought away with a little shake of his head. He didn't have time to feel sorry for Roscoe Goldsmith.

"Listen to me," he said. "I didn't kill that girl."

"Doesn't matter," Goldsmith said. "My job is

143

to . . . to give you the best possible defense."

"It matters to me," Matt snapped. "This is all Cyrus Longacre's doing. He wants to get me out of the way, but he's using the law to do it for him. His cronies back in Washington are probably pressuring him to make things appear to be legal, whether they really are or not."

Goldsmith belched again. "That's what those people in Washington do, all right. Biggest bunch of thieves and guttersnipes—"

"Get Colin Ferguson and bring him over here to see me," Matt broke in. "Can you do that?"

"Colin's a good man. Good friend."

"Get him," Matt said again. "We've got to start figuring out some sort of strategy for the trial."

"Better hurry, then. Trial . . . trial's this afternoon."

Matt's eyes widened in surprise. "This afternoon!" he repeated.

"Judge Dunwoodie says . . . no need to wait. Every man entitled to . . . a speedy trial. Law says so."

Matt bit back a curse. "Get Ferguson *now.*"

Goldsmith drew himself up. "See here, young man . . . I'm the attorney, not you. I . . . I . . ." His voice trailed off as a sick look came over his face. He suddenly twisted away from the cell door, stumbled a couple steps, and threw up in the corridor.

"Sheriff!" Matt called, shaking his head in

144

disgust. He stepped to the cell's single window where the air was a little fresher.

Sanger came in, saw what had happened, and muttered, "Son of a . . . I ain't cleanin' that up, Roscoe."

Goldsmith stood bent over with his hands braced on his knees, breathing heavily. After a moment he was able to straighten up. He turned toward the cell, wiped the back of a hand across his mouth, and said, "I'll get Colin." Then he stumbled out.

"I ain't cleanin' that up," the sheriff said again.

"Roscoe's really a smart man and a good lawyer, when he hasn't had too much to drink," Ferguson said as he and Matt conferred through the barred door a short time later. "It's just that once every week or ten days, almost like clockwork, he goes on a bender. It's been that way ever since his wife died. Poor fellow's never gotten over it."

"I might feel more sorry for him if I wasn't behind bars," Matt said.

"Tell me what happened," Ferguson said. "Go through the whole thing."

When he finished telling Ferguson everything he knew about Virginia's death, Matt said, "What I can't figure out is why anybody would think I even had a reason to kill her."

"Oh, well, that's easy enough. There's lots of talk around town about it this morning. Everybody thinks you and the girl were, ah, romantically involved. People have seen you talking to her on several occasions. And there were witnesses to the fight you had with her last night."

"What fight?" Matt asked, then closed his eyes and tried not to groan. "When she slapped me on the boardwalk in front of the milliner's shop."

"That would be the one."

Matt gazed through the bars at Ferguson again. "That didn't make any sense to me at the time, but it does now. She had orders to make it look like we were fighting."

"Wait a minute." Ferguson frowned. "She helped set up the motive for her own murder?"

Matt shook his head. "I don't know what she thought the plan was, but Longacre—or more likely, Talley carrying out Longacre's orders—told her what to do. She probably didn't have any idea the whole thing would wind up with her getting her throat cut."

"Well, it appears they've got the whole thing sewn up quite neatly. They've got a motive, far-fetched though it may be"—Ferguson paused —"it *is* far-fetched, isn't it? You weren't dallying with that girl?"

Matt shook his head. "I give you my word, Colin, there was nothing between me and Virginia Barry."

"All right, then. I believe you. But they have

motive, they have the clerk's testimony that he heard the woman scream, and they have the sheriff finding you there with her body and her blood on your knife. Even an honest, unbiased jury might have a hard time returning a verdict of not guilty, lad."

"It's unlikely there'll be an honest, unbiased jury in Halltown these days," Matt said with a bitter edge in his voice.

"You speak more truth than you know," Ferguson replied. His narrow face was grim "Judd Talley and more than a dozen gunmen rode in this morning. The whole town's scared. Talley acted surprised when he heard what happened to the Barry woman, and he and his friends are going around saying that if justice isn't done, the town will pay the price."

Matt grunted. "Why don't they just go ahead and start building the gallows?"

"Well . . ."

Matt stared at him. "They are, aren't they?"

"They're getting the wood together. Everybody, ah, everybody's expecting that the trial won't take long. They think there'll be a verdict by the end of the day."

"And a hanging tomorrow," Matt said.

And that was the way it was. The trial was a joke, with Longacre's tame judge overruling every objection and denying every motion Roscoe

Goldsmith made. The only defense Goldsmith could mount was to put Matt on the stand to tell his story. Matt had told the truth, laying Virginia Barry's killing at the feet of Judd Talley, who sat in the front row of spectators with a confident smirk on his face.

The nervous-looking jury hadn't even withdrawn to consider their verdict. They had talked among themselves for a few moments, then one of them stood up and announced to Judge Dunwoodie, "We find the defendant guilty of murder, Your Honor."

That had caused a little stir in the courtroom, but not much. Dunwoodie, a thick-bodied man who reminded Matt of a fat old bullfrog, rapped his gavel for quiet and said, "That being the case, I have no choice but to pronounce a sentence of death, in accordance with the laws of this state, said sentence to be carried out forthwith, at noon tomorrow, defendant to be hanged by the neck until dead." The gavel cracked again, even as Roscoe Goldsmith lumbered to his feet to make some feeble, last-minute objection.

"Court's adjourned!" Dunwoodie bellowed over him.

So there was nothing left but to wait for the gallows to be finished. Matt sat on the bunk in his cell, aching from the beating Talley and the other hardcases had given him, thinking he should have made a break for it when he'd had the chance, law or no law. He had expected to be railroaded, but he hadn't known his enemies would do such a swift, efficient job of it.

They weren't going to hang him. He made that vow to himself. He would get his hands on a gun somehow, and even though he would wind up riddled with slugs, before he went down he would get lead in Judd Talley. Count on it.

He had told himself Smoke and Preacher would show up in time to help him, but the minutes were slipping away too fast. They would be there, sooner or later, and when they found out what had happened to him, all hell would break loose. Cyrus Longacre was going to be mighty sorry he had ever heard the name Jensen.

That thought made a bleak smile tug at Matt's swollen lips as he waited for someone to come get him and march him to the gallows. Or try to, anyway.

BOOK TWO

CHAPTER 15

Big Rock, Colorado

"Be careful, Monte," Smoke Jensen called to his friend. He grinned. "You don't want to fall and break your neck."

"I'm not gonna fall and break my neck," Sheriff Monte Carson replied from the top of the ladder. "And if I do it's gonna be your fault, you dang chucklehead."

Smoke laughed. Monte Carson could get away with talking to him like that because they were old compadres, men who had ridden the river together.

Most hombres, though, would be a mite leery of insulting a man widely considered to be one of the fastest and deadliest gunfighters to ever ride the frontier.

Smoke hadn't set out to acquire that reputation, but he had never run away from trouble. He was what he was and never saw any point in denying it.

Fortunately, the gunman was just part of the man who had been born Kirby Jensen. He was also the loving, devoted husband to Sally, the successful rancher who owned the spread called

Sugarloaf, the boss to loyal hands like his foreman Pearlie and young Calvin Woods, the good friend to the citizens of Big Rock such as Sheriff Carson and gambler Louis Longmont, who owned one of the local saloons. Smoke was all those things and more.

Right then he was the fella holding the ladder while Monte Carson repaired the damage done to the jail's roof when a bad windstorm had blown through the area the day before. The ferocious gusts had ripped some of the shingles off. Carson was attempting to hammer new ones in place.

Holding a hammer instead of a six-gun, the sheriff leaned far to one side and muttered, "I think I can reach one more before we have to move the ladder."

"Monte, be careful," Smoke said again, but he was serious. "You're going to—"

With a startled yell, Carson lost his balance. He dropped the hammer and grabbed for the edge of the roof to steady himself, but his frantic lunge came up short. Smoke reached up and tried to catch hold of the sheriff's belt, but Carson had already toppled out of reach. With a heavy thud, he crashed to the ground in the alley beside the jail.

Smoke heard the sharp cracking sound, like a tree branch breaking, and knew what had happened. Carson confirmed it by clutching at his right leg and howling in pain. Smoke knelt beside him. "Well, I was wrong. I said you were going to break your neck, and it's only your leg you broke."

Eyes wide with pain, Carson looked up at his friend and said between clenched teeth, "I'll . . . get you . . . for that . . . Smoke. You better . . . fetch the doctor."

"That's what I was thinking." Smoke gave his friend a reassuring squeeze on the shoulder, then hurried to the mouth of the alley. He spotted Pearlie across the street, leaning against the ranch wagon parked in front of the general store. The lanky cowboy had a grin on his face as he watched Cal struggle to load boxes of goods into the wagon.

"Pearlie!" Smoke called. When the Sugarloaf foreman turned to look at him, Smoke went on, "Go find Doc Simpson! Sheriff Carson's hurt!"

Pearlie's dark, bushy eyebrows jumped in surprise. He normally moved in a slow, loose-jointed manner, but he didn't let any grass grow under his feet as he hurried off down the street in search of the sawbones. Cal put the box he was carrying in the wagonbed, then trotted over to the alley to join Smoke.

"What happened?" Cal asked. "Did the sheriff fall off the ladder and break his neck?"

"No, just his leg, but I wouldn't advise pointing that out to him," Smoke said with a smile.

"I heard that!" Carson said.

Smoke was more worried about the lawman than he let on. If a broken bone received prompt medical attention, it usually healed all right, but sometimes despite everything a doctor could do, the affected limb was never the same. Big Rock depended on Monte Carson to keep the peace and a lot more. He was one of the pillars of the community. It didn't take long for Pearlie to return with the doctor, and when they hurried into the alley, they were trailed by a small group of townspeople who had figured out that something was wrong. Smoke knew the word that the sheriff was injured would spread quickly through the settlement.

Dr. Hiram Simpson knelt next to Carson, set his black bag down and opened it. He cut away the leg of Carson's trousers to expose the injury. Smoke winced as he saw the unnatural way the leg was bent and the ugly lump under the skin where the broken bone was pressing against it.

"Well, at least the bone's not sticking out," Simpson said. "We should be grateful for small favors, eh, Sheriff?"

"You can . . . be grateful . . . if you want," Carson said. "I don't plan on . . . bein' too happy about any of this."

"You'll make a quicker recovery this way," Simpson told him. "I'll get the bone stabilized and splinted, and then we can take you down to my surgery and put a cast on that leg."

"A cast? That means I'll be laid up for a while!"

Simpson nodded. "That's what usually happens when you break your leg." He looked up at Smoke, Pearlie, and Cal. "I'll need a couple of two-by-fours for splints, probably about a foot and a half long."

"We'll go see what we can find," Pearlie said.

Carson let out a groan.

Smoke asked, "Hurting pretty bad, Monte?"

"Of course it hurts, but I groaned because I'm worried. I've got a couple deputies who can handle the usual problems, but if there's any real trouble, Big Rock's gonna need a real sheriff." He gave Smoke an intent look.

Smoke lifted both hands. "Hold on, Monte—"

"You're worn a star before."

"Not that often, and I was never all that comfortable with it. Have you forgotten I was a wanted man myself for a while?"

"You were never a real outlaw and you know it," Carson insisted. "The charges against you were trumped up."

"Plus I've got a ranch to run."

"And a fine crew to run it," the sheriff pointed out. He winced as Dr. Simpson moved his leg slightly. "Lord, Doc, if you're gonna twist it like that, why don't you just go ahead and saw it off!"

"Settle down," Simpson advised. "I'll give you some laudanum before I actually set the leg."

Carson turned his head to look at Smoke again.

157

"What about it, Smoke? Just take over for a while, until I get back on my feet. Shouldn't be more than a week, should it, Doc?"

"Six weeks, maybe longer," Simpson said. "You won't be back to full strength for several months."

Smoke hunkered on his heels next to Carson and thumbed his hat back on his close-cropped, ash-blond hair. "Tell you what I'll do, Monte. I'll send a telegram to the governor and ask him to see about getting a real lawman down here to take over for a while. Maybe a deputy U.S. marshal or somebody like that. That shouldn't take very long, maybe a week or so, and I'll keep an eye on things until then. Deal?"

"Deal," Carson said, gratitude in his voice. Even though he was in great pain, he raised his hand and shook with Smoke. "I feel better already knowing somebody's gonna be watchin' over the town while I can't."

Pearlie and Cal came back with several boards for Dr. Simpson to choose from. The doctor straightened Carson's leg, causing the sheriff to groan again and ask bitterly, "Why didn't somebody think to give me a few slugs of whiskey first?" Then Simpson bound a couple boards in place as a crude splint and stepped back so Smoke, Pearlie, Cal, and a couple townsmen could pick up Carson and carefully carry him down the street to the house were the sawbones lived and practiced.

The men from Sugarloaf came out of the house a short time later and paused on the porch. With a sly smile, Pearlie said, "You know, Cal, when Doc saw it was me who came runnin' in, he figured I'd come to fetch him 'cause you'd been shot again."

"I haven't been shot *that* many times," the youngster protested.

Pearlie snorted. "Heck, you catch lead in just about every fracas that comes along. We've had to dig so many slugs outta you, you're practically a lead mine!"

"Well, you've been shot a time or two yourself, as I recall."

"Yeah, but at least I've got sense enough to duck when the bullets commence to flyin'—"

"That's enough, you two," Smoke said, knowing they would squabble happily for hours if nobody put a stop to it. "You can take those supplies we bought back on out to the ranch and tell Sally I'll be staying in town for a while."

Pearlie frowned. "You're not comin' back to Sugarloaf with us?"

Smoke explained about the promise he'd made to Monte Carson. "I'll walk down to the train station and send a wire to the governor. It shouldn't take long to get somebody down here to take over."

"But until then you're the law in Big Rock, eh?"

"Monte's deputies are the law," Smoke corrected. "I'm just keeping an eye on things for the time being. I don't plan on pinning on the sheriff's badge unless there's some real trouble. The Good Lord willing, there won't be."

The two men lounging at the bar in one of the town's saloons were strangers to Big Rock. They had ridden in earlier in the day, taken a good look around—especially at the bank—and then with-drawn to have a drink. They were big, hard-faced, beard-stubbled men, and the coating of trail dust on their clothes testified to the fact that they'd done some long, hard, fast traveling in recent weeks.

One of the men tossed back the whiskey that remained in his glass and motioned for the bartender to refill it. His companion shook his head, and put his hand over the empty glass. If the meaning of the gesture wasn't obvious enough to start with, he said, "You've had enough, Crandell."

The stocky Crandell scowled. "Blast it, Burke, you got no right to tell me how much I drink."

"You want to argue about who's got what right?" Burke asked in a soft but somehow dangerous tone.

Crandell grimaced and shook his head. "No, no, don't get me wrong. I ain't lookin' for trouble."

"We need to go."

"Sure, whatever you say."

Burke led the way out of the saloon. Nobody paid any attention to him and Crandell as they untied their horses from the hitch rail, swung up into their saddles, and rode slowly out of town. They were just two more drifting cowpunchers, the sort of men who passed through Big Rock all the time looking for work on one of the ranches in the lush southern Colorado rangeland that surrounded the town.

It would take a closer look for anybody to notice the cold, flintlike hardness of their eyes or the well-worn walnut grips on their revolvers.

"So long, Big Rock," Burke drawled as they left the settlement. "We'll be back."

"I thought you said it would be too risky to hit the bank here, since the place has got a tough hombre like Monte Carson as its sheriff."

"You weren't paying attention to the talk in the saloon, Crandell. I was." A smirk curved the normally grim slash that was Burke's mouth. "While you were pouring whiskey down your throat, somebody came in and said that Sheriff Carson fell off a ladder and broke his leg."

Crandell's eyes widened as he looked over at his companion. "Really? I'll bet he's got deputies, though."

"A couple." Burke nodded. "But from the sound of everything I heard, they're nothing for us to worry about. They won't be any match for us. We'll rendezvous with Stonebreaker

161

and the rest of the boys, and then in a day or two, we'll pay Big Rock another visit."

Crandell laughed. "And leave with all the money in the bank, eh?"

Burke nodded again. "And leave with all the money in the bank. And if those deputies or anybody else try to stop us, it'll be their funeral."

CHAPTER 16

When she heard the creaking of wagon wheels drifting through the open window, Sally Jensen looked up from the plate of bear sign she had just taken out of the hot grease and set aside to cool. She turned to the window and moved the curtain aside, expecting to see her husband on the big 'Paloose horse he rode as he accompanied the wagon.

Instead she saw only Calvin Woods sitting on the wagon seat, hauling back on the reins to bring the team to a halt. Pearlie rode alongside on horseback. No sign of Smoke or the 'Paloose he had ridden into town.

For a second, she felt a tingle of fear that something had happened to Smoke. But Pearlie and Cal were grinning and laughing as they gibed at each other about something, and that wouldn't be the case at all if Smoke was hurt.

Despite the fact that she was an educated, highly intelligent woman, most of the time she felt like there was nothing in the world that could hurt Smoke Jensen. Some folks would say he led a charmed life.

Of course, that wasn't true at all. He had been wounded many times, some of them seriously. His heavily muscled, broad-shouldered body was covered with scars from gun and knife, as Sally had good reason to know. Not only that, but Smoke had known considerable tragedy in his life. His older brother Luke had been killed during the Civil War, his father Emmett had been cut down by gold-hungry outlaws, and his sister Janey had come to a bad end as well. Smoke's first wife Nicole and their infant son Arthur had been murdered by owlhoots. You might say much of Smoke's life had been dogged by death. In fact, when Sally had first met him, in the Idaho town of Bury, where she had come from New Hampshire to teach school, he had been on the run from the law himself and using the name Buck West.

Sally's life had taken a turn for the better the day she met Smoke, and she liked to think the same was true for him. They had been through a lot together. They had fought Indians, badmen, and the elements to forge a life for themselves on Sugarloaf. She had tended to his wounds when he was shot up. She had killed men who needed killing. And even when things had looked the worst, she had never given up.

So the worry she felt when she saw that Smoke wasn't with Pearlie and Cal lasted only a fraction of a heartbeat. She told herself he had either gotten sidetracked on the way back to the ranch or had stayed behind in Big Rock for some reason.

The two ranch hands came into the kitchen a moment later, each carrying a box of supplies. Cal said excitedly, "I told Pearlie I smelled bear sign!"

"You can eat your fill as soon as it cools off," Sally told him, "and as soon as you tell me where Smoke is."

"He's still in town," Pearlie explained. "Sheriff Carson was tryin' to patch up some damage to the roof of his office from that big windstorm yesterday."

"And?" Sally prodded when Pearlie paused and didn't go on. Sometimes getting information out of those laconic cowboys was like the proverbial pulling of teeth.

"Oh, he fell off the ladder," Pearlie said. "Didn't I tell you that part?"

"No," Sally said patiently. "You mean Sheriff Carson fell off?"

"Yeah, Smoke warned him," Cal put in. "Told him he was going to break his neck."

"Oh, my goodness!" Sally exclaimed as her eyes widened in alarm. "Monte broke his neck?"

"No, ma'am, I never said that."

164

"He broke his leg," Pearlie added. "Busted it clean in two."

"Oh." Sally felt relieved, even though she hated to hear that Monte Carson was hurt. "Is he going to be all right?"

"Yeah, but Doc Simpson says he's gonna be laid up for a good long while."

"Sheriff Carson got Smoke to promise he'd sorta look after the town," Cal said.

"For how long?" Sally was used to Smoke being away from Sugarloaf for weeks or sometimes months at a time, but she didn't have to like it.

"Doc claims it'll be six weeks before the sheriff can even start gettin' up and around again," Pearlie said. "Could be several months before he's plumb back up to snuff."

Sally sighed, then perked up slightly. Big Rock wasn't far away. If Smoke couldn't come back to the ranch, maybe she would go and stay in town with him, or at least visit frequently. No matter how competent Pearlie and Cal and the other hands were, someone would still need to keep an eye on what was happening at Sugarloaf.

"But you don't have to worry," Cal said. "Smoke won't have to stay there the whole time. He was gonna send a wire to Denver and ask the governor to send somebody down to take over for Sheriff Carson, you know, until the sheriff's back on his feet."

That was even better, Sally thought with a

smile. Smoke had done more than one favor for the governor in the past, so she knew the man would act quickly to handle the request. He would probably be home in a few days, or a week at most.

"Uh, how long do you reckon it'll be before that bear sign's cooled off enough to eat?" Cal asked.

"It might be ready by the time you and Pearlie finish bringing in the supplies," Sally said pointedly. "Aren't you worried you'll ruin your appetite for supper?"

"Trust me, ma'am," Pearlie said. "That ain't never gonna happen!"

They went out, swatting at each other with their hats, and Sally laughed at their antics. She wasn't worried anymore. Big Rock was a pretty peaceful place these days, so Smoke staying there to help out the sheriff was just a precaution. He probably wouldn't have to do a thing.

The man standing off a ways from the campfire was big, but there was something more than sheer size that drew the eye to him. He had that magnetic quality that all great leaders have, a certain intangible aspect that made men want to follow him out of a mixture of respect, awe, and even a little fear. He might have been a military general or a statesman or a titan of industry.

Of course, not all men who possessed that quality rose to such heights. Oliver Stonebreaker

166

didn't lead an army or a political party or a business. He led a motley gang of outlaws. His circumstances in life—a petty thief for a father and a whore for a mother, neither of whom had lived until young Oliver's eighth birthday—had robbed him of his true destiny.

So Oliver robbed, too. He killed, as well, when anyone got in his way, and raped when the mood struck him. His men knew to steer clear of him when one of his increasingly frequent rages was upon him, but they never gave any thought to leaving him. He was smart, and since he had started running the gang and planning their jobs, they hadn't even come close to getting caught. They had plenty of loot to divvy up, and whenever it started to run low, why, they just found themselves another bank to rob.

Or rather, Stonebreaker did. He picked out the targets, and like the great general he might have been, he sent men to scout them and get the lay of the land before he acted. If a job looked like it would be too dangerous or not profitable enough, the Stonebreaker gang passed it by and waited for something better. That way they stayed out of prison and more important, stayed alive.

Southern Colorado wasn't Stonebreaker's usual stomping grounds. He didn't know the name of the settlement he'd sent Burke and Crandell to to check out the bank. They weren't back yet and he worried they might have gotten into trouble.

He wasn't particularly concerned about something bad happening to them, but if they had run afoul of the law, they might sell out the rest of the gang to save their own hides. Unfortunately, he couldn't really trust a bunch of cold-blooded, bank-robbing murderers.

The sound of hoofbeats approaching in the night made Stonebreaker swing around toward the fire. He was an impressive figure in a black frock coat, with a gray-shot spade beard that stuck out from his massive jaw. He never wore a hat, so the night wind stirred the long, wild thatch of dark hair that hung to his shoulders. The only spots of lightness about him were the pearl-handled revolvers that rode butt-forward in his holsters. He knew the guns were fancy, but he liked them. More important, he was good with them.

Close to a dozen men sitting around the fire got to their feet as they heard the horses. Some of them picked up rifles leaning against the rocks near the fire. Others rested their hands on their holstered guns. The riders were probably their fellow outlaws Burke and Crandell, but men who rode the dark, lonesome trails knew it never paid to take chances.

The hoofbeats came to a halt. A voice called out, "Hello, the camp!"

Stonebreaker strode forward. "Come on in, Burke!" he rumbled. The rest of the men relaxed. They had recognized the newcomer's voice, too.

Burke and Crandell rode into camp and dismounted. A couple men took their horses to unsaddle them and picket them with the others. Another man handed them cups of coffee. Burke nodded his thanks. Crandell was more sullen, but then, he always was.

Stonebreaker waited until the men had swigged down some of the Arbuckle's, but couldn't contain his impatience any longer. "Well?" he demanded, "What did you find out?"

"The bank looks pretty prosperous," Burke reported. "Impressive building. Brick, two stories."

"That doesn't mean there's any money in the vault," Stonebreaker snapped.

"There ought to be. There are several big cattle spreads in the area, and it's getting on toward the end of the month. Be payday for the hands soon. The businesses in the settlement seem to be doing pretty well, too. The saloons alone probably make some big deposits. Throw in all the stores and the other businesses, and there'll be money in the vault, all right."

Stonebreaker nodded. "Sounds promising," he admitted in his deep, rumbling voice. "What about the law situation?"

A grin spread across Burke's lean, sardonic face. "That's even better. The local sheriff fell off a ladder and busted his leg while we were in town. He's going to be laid up for a while. And that's a good thing, because he's Monte Carson."

169

Stonebreaker's bushy eyebrows drew down in a frown as he shook his head. "I don't recognize the name."

"I never met him, but I've heard of him," Burke explained. "He used to be a hired gun, years ago. Pretty tough hombre. I guess that life got to be too hard for him. He settled down and started packing a star instead. He's probably lost some of his edge, but I'd just as soon not have to find out. With him laid up, all we have to worry about is a couple green deputies who won't be any real threat to us."

Stonebreaker suppressed the impulse to rub his hands together in anticipation. "From the sound of it, we can not only empty the bank but take over the rest of the town as well."

Burke nodded. "I think you're right, boss. We can pick the whole settlement clean if we want to. Might even be a good place to hole up for a little while."

"I'll decide things like that," Stonebreaker snapped.

"Sure," Burke said. "I never figured otherwise."

Mollified by the man's quick response, Stonebreaker nodded in satisfaction and started to turn away, asking over his shoulder, "By the way, what's the name of this place?"

Crandell chuckled. "You'll like this, boss, because of your name. It's called Big Rock. Big Rock, Stonebreaker, you get it?"

Stonebreaker froze as his muscles stiffened

and his breath caught in his throat. He stood like that for a moment, then slowly swung around. "What did you call it?"

Crandell swallowed hard, aware that he had said something to disturb the boss but unsure of what it might be. "Big Rock. But I didn't mean nothin' by it—"

"You never heard of Big Rock before?"

Crandell shook his head, and glanced at Burke who said, "No, I don't think so. Should I have?"

"Something rung a bell when you mentioned Monte Carson, but I wasn't paying any attention. Tell me, while you were there did you see a man who stands maybe a couple inches over six feet, with shoulders about as broad as an ax handle? He wears two guns, one holstered the regular way on the right, the one on the left butt-forward. He has ash-blond hair, sort of the color of . . . smoke."

"I don't recall seeing anybody like that," Burke said, and Crandell shook his head again. "Who is he? An old enemy of yours?"

"Not really. I saw him in action once, over in Kansas. That's how I know what he looks like. But he wasn't gunning for me. He killed four men in less time than it takes to tell it."

Crandell let out a low whistle of appreciation. "Sounds like quite a gunslick."

"You could say that." Stonebreaker's voice suddenly rose to an angry roar. "He's Smoke Jensen, you idiot!"

A stunned silence hung over the camp after Stonebreaker's shout. Burke finally broke it by saying, "Smoke Jensen. I've heard of him."

"Of course you have," Stonebreaker said with a withering glare. "He has a ranch near Big Rock, Colorado. He's friends with Monte Carson, that old gunfighter-turned-lawman. If Carson's laid up, there's a good chance he's asked Jensen to help keep peace in the town for a while."

"We can't know that for sure," Burke argued. "From what I've heard about Jensen, he roams around a lot. He might not even be in these parts right now."

Stonebreaker got control of his anger and nodded. "He might not be. But we have to find out before we decide what to do."

Crandell asked, "What're we gonna do if he *is* around? Just forget about that bank and turn tail and run?"

Stonebreaker moved with blinding speed for such a big man. His arm shot out, swinging around like a freight train. The back of his hand cracked across Crandell's face with such force the blow sent the stocky outlaw flying backward. His coffee cup went high in the air and came down with a clatter as it bounced toward the fire. One of the other outlaws caught it before it landed in the flames.

Crandell lay on his back. He pushed himself up on his elbows and looked groggy. With one hand, he took hold of his jaw and worked it back and forth to see if it was broken.

"No, we're not going to turn tail and run," Stonebreaker said. "We're not going to forget about that bank, either. But we have to find out if Smoke Jensen is in Big Rock, and if he is, we'll have to deal with him before we make our move."

"How are we going to do that?" Burke asked.

Stonebreaker's lips curved in a vicious smile under the thick mustache that drooped over them. "Like I said, Jensen's got a ranch, and on that ranch is his pretty little wife. Threaten something that a man loves, and he'll usually come a-runnin' . . . even if he's charging right into a trap."

CHAPTER 17

The back room of the sheriff's office and jail held a cot where Monte Carson sometimes spent the night when he had a reason to. Smoke stayed there, although he could have gotten a room at the hotel. The cot wasn't as comfortable as his bed in the ranch house, partially because Sally wasn't in it, but he had slept in a lot worse places. He had asked Pearlie to ride back into town the next day to bring him clean clothes and other personal things he would need to get through the rest of the week or so.

In the morning, he went to Dr. Simpson's home to check on Carson. The lawman was sort of doped up. The broken leg was swathed in a white cast and propped up in the bed where he lay.

"He spent a fairly quiet night," Simpson told Smoke.

"Expect him to start complaining when he wakes up more," Smoke advised the doctor with a smile. "He's not going to take kindly to being cooped up."

Simpson nodded and sighed. "I know. He's already started talking about getting some crutches so he can walk around. He can't seem to grasp the idea that he's not going to put any weight on that leg for several weeks."

"He can grasp it, he just doesn't like it." Smoke clapped a hand on Simpson's shoulder. "Good luck, Doc. I have a feeling you're gonna need it."

Smoke returned to the sheriff's office and found both of Carson's deputies waiting for him. Smoke knew both men, although not well. He had spoken to them briefly the evening before, telling them to go ahead with their normal routine and make their rounds as they usually did.

"Mornin', Smoke," one of the men said. "Town seems pretty quiet."

Smoke nodded. "That's what I thought. I'm hoping it stays that way. I'll be either here or some-where around town if you need help, but you fellas are in charge. I figure you know more about how Monte would want things done than I do."

"Thanks." The man grinned. "I've got to admit, knowin' we've got Smoke Jensen to call on if a bad ruckus breaks out makes me feel a mite better."

"I plan on moving over to the hotel today," Smoke continued. "That way whichever one of you normally works nights can get back on your regular schedule."

They chatted for a few minutes longer, then Smoke left the office and walked down the street to the livery stable where he had left his 'Paloose. The big spotted horse whickered a warm greeting to him.

Smoke chewed the fat with the elderly hostler for a while, then went over to the hotel and made arrangements for a room. As he was leaving the hotel, he spotted Pearlie riding into Big Rock with a warbag tied to his saddle. Smoke lifted a hand in greeting, took the gear Pearlie had brought him, and listened to his foreman's brief report on the state of things at Sugarloaf.

"The ranch is just fine. Miz Jensen was a mite surprised when she heard you weren't comin' home for a while, but she didn't seem upset."

"That's good." Smoke nodded. Sally was a little more adaptable than some women, he thought. Unexpected developments seldom threw her for a loop, which was good. Sharing a life with him had never been what anybody would call predictable.

"You missed out on some mighty good bear sign," Pearlie went on. "Cal says it was some of the best he's ever eaten, and he sure stuffed his belly full to prove it."

Smoke grinned and let out a mock groan of disappointment.

"How're things here in town, Smoke? You need any help?"

"Quiet," Smoke replied. "Mighty quiet. If things keep up like this, the main thing I'll have to worry about is getting bored."

"We wouldn't want that to happen. Maybe you'll get lucky and things'll start to pop."

"Yeah," Smoke said, giving a friendly nod to a stranger who rode by in the street. "Lucky."

That was Smoke Jensen on the boardwalk, talking to some lanky cowboy. No doubt about it, thought Wylie Fisk. Stonebreaker had described the famous gunfighter to a *T*.

Fisk smiled and returned the nod Jensen gave him, but he didn't slow his horse. He kept moving, angling toward a saloon on the other side of the street. THE LONGMONT SALOON, a sign over the boardwalk on the front of the building announced.

Fisk was a small, inoffensive-looking man with eyes so pale blue they were almost colorless. His battered Stetson was pushed back on fair hair. The gun on his hip was old but well cared for. Looking at him, nobody would ever guess he had killed eight men, two during shoot-outs that followed some of the gang's bank robberies, the other six gunned down from behind. Fisk had tortured a couple Mexicans to death, too, but he didn't count those in his total.

He dismounted and tied his horse at the hitch rail in front of the saloon. It was early enough in the day the place wasn't doing much business, but a few men stood at the bar drinking. A poker game went on at one of the tables. Fisk considered sitting in on the game—he had a weakness for cards—but Stonebreaker had sent him into Big Rock for information, not to risk his luck on the pasteboards. He went to the bar and told the bartender to fetch him a beer.

As the man set the mug in front of him, Fisk said, "Looks like a nice little town here."

The bartender nodded. "Yeah, Big Rock's a good place to live. You a stranger in these parts?"

Fisk took a swallow of the cool beer and licked his lips appreciatively. "That's right."

"Looking for work?"

"I might be," Fisk allowed. "Any of the spreads around here hirin' right now?"

"Well, since it's not round-up time, I don't really know," the bartender replied with a shrug. "But you could ask around. Never can tell when somebody might need an extra hand."

Fisk took another swallow of the beer, then said easily, "I've heard about a ranch called Sugarloaf

177

that's supposed to be in this part of the country."

The bartender grinned and nodded. "Sure, Sugarloaf is Smoke Jensen's spread."

"Smoke Jensen?" Fisk repeated. "The gunfighter?"

"Oh, he's got quite a rep, sure, but these days Smoke's more rancher than gunfighter. He comes in here all the time, you know. Him and Mr. Longmont are good friends." The bartender nodded toward the table where the poker game was going on.

Fisk looked at the players, his gaze lingering on a well-dressed hombre with sleek dark hair and a thin mustache. He looked like a professional gambler, and Fisk recalled hearing talk about a gambler and gunman named Longmont. Louis Longmont, that was it. One more bit of information Stonebreaker would want, Fisk told himself.

"Smoke will probably be in later," the talkative bartender went on. "He's staying in town right now because our sheriff, Monte Carson, busted his leg yesterday. Smoke's filling in for him."

"Do tell," Fisk murmured. That was the very thing Stonebreaker had been worried about.

Fisk knew he'd been lucky. He had come to the right place when he rode up to the Longmont Saloon. That big-mouthed drink juggler had told him everything he needed to know. Almost everything, he amended.

"How do I find that Sugarloaf spread? I might ride out there and see if they need any hands."

"You could wait and just ask Smoke if you want," the bartender suggested. "Like I said, he'll probably be in here after a while."

"Oh, I don't want to bother a busy man like that. He's probably got a lot on his mind if he's takin' the sheriff's place. I'll just talk to his foreman."

"That'd be a fella name of Pearlie."

"Pearlie," Fisk repeated. "I'm obliged. And where do I find the place?"

The bartender gave him directions to Sugarloaf. Fisk listened carefully, then took a coin from his pocket and slid it across the hardwood to pay for the beer, handling it as if he didn't have too many and was reluctant to let it go. He didn't want the bartender remembering him as anything except another harmless saddle tramp.

He drained the last of the beer from the mug, nodded his thanks to the bartender, and turned to leave. He was almost at the door when a broad-shouldered figure appeared, blocking the entrance as he pushed back the batwings.

"Oh, howdy, Smoke," the bartender called as Fisk's spirits abruptly sank. "Say, that fella there was just asking about you and Sugarloaf. He's looking for work."

"Is that so?" Smoke recognized the man in the saloon as the one who had ridden past a short time earlier while he was talking to Pearlie, before he had taken the warbag up to his hotel room. He held out his hand to the stranger. "Smoke Jensen. Pleasure to meet you."

The stranger hesitated for a second, but Smoke didn't think anything about it. A lot of people had heard of him, had heard all the stories about how many men he had killed and how fast he was on the draw. When they met him they weren't quite sure what to make of him.

"Wiley Fisk," the man said as he gripped Smoke's hand. Fisk had nothing to distinguish him. He was the sort who wouldn't be noticed in a crowd.

"You say you're looking for work? A riding job?"

Fisk nodded. "Yes, sir. I'm a pretty fair hand."

Smoke inclined his head toward Pearlie, who had come into the saloon behind him. "This is my foreman."

Fisk nodded to Pearlie. "Howdy."

"Howdy, your own self," Pearlie replied. "Sorry to disappoint you, amigo, but Sugarloaf ain't hirin' right now. You might try some of the other spreads around here, or check with us again in the fall. We're likely to need some extra hands then to bring all the stock down from the high pastures."

"Yeah, I understand," Fisk said. "I'm obliged to you, anyway." He smiled, slid past them, and left the saloon.

Pearlie went on toward the bar to wet his

whistle, but Smoke turned and looked out over the batwings, watching as Fisk mounted up and rode out of Big Rock, heading back in the direction he had come from.

When the stranger was out of sight, Smoke ambled over to the bar. "Strange little fella," he commented to Pearlie, who signaled the bartender for a beer.

"Who? Oh, you mean that saddle tramp who was lookin' for a job. What was strange about him? Looked pretty common to me. We see a bunch of 'em passin' through here."

"Maybe . . . but that was a pretty good horse he rode out on. A better looking piece of horseflesh than you usually see being ridden by a down-at-the-heels drifter like that."

Pearlie blew the foam off the mug of beer the bartender set before him and took a healthy swallow. "Horse is probably worth more'n the rest of the hombre's outfit put together. I've known fellas like that."

"So have I," Smoke agreed. "His name mean anything to you?"

"Shoot, I don't even remember his name."

"Wylie Fisk."

"Fisk, Fisk . . . Nope, can't say as it does. How about you?"

Smoke shook his head. "Not really."

"Well, we don't have to worry about him. He pulled his freight, didn't he?"

"Yeah. Rode out of town."

"There you go," Pearlie said. "Probably never see him again."

Smoke knew his friend was right, and yet some instinct still stirred inside him, some vague hunch that not everything was right.

Smoke trusted his instincts, but nothing seemed amiss. He talked to Pearlie for a while longer, then the foreman headed back out to the ranch. Smoke ate some lunch and drifted around town the rest of the afternoon, talking to friends and acquaintances in the various businesses. He stopped by Doc Simpson's again but found that Monte Carson was sleeping. There was no need to wake him.

It was late in the day before Smoke went back into the sheriff's office and found one of the deputies sitting behind the desk. The man started to get up, but Smoke waved him back into his chair. "Keep your seat. Everything under control?"

The deputy grinned at him. "How could it not be, with Smoke Jensen circulating around town all day? Nobody's gonna start any trouble as long as you're around, Mr. Jensen."

Smoke gestured toward the desk. "Monte's got a drawerful of wanted posters and reward dodgers in there, doesn't he?"

"That's right. You want to take a look at them?"

Smoke's hunch had grown stronger during the afternoon, until he could no longer ignore it. "Yeah, I do. Don't get up, just hand them here."

The deputy opened a drawer and took out a thick stack of papers. He gave them to Smoke, who took them over to the lumpy couch along the front wall and sat down to go through them.

He had flipped through several dozen posters depicting assorted outlaws, killers, and dealers in depravity before his hand abruptly tightened on the one he held. There was no drawing or tintype on that one, just a name and description, and a recital of the charges against the man—bank robbery, stagecoach robbery, and murder and the reward offered for his capture by authorities in Kansas, Nebraska, Missouri, and Arkansas. The description was that of a small, fair-haired man with pale blue eyes, whose name was Wylie Fisk.

And that man had been in Big Rock, asking about Sugarloaf.

Smoke was about to toss the other reward posters aside when a note caught his eye. It said that Fisk was thought to be traveling with a gang of outlaws led by somebody called Oliver Stonebreaker. That name was familiar, and Smoke rummaged through the posters he had already looked at until he found the one he was thinking of. A drawing of a man with a prominent black beard stared up at him. According to the poster, Stonebreaker was the leader of a gang of at least a dozen desperadoes.

He was wanted on the same charges and in the same places as Fisk, but the law was looking for him in Texas, the Indian Territory, and Dakota Territory, as well, He had a more widespread and even more violent career as an owlhoot. In addition to murder and robbery, he was wanted for rape and assault.

That was the man who might be on his way to Sugarloaf.

The deputy at the desk wasn't paying much attention. He heard a little noise, saw a blur of motion from the corner of his eye, and looked up to see that the sofa was empty. The stack of wanted posters lay scattered on the floor. "Mr. Jensen? Smoke?"

But Smoke Jensen was gone.

CHAPTER 18

"Are you sure that's the place?" Burke asked Wylie Fisk as the two men sat on their horses looking down a hill at the ranch buildings. Dusk had begun to settle, and lamplight glowed warmly in some of the windows.

"That's it, all right," Fisk insisted. "That blabber-mouthed bartender in Big Rock gave me good directions."

Burke nodded. Crandell and another man, a half-breed who called himself Kiowa Smith, were right behind him and Fisk. Stonebreaker had sent the four of them to Sugarloaf. Burke would have preferred to ride with Stonebreaker and the rest of the men who were going to Big Rock, but he knew he and his companions had an important job to do. They were going to make sure Smoke Jensen wasn't in town to interfere when Stonebreaker and the others hit the bank.

"Do you know how many hands are here?" Burke asked.

Fisk shook his head. "No, but that cowboy Pearlie said they weren't hirin'. Half a dozen, maybe, given the time of year."

"Then we'll likely be outnumbered."

Behind Burke, Crandell snorted. "Half a dozen cowhands aren't gonna be any match for us, and you know it, Burke. Plus we'll be takin' 'em by surprise. They won't have a chance."

"Maybe so, but I want to wait a little while longer," Burke said.

"What for, blast it? I say we just ride down there and kill 'em all except the woman."

"I like to know as much as I can about an enemy—"

As if to reinforce what Burke was saying, at that moment a figure stepped out on the front porch of the ranch house. A second later, a clangor rang out as whoever it was banged on an iron triangle to summon the hands to supper. Men began to emerge from the bunkhouse and head toward the main house.

As the triangle rang, Burke quickly lifted a spyglass to his eye and peered through it. Light spilling through the open door of the house revealed the woman who was banging on the triangle. She was well-shaped, with long dark hair that streamed over her shoulders. Even though Burke couldn't make the details of her face, he saw enough to make a pang of lust go through him. She had to be Jensen's wife.

"Looks like the lady cooks for the hands, and they eat in the house," Burke said as he lowered the spyglass. "That's good. That way they're all in one place."

"So there's no need to wait," Crandell said.

Burke closed the spyglass and stuck it back in his saddlebags. "No. No reason at all."

It seemed unlikely that anybody could get lonely with these rollicking cowhands around, Sally thought as she watched the men dig into the food she had placed on the table, but she definitely missed Smoke, now that he had been gone for more than a day. Of course, that was nothing new. They had been separated for much longer on numerous occasions in the past. She knew she would be all right until he got back.

Still, it would have been mighty nice to see his face and hear his laugh.

When the men were all eating, Sally took her place at the head of the table. Pearlie was to her right, Cal to her left, and the other four hands ranged along the sides of the table. There was a lot of talk and laughter as Pearlie and Cal joshed with each other as usual and the other men joined in. Sally smiled. They were good company.

The sound of glass shattering made Sally's head jerk up in shock. A crash followed less than a heartbeat later as someone kicked the door open. Guns began to roar even as the men at the table leaped to their feet and clawed at their weapons.

Horrified, Sally saw two of the Sugarloaf hands crumple with blood spouting from the wounds where slugs had torn through them. She stood as her hand dove into the pocket of her dress where she kept a small pistol. It wasn't the first time she had been caught in a gunfight. She knew what to do. She whirled toward the door and brought the .32 up. It cracked wickedly in her hand as she fired at the man who stood there holding a smoking revolver.

He jerked as Sally's bullet ripped across the outside of his upper left arm, leaving a painful burn but not doing any significant damage. The gun in his hand blasted again, and another of the cowboys went down. The men at the windows continued to fire, flame lancing from the muzzles of their guns.

Somebody grabbed Sally and hauled her to the floor. "Stay down!" Pearlie shouted as he loomed over her, gun in hand. He fired toward the intruders, then grunted and went over backward as at least one slug struck him.

"Pearlie!" Sally cried.

Cal had his gun out, and snapped a couple shots at the windows as he scrambled toward his fallen friend. "Pearlie! Pearlie! Blast it, it's me who's supposed to get—"

The impact of a bullet twisted him in mid-air and drove him to the floor. Sally screamed.

All the Sugarloaf men were down. The massacre was complete—almost. Sally still had her gun, and she intended to go down fighting, just as Smoke would have. She lurched to her feet and tried to lift the pistol, only to have a snake-quick little man with pale blue eyes bring his own gun down in a chopping blow that caught her on the wrist. She cried out in pain as the .32 fell from her numb fingers and thudded to the floor.

The man who had kicked the door open came toward her, scowling. "You shot me, Mrs. Jensen. You *are* Mrs. Jensen, aren't you?"

"Go to hell!" she blazed at him.

The little man with colorless eyes caught hold of her arm. "No need to talk like that, missy," he told her with a smirk. "We're not gonna hurt you—too much. We need you alive."

"Shut up," the wounded man snapped. His mouth was an almost lipless slash across his grim face. "Check on the others. We want one of them alive."

All four of the attackers had crowded into the room. One of them, a dark-faced man who looked like he had Indian blood, knelt next to Pearlie. "This one's still breathing. Got a crease in his side, but it don't look too bad. He'll live."

"That's good," the man with the colorless eyes said. "He's the foreman."

The 'breed rolled Pearlie onto his back and drew a knife, resting the blade on the foreman's throat hard enough so that a trickle of blood rolled down Pearlie's turned neck. Pearlie groaned as his eyes flickered open.

The wounded man stood over him. "Listen to me. You're going to take a message to Smoke Jensen for us, understand? Tell Jensen we have his wife, and if he ever wants to see her alive again, he'd better bring five thousand dollars to Hampton Peak by sunup tomorrow morning. Got it?"

Pearlie started to curse. The man with the knife pressed harder with the blade, increasing the flow of blood from the cut.

"Pearlie, don't," Sally said. "Don't make them kill you."

"But ma'am—" he began in a choked voice.

"Do what they tell you." Sally's chin lifted defiantly as she glared at the man she had wounded. "Didn't you hear them? They need me alive."

"Now you're being smart." The man glanced at

the fourth raider, an ugly, stocky man. "Any of the others still alive?"

"This kid's breathin'," the outlaw replied, gesturing with his gun at Cal. "The other four are dead as stumps."

Sally was grateful to hear that Cal was still alive, even though her heart broke over the deaths of the other hands.

"You hear that?" the wounded man asked Pearlie. "You either cooperate and deliver that message for us, or my friend here will slit your throat and we'll get the other survivor to deliver our message."

Pearlie blew out his breath. "I'll carry the word to Smoke. And I'll ride with him when he comes after you varmints. I want to be there when the whole bunch of you get your lights blowed out for good."

The man smiled. It didn't make his face look any less grim. "You keep on thinking that. See what good it does you." He nodded to the man who had hold of Sally. "Get her out of here."

Her captor dragged her toward the door. The stocky outlaw went out in front of them. He headed for the barn and came back a moment later with a couple horses already saddled. The raiders had readied the mounts before they broke into the house and started shooting.

"Get on," the man with the colorless eyes told Sally. She knew she couldn't fight them, so the best thing to do was to play along for the time being and wait for a chance to take them by surprise. She swung into the saddle, hiking her skirt as she did so. It was no time for false modesty.

The other two men brought Pearlie out of the house. The half-breed had put away his knife, but he had his gun out. Pearlie was unsteady on his feet, but managed to stumble to the horse they had waiting for him, and climbed into the saddle. He sat hunched over from the pain of the bullet crease in his side.

"If you know what's good for your boss's wife, you'll head straight to Big Rock," the leader warned. "Remember, five grand, Hampton Peak, sunup tomorrow."

"I got it," Pearlie mumbled. He lifted the reins and heeled the horse into motion. Urging the animal into a run, he pounded off into the shadows, even though the gait caused him pain. Full night had fallen.

"All right," the leader went on. "Everybody mount up. We're getting out of here."

Sally said, "You're fools, you know that, don't you? You might live to see the sun rise tomorrow morning . . . but you'll never see it set again."

"You let us worry about what we see and don't see, Mrs. Jensen," the man advised her. He took the reins of her horse and rode away from the ranch house. The other three followed, closing in around Sally so there was no way she could try to escape.

Smoke was still several miles away from Sugarloaf's headquarters when he heard a faint popping sound drifting to him on the evening breeze. He stiffened in the saddle but didn't slow the 'Pa-loose. He recognized gunshots when he heard them, and knew they were coming from the direction of his home.

Cold fear clutched at his belly. He never knew fear for his own sake, but threaten his loved ones or his friends and he experienced it, mixed with a fierce anger. He had still been a young man when Preacher taught him how to control his emotions, rather than letting them control him, and how to use them to his own advantage. He drove himself and the 'Paloose on, covering the ground with swift efficiency. He was on Sugarloaf range and knew every foot of it.

The shooting was fast and furious but didn't last long. That wasn't a good sign, Smoke thought. He couldn't figure why Oliver Stonebreaker and his gang would raid the ranch—they had no real history as rustlers, although they had stolen a few horses in the past—but Smoke was convinced that's what was happening. The little outlaw named Fisk had ridden into Big Rock, found out where Sugarloaf was located, and knew Smoke was in town rather than at the ranch. The gang must have thought they would have a free hand for their raid.

The gunfire meant Smoke hadn't tumbled to what was going on in time to get there before Stonebreaker and his men attacked. But maybe Pearlie, Cal, and the other hands had been able to hold them off. Maybe the outlaws had abandoned the assault and ridden away.

Smoke didn't believe that. The icy hand clutching his stomach told him otherwise.

Suddenly he heard hoofbeats in the darkness ahead of him. Reining to a halt, he drew his Colt. If the outlaws were riding in his direction, they would have a hot lead welcome waiting for them.

It was only one horse, Smoke realized a moment later. He drew his own mount to the side of the trail, in the shadow of a looming slab of rock, and waited.

The lone rider burst into view. Even in the bad light, Smoke saw how the man was swaying back and forth in the saddle as if he were injured. Smoke sent the 'Paloose lunging in front of the other horse. The animal shied away, causing the rider to tumble off. The man hit the ground hard, rolled over a couple of times, and came to a stop on his back.

The light from the stars and a half moon was strong enough for Smoke to recognize Pearlie's rawboned countenance.

Smoke was out of the saddle in the blink of an

eye, pouching his iron and kneeling beside his friend. "Pearlie!" He caught hold of the foreman's shoulders. "Pearlie, what happened?"

Pearlie blinked and stared up in Smoke's general direction, clearly having trouble focusing on his employer. "Sm-Smoke? That you?"

"Yeah, it's me. Sorry I spooked your horse like that. I didn't know who you were. How bad are you hurt?"

"It's nothin' . . . just a scratch . . . but Sally . . . you gotta help her!"

That cold, clutching fear was back. "Where is she?"

"They . . . they took her. Four hombres . . . badmen . . . one of 'em was . . . that little fella you talked to . . . in the saloon."

"You mean Fisk?"

"Yeah . . . Don't know why I can't . . . ever remember his name."

That confirmed it was Stonebreaker's gang that had raided the ranch, although Smoke thought there would have been more than four men.

"They kidnapped Sally?"

"Yeah . . . Said you was to bring . . . five thousand dollars . . . to Hampton Peak by sunup . . . tomorrow mornin' . . . They'll meet you there . . . with her."

Smoke's jaw tightened. He had no intention of paying any ransom for Sally, and he wasn't going to wait until morning to get her back. The outlaws believed he was in Big Rock. They had no idea he was less than half an hour behind them.

He knew this country a lot better than they did. He was willing to bet a hat on that. He knew the route they would take to get to Hampton Peak. By using some shortcuts, he could get ahead of them.

Pearlie's hand came up and clutched at Smoke's arm. "The kid . . ."

"You mean Cal?"

"Yeah. He ain't . . . dead. The other boys . . . it's too late for them . . . but we gotta help Cal."

The dilemma tore at Smoke. Did he go straight after Sally and her captors, or did he detour by the ranch first to see what he could do for Cal?

He knew what Sally would want him to do. She would tell him to see to Cal first and then come after her. But it was his choice to make, not hers.

"If you'll . . . get me back on that horse," Pearlie said, "I'll go see . . . what I can do to help Cal. You can . . . get on after them varmints. . . ."

"Thanks, Pearlie," Smoke said, his heart going out to his friend. "I don't think you're in any shape to—"

"The heck I . . . ain't! Just . . . catch that nag for me . . ."

Pearlie was already struggling to his feet. Smoke took his arm and helped him up. Pearlie caught his breath, and seemed a little stronger, although he was still unsteady on his feet. The horse he had been riding hadn't gone far. Smoke

195

caught the animal easily and led him over to the foreman. He helped Pearlie climb into the saddle.

"You go on now," Pearlie said. "You got to help Miss Sally. If anything was to . . . happen to her . . . we wouldn't get no more bear sign . . . and Cal'd never let me hear the end of it!"

Despite the desperate situation, a hint of a smile flickered over Smoke's rugged face. "Once I get Sally home, I reckon you and Cal will get all the bear sign you can eat from now on."

"One more thing," Pearlie grated. "I promised those no-good skunks . . . you'd blow their lights out for good."

"I'll keep that promise for you," Smoke said.

CHAPTER 19

Burke's hunch about Sally Jensen was confirmed as soon as he got a good look at her: she was a mighty handsome woman. And a mighty brave one, too. Even with bullets flying around, she had stood coolly, whipped out a gun, and shot him. The pain he felt from the bullet burn on his arm was tempered by the admiration he felt for her. He would have enjoyed getting to know her better, in more ways than one.

Too bad she wasn't going to live much longer.

Burke wanted to get well out of earshot of that puncher he had sent to Big Rock with the message for Smoke Jensen. If the man heard a single gunshot, he might figure out what was going on. It was unlikely, but Stonebreaker didn't like to take any chances and insisted that the men who rode with him follow his plans to the letter.

Once Mrs. Jensen was dead, they would hide her body so her husband couldn't stumble over it, then Kiowa Smith would ride on to Hampton Peak and set up an ambush for Jensen. The 'breed was the gang's best shot with a rifle. As soon as he could see Jensen, he would put a slug from his Sharps through the gunfighter, and that would be the end of the notorious Smoke Jensen.

In the meantime, Burke, Crandell, and Fisk would hightail it back to Big Rock to join forces with Stonebreaker and the rest of the gang for the raid on the town. It would be a night of blood, death, and fire, Burke thought, and when he and the others rode away, they would be considerably richer. It was a good plan . . . but Burke still wished Sally Jensen didn't have to die so soon.

He had a lot of wishes in life he told himself as he slipped his Colt from its holster. A little farther, he thought. A little farther, and then he would bring his horse to a stop, turn around in the saddle, and shoot Sally Jensen in the head before she knew what was going on.

It was the merciful thing to do.

• • •

The 'Paloose responded gallantly, as Smoke had known it would. Some folks didn't like the big, spotted horses bred by the Nez Percé, claiming they were too high-strung and lacking in stamina. Smoke had ridden many Appaloosas over the years and knew that to be false. There were good and bad horses among every breed, but in general he had found the 'Palooses to be valiant, dependable animals.

They were sure-footed, too, which was a good thing. Smoke was in a hurry and a misstep could be disastrous. He circled to the south, through a series of narrow canyons along the edge of Sugarloaf range that not many people knew about. Preacher had known an old Indian war trail ran through there, and he had told Smoke. Since then, Smoke had explored the route on numerous occasions.

The trail ended in a steep, rocky slope. The 'Paloose swarmed up it like a mountain goat. Smoke held his breath a few times when it seemed like the horse might topple over backward, but the 'Paloose struggled on and finally reached the top. Smoke reined in and listened for the sound of hoofbeats that would tell him Sally's kidnappers were close by.

Not hearing anything, he rode quickly across the shoulder of ground that tailed off into the rocky slope behind him. On the far side of the open space was another slope covered with a thick growth of pines. Smoke rode into the trees. Sally's captors would have to come along there to reach Hampton Peak, which bulked darkly in the night several miles to the west. Concealed in the pines as he was, they wouldn't be able to see him until it was too late.

Smoke couldn't be a hundred percent certain his quarry hadn't passed by already, but he knew he ought to be in front of them. Never having been one to brood about such things, he pulled his Winchester from the saddle boot, levered a round into the chamber, and waited.

Minutes stretched out nerve-wrackingly, and he was mighty glad when he finally heard the steady sound of hoofbeats approaching. He edged the 'Paloose forward a little.

The riders came into view about fifty yards away, moving from left to right in front and slightly below him. They were far enough away that shooting would be tricky in the bad light, but he brought the Winchester to his shoulder and sighted over the barrel.

"You must not value your lives very highly," Sally said to the man riding in front of her as they started along an open stretch of ground with a heavily-wooded slope rising to the right. To the left the terrain dropped away ruggedly into a deep, vast pool of blackness. "Five thousand dollars split four ways doesn't really add up to much. Not that you'll get even that much. Smoke won't pay any ransom for me."

"Are you saying your husband doesn't love you, Mrs. Jensen?" the leader asked over his shoulder with a mocking tone in his voice.

"I'm saying he'll think it's easier and cheaper to kill you."

The man laughed. "He can try."

"When Smoke Jensen tries to kill somebody, he generally succeeds."

"There's always a first time for a man to fail."

"Maybe. But not tonight. Not for Smoke."

The man reined in, bringing his horse to an abrupt stop right in front of Sally's mount. The other three crowded up around her. The leader twisted in the saddle, and Sally felt her heart drop when she saw moonlight reflect off the pistol he held. As the pistol came up, the man said, "You're wrong."

Sally wanted to close her eyes so she wouldn't see it coming, but she was too stubborn to do that. She was going to be looking right at the man when he shot her.

The whipcrack of a shot tore through the night.

Smoke bit back a curse when he saw the riders stop suddenly and close tighter ranks around Sally. Under better circumstances, he might have risked trying to blow them all out of their saddles

200

before they knew what was happening, but in the uncertain light, a missed shot might hit her.

He shifted his aim to a bigger target, the leader's horse, and pressed the trigger. The Winchester kicked hard against his shoulder as the shot rang out.

Instantly, Smoke dug his heels into the 'Paloose's flanks and sent the horse leaping out of the trees. He jammed the rifle back in its sheath and drew both Colts as he guided the 'Paloose with his knees.

"Sally, go!" he bellowed. "Straight ahead!"

The leader's horse was down, thrashing around as its life's blood poured out from the wound in its breast. A hideous scream of pain had come from the animal as it fell, blending in with the shot its rider had fired as he was thrown from the saddle. Smoke prayed the bullet hadn't found Sally.

Only a handful of heartbeats had passed, but Smoke's quick action and the swift, lunging strides of the big, spotted horse had closed the distance between him and the kidnappers by half. His spirits soared as he saw Sally's horse leap forward, past the horse he had shot. She was leaning over, riding low in the saddle to make herself a smaller target.

The leader scrambled to his feet and flung a shot after her while his companions clawed their guns from leather and opened fire on Smoke. He veered the 'Paloose from side to side as bullets whipped around his head. The Colts in his hands began to roar, orange flame spewing from their muzzles as he triggered again and again. One of the riders threw his hands in the air and pitched off his horse as Smoke's lead found him.

The leader snapped a couple shots as he dashed toward the riderless horse. He managed to grab the reins and got a foot in the stirrup. The horse bolted, but the man hung on for dear life and struggled up into the saddle. In the face of that furious charge, the other two broke and ran, wheeling their horses and kicking the animals into frantic gallops.

Smoke let them go. He could always track them down later—and he would. His only concern at the moment was Sally.

She had ridden a couple hundred yards away from the scene of the fight, then reined in and turned her mount. When she saw Smoke coming toward her, she raced to meet him. They called each other's name at the same time.

Smoke wanted to dismount, grab her out of the saddle, and hold her close. But the men who had fled still represented a threat. They might double back. Smoke's goal was to make sure Sally was safe, so he stayed on the 'Paloose, holstered his revolvers, and drew the Winchester again.

"Sally!" he said as their horses came alongside one another. "Are you all right? Were you hit?"

"I'm fine, Smoke," she told him breathlessly. "What about you?"

"They didn't get me." He kept his eyes on the spot where the trail twisted around a ridge, where the three men had disappeared.

"Do you think they're coming back?"

"I don't know, but I intend to be ready if they do."

"I knew you'd come after me."

A grim smile touched Smoke's mouth. "Did you ever doubt it?"

"Not one bit."

"I'd better go check on the one I downed."

"I'm coming with you," she declared.

Smoke knew better than to argue. "Just stay behind me." If he could get her to do that, he'd be doing good.

He guessed she realized just how close she had come to dying. As they rode slowly toward the fallen man with Smoke in the lead, he said, "Do you know who those varmints were?"

"I don't have any idea. They never called each other by name."

"I'm pretty sure they're part of a gang led by an hombre named Stonebreaker."

"Never heard of him."

"Neither had I until today." Smoke told her quickly about the encounter he and Pearlie had had in town with Wylie Fisk, and how he had figured out those at the ranch might be in danger.

"Pearlie!" Sally exclaimed. "He was shot, and so was Cal. Oh, Smoke, we have to help them—"

"I already ran into Pearlie. Once he told me what was going on, he headed back to the ranch. He and Cal better be all right, otherwise I'll have some more scores to settle with Stonebreaker and his bunch." Smoke grimaced. "Of course, I can only kill 'em once."

"Sometimes that's a real shame," Sally said with a touch of the savagery that usually cropped up in her when those she cared about were hurt.

Smoke nodded. "Was it just a kidnapping scheme? There are more than four men in Stonebreaker's gang."

"Maybe these men weren't riding with Stonebreaker anymore."

"Maybe if this varmint is still alive," Smoke said with a nod toward the man on the ground as they brought their horses to a stop, "we can find out." He handed the rifle to Sally, knowing she could handle it. "Keep him covered." He swung down from the saddle and cautiously approached the man he had shot.

Sally circled around on the other side so she would have a clear shot at the man if he tried anything. She lifted the rifle and aimed it as Smoke got the toe of his boot under the man's shoulder and rolled him onto his back. The man let out a groan.

Smoke wasn't surprised that he recognized the

man. Wylie Fisk had lost his hat when he fell off his horse. The evening breeze plucked at the lank strands of his thinning hair. The front of Fisk's shirt was dark with blood.

Smoke went to a knee beside him. "Fisk, can you hear me? Wylie Fisk!"

The little outlaw's eyelids fluttered. After a moment he was able to hold them open. "J-Jensen?" he gasped.

"That's right."

"You gotta . . . help me! I'm shot!"

"I know," Smoke said calmly. "I'm the one who shot you."

"I . . . I'm sorry. I never meant to . . . hurt your wife. It was all . . . Stonebreaker's idea."

"Was he with you?" None of the men Smoke had seen looked big enough to match Stonebreaker's description on the wanted poster.

"I hurt . . . like blazes." Fisk licked his lips. "I need a drink of water . . . or some whiskey."

Neither of those things was going to help Fisk, gutshot the way he was. He was dead already. It would just take an hour or so of very painful wrestling with the Grim Reaper before everything was finished.

However, Smoke didn't point that out. He said, "I'll help you after you tell me where Stonebreaker is." Kidnapping Sally wasn't the whole plan, he sensed. Stonebreaker had some other objective in mind.

"You swear you'll . . . do what you can for me if I tell you?"

"I swear," Smoke said.

"Stonebreaker . . . Stonebreaker and the others . . . are in Big Rock. It was . . . our job to get you away from there . . . so they could hit the bank . . . and loot the town."

"Tonight?" Smoke snapped. It was an audacious plan, and it had come close to working.

"Yeah . . . They were gonna wait . . . until the rest of us . . . got back."

So murdering his ranch hands and kidnapping Sally was just a ploy to lure him away from Big Rock, Smoke thought. It made sense. The two deputies left in town were good men, but they wouldn't be any match for Stonebreaker and his whole gang.

"I told you . . . the truth . . . Jensen," Fisk went on. "Now you . . . promised to help me . . ."

"I'll get my canteen." Smoke started to straighten up.

Fisk caught at his sleeve with a bloody hand. "That ain't gonna . . . do any good . . . and we both know it. . . . Only one way . . . you can help me. . . . My guts are . . . full of lead. . . . Don't let me . . . die like this."

Smoke reached for the knife sheathed behind his left hand gun. "You want to make your peace first?"

A strangled laugh came from Fisk. "Ain't no

peace . . . for a man like me . . . to make. The Devil's been ready to . . . shake my hand . . . for a long time now!"

That was probably true, Smoke thought. The hand holding the knife made one swift move that opened Fisk's throat from side to side. The outlaw's back arched and his feet drummed against the ground, but only for a second. Then he slumped down again and it was over.

"Sorry you had to see that," Smoke said to Sally as he wiped the blade on the sleeve of Fisk's shirt. He stood up and sheathed the knife.

"You kept your promise, Smoke. You did what you could for him."

Smoke headed for his 'Paloose. "Now I've got another promise to keep. I told Pearlie I'd kill those varmints, and I intend to do it."

CHAPTER 20

Oliver Stonebreaker was not a patient man. Prodigious appetites—for food and drink, for money, for women, for power—had gripped him all his life, and that sort of drive didn't allow for patience. So a part of him was ready to attack Big Rock, to charge into the settlement with all guns blazing, as soon as darkness descended over the land.

But another part of him was cunning enough to know he needed to wait. Burke and the others weren't supposed to raid Sugarloaf until night had fallen. They'd had orders to leave one of Jensen's cowboys alive, and if all had gone as planned, that man would be galloping toward Big Rock with the news that Mrs. Jensen had been carried off by kidnappers. Smoke Jensen would go tearing after them. Stonebreaker had heard enough talk about the man to be certain of that. Once Jensen was gone it would be a simple matter to take over the town.

You wouldn't think one man could make that much difference, Stonebreaker brooded, but he knew it was true. Smoke Jensen was perhaps the best pure fighting man anywhere on the frontier, better even than Stonebreaker—and the outlaw chieftain knew how dangerous *he* was. Jensen was worth at least half a dozen good men in a battle.

But more important was Jensen's ability to rally others to his cause. The man was a natural leader. Stonebreaker had heard about how Jensen had banded together with a group of cantankerous old mountain men more than once to wipe out small armies of outlaws. With Jensen leading the defense of Big Rock, the townspeople would find courage they didn't even know they had.

Without Jensen, and without their tough old sheriff, any resistance they put up would quickly collapse. Stonebreaker was counting on that, and he was enough of a strategist to know it was true.

But as the stars came out and the moon rose and the evening passed without any sign of a cowboy from Sugarloaf galloping into town with the message for Jensen, Stonebreaker began to worry. That should have happened already. In fact, it was time for Burke, Crandell, and Fisk to be getting back, and they hadn't shown up, either.

Stonebreaker and the other eight members of the gang were waiting in a thick stand of trees on top of a hill about a quarter mile from Big Rock. The shadows were so thick no one could see them. Stonebreaker had given strict orders that none of the men were to light up a quirly or anything else. He didn't want them striking matches that might be noticed in town.

Pacing back and forth at the edge of the trees with his hands clasped behind his back, Stonebreaker muttered oaths to himself. No plan was ever perfect. Some small detail always went wrong. Usually it didn't have any effect on the outcome of things, but unaccustomed worry gnawed at Stonebreaker's brain. He had a feeling something bigger than usual was wrong.

One of the men came up behind him and whispered, "Boss, somebody's comin'!"

Stonebreaker swung around. "Burke and the others, no doubt," he rumbled.

"But what about Jensen? He ain't left town yet, has he?"

"Perhaps Burke can tell us about that."

Stonebreaker stalked through the trees, weaving back and forth around the trunks with uncanny ease though it was almost too dark for a man to see his own hand in front of his face. He heard the hoofbeats of several horses and said to his men, "Be ready for trouble, but hold your fire until I give the order." He crossed his arms over his body and gripped the pearl-handled guns in their holsters.

Burke and his companions were the only ones who should know about the rendezvous. If anyone else came along and discovered them, it would be an accident . . . a very unlucky accident for those unknown riders.

But the riders weren't unknown at all. The sound of the horses abruptly stopped, and Burke's voice called softly, "Stonebreaker?"

He exhaled in relief and returned Burke's hail. "Come ahead!"

Burke and two companions rode up. That was the right number, Stonebreaker thought, because Kiowa Smith was supposed to be at Hampton Peak, waiting to bushwhack Jensen at sunrise the next morning. Maybe all his uneasiness had been for nothing.

As Burke slid out of the saddle, he quashed that notion by saying, "It's all shot to hell, Stonebreaker. Jensen got ahead of us somehow, ambushed us, killed Fisk, and rescued his wife."

Stonebreaker stood with his feet planted wide

apart, but still swayed a little, so fierce was the wave of anger that went through him. "How?" he demanded. "How did Jensen find out?"

"I don't know," Burke snapped. "All I know is that he came close to killing all of us. He's hell on wheels, Stonebreaker, just like you said."

A chorus of gibbering demons clamored inside Stonebreaker's head. He drew in a deep breath and willed them to shut up. When they had quieted down, he said, "Where is Jensen now?"

"I don't know that. Fisk went down, Kiowa and Crandell are both wounded, and I got nicked myself earlier when we hit the ranch. We got out before Jensen could kill us."

"You mean you abandoned my plan."

"Damn it! Jensen was already between us and his wife with both guns spitting fire. What good would it have done for us to stay there and get killed?"

Burke had a point there, Stonebreaker supposed, but he was still furious his plan had gone awry. All that was left was to salvage as much of it as he could. A good general was able to think on his feet, Stonebreaker reminded himself.

"Very well. Jensen isn't in Big Rock and doesn't know what's about to happen, or he would have sounded the alarm by now. We still have time to hit the bank and clean it out."

"What about taking over the town and looting the rest of it?"

"That may not be possible. But do what you can. Four of us will go to the bank. The rest of you spread out and keep the citizens occupied. Any valuables you're able to grab will be that much more."

Burke nodded. "We still ought to come out with a good haul."

"Of course we will," Stonebreaker said. "In case Jensen comes along afterward and has any thoughts about following us, we'll make sure he's too busy for that. Put the torch to the town as you ride out. We'll burn Big Rock to the ground!"

Sally wanted to ride with Smoke to the settlement, but he wasn't going to allow it. Sometimes he knew better than to argue with her, but the reverse was true, too. He wasn't budging on that one. She needed to tend to Pearlie and Cal, he pointed out, and Sally sure couldn't argue with that.

As they galloped up to the ranch house, Pearlie stepped onto the porch with a rifle in his hands. The foreman leaned against one of the porch posts to prop himself up, but the Winchester was steady as he pointed it at the new arrivals.

Smoke called out, "Pearlie, it's us!"

Pearlie lowered the rifle. "Smoke? Miss Sally? Thank the Lord, you're both all right! You are, ain't you?"

"We're fine," Smoke assured him. Sally dismounted, but Smoke stayed in the saddle.

"How's Cal?" Sally asked as she hurried up onto the porch.

"He's lost some blood, but the bullet went straight through and I'm hopin' it didn't hit nothin' too important. I been tryin' to clean him up—"

"I'll help you," Sally broke in. She looked back at Smoke before going in the house. "Be careful."

He gave her a nod but made no promise. What he found in Big Rock would determine how careful he could be.

"What are you fixin' to do, Smoke?" Pearlie asked after Sally had gone inside. "Why do you need to be careful?"

"The gang those varmints belong to is going to hit the bank in Big Rock tonight," Smoke explained. "They may already be doing it."

Pearlie let out a low-voiced curse. "Raidin' the ranch was just a decoy to get you out of town!"

"That's the way I figure it. But I realized something was wrong earlier than they expected. Now I've got to get back there and see if I can stop them."

"I'm comin' with—"

"No, you're not," Smoke broke in. "You're wounded, and I'm sorry to say it, Pearlie, but you'd just slow me down."

"Blast it, Smoke, you can't take on a whole gang of outlaws by yourself! Why, that'd be . . ." Pearlie's voice trailed off into a grim chuckle.

213

"Just the sort of ruckus you've gotten yourself into a dozen times before, wouldn't it?"

Smoke smiled, lifted a hand in farewell, wheeled the 'Paloose, and urged the horse into a run.

Stonebreaker made sure a member of the gang named Lucas Martin was with him. Martin was their blaster, a former miner who was an expert at handling dynamite. He would be able to blow the door off the vault in the bank without wrecking the whole place. Two more men went with them to serve as guards while Stonebreaker and Martin took care of getting to the money.

The rest of the gang spread out. They would enter Big Rock by ones and twos, getting into position to terrorize the townspeople, then waiting for Stonebreaker's signal to launch the attack.

Stonebreaker had his fury tamped down, but it still smoldered inside him. He wanted vengeance on Jensen for trying to thwart his plans, and part of him hoped Jensen would show up.

But it would be better if they could get out of there without having to deal with Jensen. If they could manage that, revenge could wait.

Sooner or later, Jensen *would* pay the price for daring to get in Oliver Stonebreaker's way. Stonebreaker made that promise to himself.

The four of them—Stonebreaker, Martin, Dave Ritter and Amos Green—rode openly down Big

Rock's main street toward the bank. The town was settling down for the night, but quite a few people were still out and about. Stonebreaker knew he was a striking figure, so he wasn't surprised when some of the locals stared at him. He didn't let that bother him. Unlike some outlaws, he had never tried to conceal his identity. He was proud of the reputation as a badman he had been able to carve out.

When they reached the bank, they dismounted. Martin took his saddlebags filled with dynamite from his horse and slung them over his shoulder. With Ritter and Green leading the way, they started down the dark alley beside the bank.

As Stonebreaker was about to step into the shadows, a voice called, "Hey, mister, wait a minute."

Stonebreaker stopped and looked to his right. A man was hurrying along the boardwalk toward him. As he passed a lighted window, the glow reflected off the badge pinned to his shirt, telling Stonebreaker it was one of the deputies.

Martin and the others had paused. Stonebreaker waved them on as he turned to face the lawman. "What can I do for you?" he rumbled.

The deputy came to a stop a few feet away with his hand resting on the butt of his gun. "I saw you fellas riding into town just now. No offense, but I like to keep track of strangers, especially when they come into Big Rock after dark."

Stonebreaker smiled and said, "You think we might be up to no good, is that it?"

"Well, like I said, no offense, but you hombres look like you still got plenty of bark left on you."

"Indeed we do, Deputy," Stonebreaker said.

The man frowned. "Hey, how'd you know I'm a deputy and not the sher—"

Stonebreaker's arms shot out with blinding speed for such a big man. His right hand clamped around the deputy's neck to choke off any outcry, while his left grabbed hold of the man's wrist to keep him from drawing his gun. Jerking the deputy closer to him to get better leverage, Stonebreaker twisted hard on the unfortunate lawman's neck. The bone broke with an audible snap, and the deputy went limp in his grasp.

Stonebreaker slung the dead man into the alley like a sack of garbage and followed Martin and the other two outlaws. Green was working on the back door of the bank with a knife. Martin asked, "Any trouble?"

"You know me better than that, Lucas," Stonebreaker said. "The deputy won't trouble us."

Martin laughed. "That's what I figured."

Green broke the lock, pushed the door open, and the four men went inside. Stonebreaker struck a match, cupping the flame in his hand so that it couldn't be seen easily through the front windows. It provided enough light for them to find the vault.

Martin worked quickly, taking a couple sticks of dynamite from his saddlebags and attaching them with paste to the vault door where the hinges were located. He stuck another stick of dynamite to the lock mechanism the same way. It took him only moments to put caps and fuses on the explosives. After the blasts, the door ought to fall forward, allowing them into the big safe. The explosions would signal the rest of the gang to launch their raid.

Stonebreaker slipped a pocket watch from his vest and opened it to check the time. "Burke and the others should be ready," he said as he snapped the watch closed.

"So are we," Martin said. "Light 'em up, Oliver?"

Stonebreaker nodded. "Light them up."

Martin struck a match openly and held the flame to each of the three fuses in turn, moving quickly. The fuses sputtered to life and started throwing off sparks as they burned.

"Let's get out of here," Martin said as he dropped the match, and headed toward the back door. They would wait in the alley while the vault door blew, then rush back in and start shoveling cash and gold coins into the sacks they had brought along to fill.

Stonebreaker let the other three go ahead of him. He lingered for a second, watching in satisfaction as the fuses burned toward the dynamite.

That part of the operation had gone smoothly.

At that moment, shots rang out, roaring swiftly one after another. Stonebreaker jerked his head up and roared, "Jensen!"

CHAPTER 21

Burke, Crandell, and Kiowa Smith picked the busiest saloon in town as their target. They figured the place had quite a bundle of cash. Likely there would be customers who would put up a fight, but Burke was confident once he and his companions burst in and killed a few people, the fight would go out of the others.

The rest of the gang split up among the other saloons in town and the express office at the railroad station. Burke worried they were spreading themselves a little too thin. It would have been better if they could have quietly eliminated both deputies, as well as anybody else who represented a threat, before revealing their presence in Big Rock. Jensen's interference on the trail had ruined that. The important thing was to strike fast, grab what they could, and light a shuck out of there, leaving flaming destruction behind to insure there wouldn't be any pursuit.

Maybe Stonebreaker's plans would go better next time, Burke told himself.

He, Crandell, and Kiowa were passing the dark mouth of an alley on their way to the saloon when Crandell suddenly clutched Burke's arm.

"Look!" the stocky outlaw said. "It's him!"

Burke turned, and his spirits rose. Smoke Jensen was riding into town. It was their chance to ambush him again and put him out of the way— but that would mean jumping the gun and starting the attack before Stonebreaker had given the signal.

Before Burke had a chance to figure out what to do, Crandell took the decision out of his hands. He jerked his gun from its holster, shouted, "I'll get him!" and charged into the street to kill Smoke Jensen.

Smoke had thought about changing horses at the ranch, but he believed the 'Paloose had one good run left. That hunch proved to be correct as the horse carried him toward the settlement at a steady gallop. As he rode, he took out each Colt in turn and slipped a cartridge into the sixth chamber. Normally he carried the guns with the hammer resting on an empty chamber, but tonight he wanted a full wheel.

As he approached the town, he listened for the sound of gunfire over the 'Paloose's drumming hoofbeats. When he didn't hear any, his hopes rose. Maybe he would get there before Stonebreaker's gang started the raid.

Smoke didn't slow down as the lights of Big Rock came into view. He expected to hear all hell break loose at any second, but the town remained peaceful as he approached. He slowed the 'Paloose to a walk as he reached the end of Main Street. His eyes moved from side to side searching for signs of trouble. A few people were still on the street. Quite a few horses were tied up in front of Louis Longmont's saloon.

Smoke looked farther down the street and frowned slightly as he noticed several horses hitched to the rail in front of the bank. The building was dark. Nobody would be doing any business there at that time of night.

Nobody but outlaws who wanted to clean out the vault.

Smoke's instincts warned him the gang was already in town. He drew his right-hand gun and was about to heel the horse into one last run toward the bank when a man suddenly burst out of the shadows to his left. Catching the quick movement from the corner of his eye, Smoke saw the man raise a gun toward him. Smoke dropped the 'Paloose's reins and drew the left-hand gun with a twist of his wrist. It roared just a hair ahead of the stranger's gun.

The man got a shot off, but it went high and wild as Smoke's slug punched into his chest and knocked him backward like a giant fist. Smoke shot him again just to make sure, then left the saddle in a rolling dive as more splashes of muzzle flame ripped through the darkness.

The 'Paloose bolted on down the street, out of the line of fire, as Smoke came up on one knee. He triggered both guns, scything lead through the shadows where his enemies were. One man staggered forward and clutched at his belly for a second before he toppled over on his face. Slugs were screaming uncomfortably close to Smoke's head as he surged to his feet. Still firing, he dashed for cover behind a nearby parked wagon with its team still in harness.

Bullets chewed splinters from the wagon bed as Smoke crouched there. As he tried to return the fire, the hammers of both guns clicked on empty chambers. He knew he was in a bad position, but he had to reload. He knelt lower, holstered the left-hand gun, and started thumbing fresh cartridges into the right-hand Colt.

Shots came from behind him as more outlaws joined in the fight. A bullet sizzled past his ear and smacked into the wagon. He dived to the ground and rolled under the vehicle.

The horses hitched to the wagon were badly spooked by the gunfire and on the verge of bolting. A bullet burned across the rump of one of the leaders, and that was all it took. The horses panicked and stampeded.

Smoke jammed his right-hand gun back in the holster and grabbed hold of the braces underneath the wagon as it lurched into motion. He held on for dear life as it dragged him along the street. The dirt scraped at his back as he was pulled out of that deadly crossfire.

After being dragged a few seconds, Smoke let go and the wagon careened on down the street without him. He rolled over and came up on his knees, reaching for his gun again. He'd only had time to reload one.

The door of the bank crashed open, kicked from inside. A huge figure loomed there, filling the doorway. Smoke saw the long hair, the beard, and knew he was looking at Oliver Stonebreaker. The outlaw knew him, too. He bellowed, "Jensen!" as he opened fire with two guns.

Stonebreaker had squeezed off one shot from each gun, when flame and noise erupted behind him and the explosion threw him forward.

Smoke took advantage of that opportunity to lunge to his feet. A couple men charged toward him from up the street, and opened fire as he whirled toward them.

Out in the open like that, no one was deadlier than Smoke Jensen. His gun blasted twice, and both men went down as his lead tore through them.

Before Smoke could do anything else, something crashed into him from behind, knocking him off his feet. Arms like tree trunks went around him and closed with crushing force, pinning his arms to his sides and making his ribs creak. Breathing was out of the question. It was like being hugged by a grizzly, and he knew Stonebreaker had tackled him.

"I'm going to break you apart with my bare hands, Jensen," the outlaw growled in his ear, confirming that hunch. "You've ruined my plans, and no man can do that and live!"

While Stonebreaker was making that dramatic threat, Smoke hunched his shoulders and lowered his head, then brought it up and back with stunning force. His skull smacked into the middle of Stonebreaker's face, his nose giving way under the impact. Hot blood spurted from it. Stonebreaker howled from the blinding pain, and for a second loosened his grip on Smoke.

Smoke's own strength was almost a match for the massive outlaw's, and the momentary distraction of a broken nose gave Smoke the chance to break free. He drove his arms to the side, breaking Stonebreaker's grip. He stumbled forward a step but quickly found his feet and pivoted in time to see one of those huge arms swinging at him.

He ducked under the blow. He could have put a couple bullets in Stonebreaker's gut, but wouldn't kill a man in cold blood, not even an outlaw. Instead, he reversed his grip on the empty left-hand gun and slammed its butt against Stonebreaker's head. That staggered the big man but didn't put him down. He bulled forward, ramming a shoulder into Smoke's chest, driving him backward. His guns were jolted out of his hands.

He twisted in mid-air, caught himself on his hands, and levered himself out of the way as Stonebreaker leaped after him. If Stonebreaker had landed on him, some of Smoke's ribs would have broken for sure. He avoided that fate by inches and jerked himself around to drive a kick at Stonebreaker's face. Stonebreaker got his left shoulder up in time to block the kick. His other hand clamped on Smoke's ankle like a bear trap.

Smoke was vaguely aware that a battle was raging in Big Rock. He heard gun thunder and caught glimpses of orange muzzle flashes that lit the night like lightning. Somewhere a shotgun boomed and a man screamed.

But Smoke had his hands full with the monstrous Stonebreaker, who was trying to twist his leg out of its socket. Rolling across the dusty street to keep that from happening, Smoke got his other leg up, and snapped a kick into Stonebreaker's chest under that jutting beard. As they grappled, Smoke clubbed his hands together, bent his body upward, and brought them down with savage force against the side of Stonebreaker's neck.

The man's grip loosened, and Smoke pulled his leg free, ignoring the pain. He rolled over, pushed himself to his feet, and swung a right and a left as Stonebreaker surged after him. Both blows landed solidly and rocked the outlaw's head back and forth, but he didn't go down. Roaring like a maddened bull, he crashed into Smoke again and forced him back against a hitch rail. Agony filled Smoke as he was bent backwards almost double.

He brought his knee up into Stonebreaker's groin. Stonebreaker grunted but continued to heave against Smoke, obviously trying to snap his spine over the hitch rail. Smoke cupped his hands and slammed them against Stonebreaker's ears, hoping it would do some good even with that wild thatch of hair around the man's head.

The pressure eased. Stonebreaker shook his shaggy head, seeming a little disoriented. Smoke got a hand under the outlaw's chin and shoved up as hard as he could, forcing Stonebreaker to take a step back, giving Smoke room to slip out of the trap.

Stonebreaker was bigger, but Smoke was faster. He hammered two punches into the outlaw's face before Stonebreaker could get his hands up, landing both blows on his already crushed and bleeding nose. Stonebreaker roared again and shook his head, slinging gore everywhere. He flailed punches at Smoke, but none of them connected.

Smoke could feel the tide of the battle turning. He backed up, forcing Stonebreaker to come lumbering after him. A quick dart to the side sent the outlaw stumbling past him. Smoke clubbed his hands again and swung them at the back of Stonebreaker's neck. The powerful blow toppled Stonebreaker and sent him crashing face-first to the street.

Smoke landed on top of him, driving both knees into Stonebreaker's back. He grabbed Stone-breaker's head, tangled his fingers in the man's hair, and jerked his head up. Smoke slammed Stonebreaker's face into the ground with stunning force, again and again, and yet again. His lips pulled back from his teeth in a grimace. *Threaten Sally, would he?* Hot rage coursed through Smoke. He sent Stonebreaker's face crashing into the dirt twice more.

"Smoke!"

The urgent voice cut through the red haze in Smoke's brain. He didn't know how many times it had already called his name. Chest heaving, he straightened and turned his head to look around. Louis Longmont stood there, as slim and elegant and deadly as ever, smoke curling from the barrel of the revolver he held.

"He's either dead or out cold, Smoke," the gambler said. "You might as well stop."

Smoke looked around dazedly. The shooting had stopped. He saw bodies sprawled here and there. Men he recognized as citizens of Big Rock moved among them, holding rifles, pistols, and shotguns.

"The rest of the gang . . ." Smoke said.

"Either dead or begging for mercy," Longmont said with a sardonic smile. "I don't know how many of them you accounted for, but with you out here fighting that behemoth of a man in the middle of the street, the rest of the town wasn't going to stand by and do nothing."

"How many of them did you get?"

Longmont raised one shoulder in a half-shrug. "Who keeps count at a time like this? The important thing is, the fight's over." The gambler holstered his gun and extended a hand to Smoke. "Let me help you up."

Smoke clasped his friend's hand and let Longmont help him to his feet. As they looked down at Stonebreaker, the rasp of air through the ruined nose told them that the boss outlaw was still alive.

"You reckon I can get some volunteers to drag him down to the jail?" Smoke asked.

"I don't think that'll be a problem at all," Longmont said.

Once Stonebreaker and three other surviving members of the gang were locked up, Smoke rode back out to Sugarloaf. Longmont had agreed to help the remaining deputy keep an eye on the prisoners. The other deputy's body had been found in the alley beside the bank, and there was no doubt in Smoke's mind that Stonebreaker had snapped the man's neck.

Two more outlaws were down at Dr. Simpson's place, shot full of holes. If they lived through the night, it would be a surprise. The other six were already dead. Big Rock's undertaker was going to be mighty busy for a while.

When Sally heard the 'Paloose's hoofbeats, she stepped onto the porch with a rifle in her hands. She let out a happy cry and set the gun aside as she recognized Smoke. She rushed into his arms as soon as his boots hit the ground and held him tight. He did likewise.

"You're all right?" she whispered.

"I'm all right. I might be a little stiff and sore tomorrow . . ."

Sally lifted her head. "Then you'd better come inside and convince me you're still fine now."

"Pearlie and Cal . . . ?"

"In the bunk house. I want to take them to town in the morning so the doctor can take a look at them, but they're going to be all right."

"In that case," Smoke said with a grin, "I'd be happy to oblige."

By the middle of the next day, most of the damage in Big Rock had been cleaned up, although it was going to take some time to repair the bank vault. In the meantime, the bank's cash on hand was locked up in the huge safe in the Wells Fargo office in the railroad depot.

Sally had driven the ranch wagon into town

with Pearlie on the seat beside her and Cal stretched out in the back. Smoke had already buried the four cowboys murdered in the attack on Sugarloaf. After examining the two wounded men, Dr. Simpson said that he wanted to keep Cal at his home for a few days, but Pearlie would be all right to return to the ranch as long as he took it easy and Sally kept fresh bandages on the crease in his side.

"Don't worry," Sally said. "I'll take good care of him."

"Probably stuff him full of bear sign, and I won't get any," Cal grumbled from the bed where the doctor had put him.

Sally laughed. "I'll make some and bring it into town for you, how's that?"

Cal grinned. "I reckon that'd help me recover from this wound, all right."

"Now I figure out how come you get shot all the time," Pearlie said. "You're just lookin' for bear sign and sympathy."

"You got shot, too."

"Yeah, but I'm still up and around."

Sally left them sniping at each other and went to the sheriff's office, where she found Smoke sitting at the desk going through Monte Carson's collection of wanted posters.

"Got to match up all these reward dodgers with the bodies down at the undertaker's," he explained as he glanced up at her.

"Are you planning on claiming the rewards?"

"You bet I am. That money ought to go to the family of the deputy who got killed."

Sally smiled. "Of course. What was I thinking?"

The sound of a train whistle made Smoke look up again. He pushed the papers aside. "I can do this later. You want to go down to the station and watch the train come in?"

"That sounds like a fine idea."

Arm in arm, they walked to the depot, arriving just as the big Baldwin locomotive rolled past the platform, belching smoke from its diamond stack. Smoke and Sally walked through the station and onto the platform. With only the deputy, Smoke had more responsibility for keeping the peace, and that meant keeping track of who got off the train.

He stiffened as he saw a tall man carrying a valise swing down from one of the passenger cars. The man wore a black suit and a wide-brimmed black Stetson with a Montana pinch. His hair was prematurely white under the black hat, his face rugged and youthful.

"What is it, Smoke?" Sally asked.

"That hombre looks like he might be trouble." Smoke nodded slightly toward the stranger.

The man noticed them then and came toward them, but he didn't seem to be looking for trouble. In fact, a friendly smile broke out on his face. "Smoke Jensen?" he asked as he came up to Smoke and Sally.

"That's right." Smoke moved so that he was between Sally and the stranger.

"My name's Boyd," the man introduced himself. "U.S. Marshal from up Montana way. I happened to be here in Colorado delivering a prisoner when your governor got hold of the chief marshal in Denver and asked for some help. The chief thought maybe I'd like to give you a hand. He said I could consider it a vacation," Boyd added dryly.

"I wasn't expecting anybody for another week or so," Smoke said.

"With the telegraph, things don't take as long as they used to." Boyd laughed, a hearty sound. "The wonders of modern communication."

"You happen to have any proof of who you are?" Smoke asked.

"Sure." Boyd took a wallet from inside his coat and showed Smoke his badge and identification papers. Satisfied, Smoke nodded and shook hands with the man.

"I'm glad you're here," he told Boyd. "We've had some trouble. A gang of outlaws hit the bank last night."

Boyd frowned. "Did they get away with much?"

"They didn't get away. We've got four prisoners locked up in the jail, including the leader of the gang."

"And the others?"

"I reckon the burials will be later today."

Boyd nodded knowingly. "I'm not surprised,

given the things I've heard about you, Smoke. You don't mind if I call you Smoke, do you?"

"Not at all. This is my wife, by the way."

"I was beginning to wonder if you were going to get around to introducing me." Sally held out a hand to the newcomer. "Sally Jensen, Marshal."

"It's an honor and a pleasure, Mrs. Jensen," Boyd told her as he took her hand.

Before they could say anything else, someone came up behind Smoke and said, "Mr. Jensen?"

Smoke turned to see the telegrapher standing there. The bespectacled man held out a yellow flimsy. "I just got this message for you and happened to see you standing out here. It came addressed in care of Sheriff Carson, but I figure it'll be all right just to give it to you."

Smoke nodded his thanks as he reached out to take the telegram. He stiffened again as his eyes scanned the words printed on it.

Sally noticed his reaction. "Smoke, what's wrong?"

"This wire is from Matt. He wants me to find Preacher and get to a place in Nevada called Halltown as fast as I can." Smoke looked up from the message and met Sally's eyes. "I don't know if I ought to—"

"Of course you should go," she said without hesitation. "Marshal Boyd's here to keep an eye on things now, and Louis can help out, if need be."

"But what about the ranch? With Pearlie and Cal laid up—"

"I'll hire some extra hands," Sally said. "You know Matt wouldn't ask for help unless it was something serious."

Smoke glanced at Boyd, who stood there trying not to look too curious. Smoke knew what the wire meant, all right. Matt wouldn't have sent out a call for help to him and Preacher unless the trouble had something to do with the Indian Ring. Sally knew all about that, but Smoke didn't want to say anything in front of Boyd. The man was a federal marshal, after all, and the Ring had a lot of power and influence in Washington. It was hard to know who could be trusted and who couldn't.

"You're right." Smoke nodded. "I guess I'd better find Preacher and light a shuck for this Halltown, wherever that is."

"Do you even know where to start looking for Preacher?"

Smoke grinned. "As a matter of fact, I happen to have a pretty good idea what that old hell-raiser is up to right now."

BOOK THREE

CHAPTER 22

Preacher looked at the beautiful woman stretched out on the divan in a scandalously small amount of clothing. "No offense, Your Countess-ship, ma'am, but I'm old enough to be your grandpappy. Shoot, I reckon these buckskins o' mine are older'n you are. This ain't right." He shook his head. "No, ma'am, it just ain't right."

"Why don't you let me worry about that, Preacher?" Countess Helena Markova asked.

"Because it's pretty clear to me that you're plumb outta your mind!" the old mountain man said. "Why, if the count was to come in right now, with you dressed like"—he waved a gnarled hand at her skimpy attire—"like that. I reckon he'd probably shoot us both!"

"Do you really think Alexi cares what I do?"

"If he don't, he's a gol-dang fool, that's for sure."

The way Helena arched one finely plucked eyebrow told Preacher she agreed with him on one point, anyway. Her husband *was* a gol-dang fool.

Count Alexi Markova was just the latest in a long line of fools as far as Preacher was concerned. Russian aristocrats had been coming to the American frontier to shoot wild game for nigh on to fifty years, and Preacher had yet to see the point in it. Why couldn't they just shoot something in that Siberia place that was part of their own country?

Preacher cast a worried glance at the door at the end of the railroad car. The count might come through there at any moment. Preacher wasn't afraid of the man—even at his advanced age, he knew he was a match for most fellas—but if Markova pitched a fit, that would cast a pall over the whole trip and embarrass Preacher's old friend Hank Wilkerson, who was in charge of guiding the hunting party. Preacher didn't want that.

"You don't really think I'm trying to seduce you, do you, Preacher?" Helena asked from the divan. She was in her late thirties, a very attractive woman with a lot of blond hair pinned up on her head in an elaborate arrangement of curls. She had lived a life of luxury and ease in Russia, and as a result she didn't look her age. She went on, "I simply wanted to ask you a question. I want to go along on the hunt this afternoon."

"You mean that's why you sent for me?"

"I'm sorry if I've disappointed you."

Preacher shook his head. "Not hardly, ma'am. It's just when I, uh, saw you dressed like that—"

Helena waved a hand. "I have never been a believer in false modesty. I'm proud of my body."

"You got every reason to be, I reckon, but I ain't the one you need to ask about goin' along on the hunt. Hank's in charge of that."

"But you and Mr. Wilkerson are good friends. I thought perhaps you might be able to influence him in his decision."

"Oh, I get it now. You've already asked him, and he said nothin' doin'."

Anger flashed in Helena's blue eyes as she sat up, abandoning her casual pose. "I can shoot a rifle every bit as well as my husband," she declared. "Probably better. There's no reason why Alexi should have all the enjoyment of this trip. He's dragged me halfway around the world to this Godforsaken wilderness—" She stopped short and took a deep breath. "I just hoped that you would put in a word on my behalf with Mr. Wilkerson, that's all."

"Personally, ma'am, it strikes me as too dangerous for you to go along. Of course, it don't seem too smart to me for your husband and them other muckety-mucks to be gallivantin' around looking for things to shoot, neither. Meanin' no offense about your husband, that is."

Helena shook her head and summoned up a smile again. "None taken. Alexi is a 'muckety-muck' as you called them, if there ever was one. You can throw in 'pompous stuffed shirt' while you're at it."

"You'd know better'n me, ma'am." Preacher eased toward the door.

Helena didn't try to stop him. He heaved a sigh of relief as he stepped onto the car's rear platform without bumping into Count Markova.

"Preacher, what in blazes were you doin' in there?" a harsh voice demanded. "You danged old goat!"

Preacher turned to see Hank Wilkerson standing on the ground next to the platform, a horrified look on his whiskery face. Swinging down from the platform to join his friend, Preacher said, "It ain't like that at all."

"I thought you was too old for such shenanigans!"

"If I was, I wouldn't admit it to the likes o' you, you ol' badger," Preacher snapped. "The countess sent for me. She wanted to ask me a question."

"What sort of question?"

"She wanted me to convince you to let her go along on the huntin' party this afternoon."

"Oh, Lord!" Wilkerson rolled his eyes. "I'm startin' to wish I'd never signed on with this bunch."

Preacher knew the feeling. He had learned from hard experience that no good usually came from agreeing to take tenderfeet into the badlands. He had been part of several such expeditions, and they invariably ended up in shooting scrapes.

He had gone along that time purely as a favor to his old friend. He and Hank Wilkerson had spent several seasons in the mountains, trapping together. They had fought the Blackfeet together, each saving the other's life more than once, creating a bond that could never be broken.

240

Even so, when Preacher had heard about the hunting expedition, put together by some newspaper back east hungry for increased circulation, he should have run the other direction as fast as his old legs would carry him. The newspaper had put together quite a bunch: politicians, business tycoons, and to spice things up a mite, Russian nobility. The famous journalist Jasper McCormick had come along, too, in order to send back dispatches to the newspaper that was footing the bill.

Preacher saw McCormick coming toward him and Wilkerson. He warned his friend, who muttered a curse and something about blasted newspaper scribblers.

"Gentlemen," McCormick greeted them. He was a relatively young man in a brown tweed suit and brown derby, clean-shaven, with dark hair and intense eyes. "Did I just see you come out of Count Markova's private car, Preacher? I thought the count was up in the dining car."

"No, you must've been mistaken," Preacher said. "I was on the other side of the train, spotted Hank on this side, and cut across on the platform of the count's car. That's all."

McCormick frowned. "But I would have sworn—"

"Then you'd be wrong." Preacher's tone of voice made it clear he didn't want to discuss the subject.

"Oh, well, it doesn't really matter. Do you

think we'll find some good game today?"

"Ought to," Wilkerson replied. "There's plenty o' game all over this part of the country."

The train was parked on a siding in southern Wyoming, serving as the headquarters for the expedition. Every day the rich, powerful men who had signed on for the hunt rode out in search of buffalo, antelope, elk, moose, and anything else they could find to shoot at. Preacher hoped fervently that wouldn't include Indians. The tribes in the area were relatively peaceful at the moment, but all it would take to put them on the warpath was some dang-fool Easterner panicking at the wrong moment and shooting a "redskin."

Preacher sometimes wondered why everybody east of the Mississippi seemed to think there were only two kinds of Indians: the mistreated, exploited, and oppressed "Mister Lo," and the bloodthirsty savage intent only on scalping and mutilating every white he came across. They couldn't seem to understand Indians were like any other group of people, some good, some bad, some smart, some dumb as rocks.

So far the expedition had been lucky. They hadn't encountered any Indians. Preacher hoped it stayed that way.

He stopped thinking about that and turned his attention back to McCormick as he heard the journalist say something about "overnight."

"What was that?" Preacher asked.

McCormick frowned at him. "I just said that maybe we'd have better luck since we'll be staying out overnight this time."

"Hold on a minute," Wilkerson said. "Nobody told me anything about that."

"Oh, it was Count Markova's idea. He wants to take tents and enough supplies for us to stay out on the plains tonight. Maybe for several nights."

"And the rest of the bunch is goin' along with that?"

"Senator Olson thought it was a splendid idea."

"That jack wagon would," Wilkerson muttered.

McCormick leaned closer. "Excuse me?"

"Nothin', nothin'," Wilkerson said quickly. "I was just sayin' it'd be easier to do that if we had a wagon."

"Oh. Well, we can use one of the saddle mounts as a pack horse, I suppose. We have a number of extras."

Wilkerson glanced at Preacher. The old mountain man knew what his friend was thinking. Hank hadn't let those pilgrims get too far away from the train, for safety's sake, and they came back to the train every night for the same reason.

"I'm not sure about this," Wilkerson said.

McCormick's voice hardened as he said, "It's been decided, Hank. May I remind you that you're an employee of the newspaper, the same as I am?"

"Your publisher's more'n a thousand miles away from here."

"And I'm his representative," McCormick snapped. His voice took on a more conciliatory tone. "I don't want this to cause a problem, Hank, but I believe it's a good idea and I know my superiors would go along with it. Why don't we try it for one night and see how it goes? If there's no trouble, maybe we can make a longer trip next time."

"Well"—Wilkerson gave the journalist a grudging nod—"all right. I reckon we can give it a try. That is, if Preacher agrees to come along." He looked at Preacher and waited for an answer.

Preacher wondered if Countess Markova had known about the overnight trip when she asked him to intercede with Wilkerson on her behalf. It seemed likely, since it was her husband who had come up with the hare-brained notion to start with.

Preacher wanted to wash his hands of the whole blamed bunch, but he couldn't do that to Hank. He sighed, nodded, and said, "Sure, I'll come along."

"Excellent!" McCormick said. "I'll pass the word for everyone to be ready to ride out this afternoon. Thank you, gentlemen."

As the journalist strode away, Wilkerson said quietly, "I hope we ain't making the biggest mistake of our lives, Preacher."

"Me, too," the old mountain man said with a slow nod. "Me, too."

CHAPTER 23

Born around the time the eighteenth century was turning to the nineteenth, Preacher had been just a boy named Arthur when he slipped out of his family's farmhouse one night and headed west to see the elephant. In the almost seven decades since then, he and that ol' elephant had become good friends. He had fought the British with Andy Jackson at the Battle of New Orleans, then accompanied some trappers into the Rocky Mountains in the first of what would be scores of such journeys.

As a young man, he had been captured by the Blackfeet, who hated him because he had killed so many of them in battle. Slated to be burned at the stake, Art had taken a desperate chance and started preaching in a loud voice, falling back on memories of a street preacher he had seen in St. Louis. He kept up the ranting for hours on end, until the Blackfeet became convinced he was touched by the spirits and therefore under their protection. They had spared his life and let him go, and as soon as the story got around, as stories always did among the mountain men, someone had dubbed him Preacher and the name had stuck. He had carried it around for so long now that sometimes it was difficult for him to remember his real name.

Age had not bent his back. He still stood tall and straight in his buckskins and moved with the vigor of a much younger man. His hair and beard were white as snow, but his eyes were clear and he could still bring down a bird on the wing with his old, long-barreled flintlock rifle. These days he carried a Winchester repeater as well, and he had traded his brace of double-shotted flintlock pistols for a pair of Remington revolvers. As a fast draw, he wasn't in the same class as Smoke and Matt Jensen, but he could get the heavy guns out quicker than most men and was still a deadly accurate shot. He knew there would come a time when the years finally caught up to him . . . but he was holding it off as long as he could.

Yes, he had seen plenty of elephants in his life, but he had never stopped looking for another one.

It was sort of a circus he was mixed up with now, he thought as he looked at the riders getting ready to set out on the hunting trip. There weren't any elephants in sight. Just jackasses.

Senator Sherwood P. Olson was all silver hair and gleaming teeth. He had a secretary and a couple aides with him; the secretary, a meek little man named Gearhart, wasn't going along on the hunting trip, but the assistants, Curtis and Jennings, were. Two Congressmen from Olson's home state were part of the group, as were Milton

Packard, the mining magnate, J.P. "Jiggers" Dunlop, who'd inherited a vast fortune from his father, the founder of the Dunlop Shipping Line, and Benjamin Skillern, the patent medicine king. There were several other rich men Preacher didn't know, and they all had their toadies with them. All told, there were almost two dozen of them.

Preacher and Hank were part of the group, along with four other plainsmen Hank had hired to come along on the expedition. They helped with the horses, skinned game, and did any other chores that needed to be done. They were all heavily armed, to protect their civilized charges.

Preacher was riding a rangy gray stallion called Horse, one in a long line of mounts he had dubbed with that name. He sat up straighter in the saddle and frowned when he saw the brightly clad figure of Countess Helena Markova ride out to join the others assembling beside the train. She rode astride like a man in a pair of tight, cream-colored trousers, a brilliant red jacket, and boots. A matching hat with a feather on it perched on her blond curls.

He looked at her for a moment, then turned Horse and rode over to where Hank Wilkerson was sitting on his mount. "I thought the countess wasn't comin' along."

Wilkerson sighed. "She insisted, and so did her husband. And of course that prissy son of a gun McCormick took their side. What can I do,

Preacher? They told me I'd be the boss on this trip, but it's plain as the nose on your face that I ain't."

"That's your horse, and this old son is mine. I see some mountains over yonder. We could just ride off and leave this bunch o' nincompoops to fend for their own selves."

"I don't take a job unless I intend to see it through," Wilkerson said stubbornly, "even when the rules get changed on me." He shook his head. "Anyway, I can't just abandon this bunch of greenhorns. They're loco enough to go off on their own, and if they did that, they might not ever get back."

Preacher glared at his old friend. He knew Wilkerson was right, but didn't have to admit it, or like it, for that matter. "All right. But this is liable to be the death of us."

Wilkerson grinned. "Tell you what, Preacher. If you wind up gettin' killed, I'll see to it that you're paid double what I promised you, all right?"

"What if you're the one who winds up dead?"

"Then I'll pay you triple!"

"Deal!" Preacher said.

To those Easterners, getting up early meant rising at ten o'clock in the morning instead of noon, so it came as no surprise to Preacher that it was well after noon before they rode away from the train. They headed north over rolling hills, into a wide valley between two mountain ranges. It was pretty country, lush with buffalo grass and wildflowers, and Preacher would have enjoyed being there if he was alone, or if it had just been him and Hank or another of his old friends.

Of course, most of his old friends were dead, he reminded himself, and the only youngsters he could stand to be around for any length of time were Smoke and Matt. One thing about living to such a ripe old age . . . it got a mite lonely sometimes. Why, he couldn't even remember the last time he'd run into any of the fellas who had gone down the mighty Mississipp' with him to fight the bloody British at New Orleans. The ones who were left were probably all sitting in rocking chairs somewhere, being coddled by their grandkids.

Not for him, by jingo. If he ever got that bad off, they could just go ahead and shoot him.

Preacher and Hank took the lead. The rich folks and their helpers came next, followed by the hired men leading pack horses loaded down with tents and supplies. Preacher wasn't sure what they needed all that gear for. This country was so lush, he could have lived off it for weeks with only a few handfuls of sugar, salt, flour, and coffee. But he supposed they knew more about how to get along in Washington, New York, Boston, and wherever the hell it was those Russians came from than he did.

Around the middle of the afternoon, Preacher and Hank spotted a herd of antelope grazing up ahead. The wind was out of the north, so the animals hadn't scented the approaching humans and horses. Hank called a halt and instructed the hunters on how to sneak up on a rise overlooking the stretch where the elk were grazing.

"Those critters ain't dumb like buffalo," he told them. "They'll take off lickety-split at the first sign of trouble, so you'll only get one shot each. Line your sights and get ready. You all fire at the same time, when I give the word."

No one argued with him. Preacher had to give them credit for doing as they were told. He sat back on Horse and watched as the hunters set up their fancy rifles on stands. Even Helena Markova had one of the long-barreled foreign weapons.

"Steady, steady," Hank said quietly. "Everybody got your bead? Speak up if you don't."

The hunters were quiet, indicating they were ready.

"Take a deep breath and squeeze the trigger a little, just a little," Hank went on. "All right . . . fire!"

Almost as one, more than a dozen high-powered rifles went off, the vicious whipcracks of their reports blending into a wicked sound. Down below, five of the antelopes leaped in the air as bullets struck them. Before the wounded animals hit the ground, the other members of the herd were streaking away, bounding over the grassy earth in a blur of motion.

"Good shootin', folks," Wilkerson told them. "We'll have us some antelope steaks tonight."

"Why don't we go after the rest of them?" Jiggers Dunlop suggested.

"Because they'll be a couple miles away before we could get mounted up," Wilkerson explained. "Anyway, you got some."

"Yes, but must of us appear to have missed," Senator Olson said.

"Well, maybe you'll be luckier next time."

McCormick spoke up, saying, "If the group wants to pursue those animals—"

"It'd be a waste of time," Preacher cut in from horseback. "Them antelope won't stop runnin' until they're ten miles from here, and it won't take 'em long to cover that much ground, neither."

"We'll find something better," Wilkerson promised. "Meanwhile, we know we've got some meat for supper tonight."

And a lot that would be left for scavengers to feed on, Preacher thought bitterly. He hated to see so much meat go to waste.

The hunters stowed their guns away—or rather, their helpers did it for them—and the party moved on. Game seemed to be scarce from that point. Preacher and Hank knew the shooting had scared it off, but neither mentioned that.

The rich folks grew impatient and irritated. "I

thought this land was supposed to be teeming with wildlife," Milton Packard complained during a stop to rest the horses. "We've hardly even seen any birds the past couple hours."

"We'll find something good," Wilkerson promised. "Just wait and see."

When the group started moving again, Preacher asked Wilkerson as they rode ahead of the others, "Are you lookin' for anything in particular, Hank?"

"I've heard rumors there are buffalo up this way, and that's what these folks really want. They've heard all about buffalo hunts. Bill Cody's made the idea mighty popular back east with those shows of his."

Preacher grunted. Bill Cody was a good hombre, and most of the exploits he bragged about had at least some basis in truth, no matter how small. But he made hunting buffalo sound like a glamorous, exciting adventure, when in reality it was a grim, bloody, sordid business. Nothing stunk worse than a field full of butchered buffalo. Somehow that never came across in Cody's extravaganzas.

Sure enough, late that afternoon Preacher and Wilkerson reined to a stop on top of a rise overlooking a vast bowl between two hills and saw that it was packed with what looked at first like a brown sea flowing slowly back and forth. It was actually a buffalo herd, and a smallish one at that. Only about ten thousand of the shaggy creatures were grazing down there, Preacher estimated.

When he was younger he had seen herds number-
ing in the millions, but so many of the beasts had
been slaughtered in the past fifteen years that
those days were probably gone for good.

"That's what I was lookin' for," Wilkerson said
with a sigh of relief. "That ought to make 'em
happy. They can set up their guns and kill buffs
for an hour."

"And leave the carcasses to rot," Preacher
pointed out.

Wilkerson shrugged "We'll skin out a few of
them to make rugs or robes or whatever the folks
want. I'm sorry about the others, but there's
nothin' I can do about it."

Preacher tried not to frown in disapproval.
Hank already knew it was wrong. He didn't need
Preacher to tell him that. If Hank could live with
it, then so be it.

"Keep an eye on the herd," Wilkerson went on.
"I'll ride back and tell the others."

"The herd ain't goin' any place."

"I know. But I'd appreciate it anyway, Preacher.
You look like you could chew nails right about
now."

Preacher jerked his head in a nod.

While he sat on the ridge, Wilkerson told the
others about the buffalo and got them started
setting up camp. Several members of the group
had to ride out and see the buffalo for themselves,
including Helena Markova and her husband. The

count was in his forties, a stocky gent with a mustache that came to a sharp point on each end. He wore a red coat and a fur hat that looked ridiculous to Preacher, but not as ridiculous as the monocle he sported.

Markova pulled out a spyglass and used it to study the buffalo. When he lowered the glass, he said, "Ugly-looking creatures, aren't they?"

"They probably think the same thing about us, Alexi," the countess said.

Markova snorted. "You give them too much credit for thinking, my dear."

"The count's right, ma'am," Wilkerson said. "There ain't many things on God's green earth dumber'n a buffalo. That's why they'll just stand there and keep grazin' while they're bein' shot down right and left. Until one of 'em gets hit, or until the smell of blood gets too strong, they don't realize there's anything wrong."

"Why don't we just go ahead and shoot them this afternoon?" Ben Skillern asked.

"We'll have more time in the morning," Wilkerson explained. "It'll be easier that way. We can shoot for a while, then skin out some of the var-mints and start back to the train with the hides."

No one put up an argument. After several hours in the saddle, the hunters were tired and looking forward to a good night's sleep before they started killing again.

The camp was half a mile downwind from the herd, which meant the air was pretty potent. No one complained about the smell except Helena. Preacher was used to it, and didn't even notice it anymore. The smell of antelope steaks frying helped some.

The servants had set up tents where their bosses would sleep. They brought out folding tables and chairs, so the politicians, tycoons, and aristocrats could sit down to eat, the way they were used to.

Preacher hunkered on his heels under a scrubby tree with his plate of food. Wilkerson came over to join him as the orange rays of the sun began to fade in the western sky.

"Well, what do you think?" Wilkerson asked.

Deliberately, Preacher finished chewing the mouthful of antelope steak before he swallowed. "I think somebody's followin' us."

Wilkerson's eyes widened. "What in blazes are you talkin' about, Preacher?"

"I've had an uneasy feelin' all day," Preacher explained, "but I figured it was because I was out here with a bunch of loco greenhorns who seem bound and determined to get into trouble. A little while ago, though, I spotted a couple riders a ways back. Looked like they was doggin' our trail."

"Indians?" Wilkerson asked in a low, worried voice.

Preacher shook his head. "I don't think so. Can't be sure, but I think they was white men."

"Two white men ain't all that worrisome. There's two dozen of us."

"Just 'cause I saw two riders don't mean that's all there is."

Wilkerson scratched at his beard. "Yeah, I reckon that's true. Why would they be followin' us?"

Preacher waved a hand at the camp. "You ever stopped to add up how much that bunch is worth, Hank?"

"No, I don't suppose I did."

"Neither did I, because I've never been that good at cipherin', but you know it's got to be a whole heap of money."

"You think somebody wants to kidnap them?" Wilkerson asked tensely.

"It's a thought," Preacher said.

Wilkerson muttered a curse. "We've gotta get 'em back to the train, and there ain't gonna be any more of these little campouts, no matter what that damn McCormick says."

"You can't go herdin' that bunch across country in the dark," Preacher pointed out. "Somebody'd be bound to get lost. Better to sit tight here tonight and head back tomorrow. Shoot, you could even let 'em kill a few buffs in the mornin', if you want to. You just need to put a good guard on the camp tonight to make sure nobody sneaks up on you."

"Yeah, I guess you're right." Wilkerson looked at Preacher with a frown. "Wait a minute. You're talkin' like you ain't gonna be here."

"I ain't."

"Blast it, Preacher, I never thought you'd run out on me the first time trouble crops up!"

"I'm not runnin' out on you," Preacher said. "I thought I'd drift back yonder and see if I can find the varmints who been trailin' us. If I can, maybe I can figure out who they are and what they want. Then we'll have a better idea how to deal with 'em."

Wilkerson grimaced and shook his head. "Sorry, Preacher. I should've knowed better."

"That's right, you should have."

"Yeah, I've heard all those stories about how you used to slip into those Blackfoot camps and cut the throats of half a dozen of their best warriors without any of the rest of 'em havin' any idea what was goin' on. Is that what you're gonna do with this bunch?"

"That was a long time ago," Preacher protested. "I was a lot younger then. Anyway, we don't know who those fellas are. Could be they're just innocent pilgrims who happen to be goin' the same direction we are."

"Do you really believe that?"

A grim smile tugged a little at Preacher's lips. "My gut don't."

"I trust your gut. So if you find out they do mean us harm . . . ?"

Preacher's hand strayed to the bone handle of the Bowie knife sheathed at his waist. "We'll see what we can do about that."

CHAPTER 24

Long ago, the Indians—specifically his greatest enemies the Blackfeet—had dubbed him Ghost Killer. At times Preacher had done things especially to convince them he was supernatural, a spirit warrior who could enter their camps as a phantom, then become real long enough to kill their greatest warriors as they slept.

Those days were behind him. The country had changed. It had been a long time since he'd been at war with the Indians, and he was considerably older.

But he could still manage some stealth when he needed it. He slipped silently through the shadows, using every bit of concealment he could find as he searched for the men who had been trailing the hunting party.

As time passed and he didn't locate them, Preacher began to wonder where they were. He wasn't the sort of man to doubt himself. He didn't question whether or not he had actually seen someone following the hunting party. He knew what he had seen. Those riders had been back there.

But where were they? He had gone at least a mile from the camp without finding any sign of them. He lifted his head and sniffed the air. No smell of woodsmoke or tobacco. Had the riders veered off in some other direction?

Or had they circled to get ahead of the hunting party?

Preacher turned his head and peered off toward the north. His eyes narrowed as he spotted just the faintest orange tinge in the night sky, low on the horizon. "Son of a—" he burst out.

He had left Horse ground-hitched a couple hundred yards away as he stalked his quarry on foot. Letting out a loud, high-pitched whistle to call the stallion, he started forward at a run to meet the horse and save as much time as he could. He had to get back to the camp right away.

He knew he might be too late already.

With a swift rataplan of hoofbeats, Horse appeared, looming out of the night in front of him. Preacher called out to the animal. Horse had barely slowed to a halt when Preacher swarmed up into the saddle, grabbed the reins, and wheeled the stallion around. Digging his heels into Horse's flanks, he sent the animal lunging ahead in a gallop.

Preacher grimaced when he saw the orange glow in the sky was a little brighter. He sniffed the air again, and the wind out of the north brought with it a slight scent of smoke.

Hank Wilkerson was no fool. He would smell that smoke, too, and know right away what the result of it would be. Preacher recalled the terrain around the camp. It was mostly flat, but there was a rocky hill several hundred yards away. If Wilkerson could get his charges up that hill, there was at least a chance they would survive the inevitable onslaught.

Preacher cursed as he raced northward on Horse. His instincts had told him something was wrong as soon as he saw those riders on their back trail, but he couldn't have predicted that whoever was following them would try to wipe out the entire hunting party. It was cold-blooded mass murder, and he couldn't see any reason for it. Senator Olson and those Congressmen probably had some political opposition, and Packard, Skillern, Dunlop, and the other businessmen were bound to have made some enemies. But would any of those enemies resort to wholesale slaughter?

All Preacher knew for certain was that somebody had started a prairie fire on the other side of that buffalo herd. As the wind carried the smoke and the flames southward, that mass of shaggy creatures would grow nervous and start to move, slowly at first, then faster and faster. Their animal instincts would force them to flee, until they were running full tilt, living engines of destruction aimed straight at the camp where those greenhorns slumbered, unaware of the danger.

Over the pounding of Horse's hoofbeats,

Preacher suddenly heard a low rumble, like thunder or the sound of distant drums. He grimaced as he leaned forward in the saddle and urged the stallion on.

The buffalo were moving. The stampede had begun.

As Preacher drew closer the smell of smoke was stronger. He veered Horse to the east. If he continued heading due north, he would run smack-dab into the stampeding buffalo. It wouldn't do anybody any good for him to get trampled. He spotted a low ridge that would probably keep him safe. Like a flooding river, the buffalo would smash over anything in their way, but they would also take the path of least resistance.

The rumble of tens of thousands of hooves pounding the ground steadily grew louder and louder until it seemed to shake the whole world. Preacher felt the terrain sloping and knew he was climbing to the top of the ridge he hoped would save his life. When it leveled out, he reined Horse to a stop and gazed off to the north. He was high enough that he could plainly see the flames of the prairie fire leaping into the air higher than a man's head.

The inferno was several hundred yards wide. The wind wasn't strong enough to send it racing southward like so many other prairie fires Preacher had seen, but the flames were making steady progress. The blaze cast a hellish orange glow over the landscape that was bright enough to reveal the sea of shaggy backs fleeing from it.

Preacher looked toward the hill he recalled, hoping to see the members of the expedition seeking shelter there. It was too far away, though, and he couldn't make out any details. The stampede was flowing around the hill, as he had thought it would, so if Wilkerson and the others had reached the top, they ought to be safe.

For the time being, Preacher was safe, but he was stuck where he was. He couldn't descend from the ridge without getting caught in the stampede. He had to wait until the buffalo were past.

They might run all the way to the railroad, he realized. The folks who had been left behind at the train would be safe enough, but they'd likely witness a spectacular scene, the likes of which they would never see again.

"Hell of a thing, Horse," Preacher said to the stallion.

The fire began to burn itself out. The hooves of the stampeding buffalo had churned up the ground so badly there wasn't much grass left to burn. The men who had started the blaze had accomplished their goal. They had caused the herd to stampede through the hunting party's camp.

The rumbling died down once the buffalo were past the ridge where Preacher waited. It seemed to take ages for all the hairy brutes to go by, but it was really less than a quarter hour, Preacher knew. As stampedes went, it was actually a small one.

But plenty deadly enough to anybody caught in its path.

Time for him to find out just how deadly it had been, he told himself as he lifted the reins and clucked his tongue at Horse. The stallion started down the ridge.

As he rode, Preacher drew his Winchester from the saddle boot, in case he encountered any stragglers from the herd. A fear-maddened buffalo bull might charge him and Horse out of sheer panic, and he would have to put it down.

The unholy smell of smoke lingered in the air as Preacher came to the spot where he thought the camp had been located. After a moment he found what was left of some tents, and then some debris that was probably a shattered table.

He saw what looked like shapeless bundles of clothing, and his mouth tightened into a grim line under his mustache. Those rags were all that was left of human beings. Several people had died there. Preacher knew there wasn't enough left to try to figure out who the bodies belonged to. He headed for the rocky knoll in hopes of finding some survivors there.

He had reached the bottom of the hill when a shot blasted out above him and a slug screamed off into the night. Somebody was up there, anyway, he told himself.

"Hold your fire!" he shouted. "Don't shoot, blast it! It's me, Preacher!"

"Preacher?" It was a woman's voice that came down to him. Had to be Countess Helena Markova. She was the only female in the bunch. "Preacher, is it really you?"

"It's me, and I'm comin' up." He added again, just to make sure she understood, "Don't shoot me."

Horse took the slope without much problem, weaving around the boulders that littered the side of the hill. When Preacher came to the top, several people gathered around him. The moon and stars cast enough light for him to recognize the Count and Countess Markova, the journalist Jasper McCormick, Milton Packard, Jiggers Dunlop, and Benjamin Skillern. Senator Olson's two aides, Curtis and Jennings, were there, along with the two Congressmen and the servants who had come along. But Preacher didn't see Senator Olson himself, or Hank Wilkerson. None of the plainsmen Wilkerson had hired to accompany the expedition were there, either. Preacher muttered a curse. It looked like Hank and the hired men had lost their lives getting those pilgrims to safety. The senator was probably a casualty, too.

Helena had one of those fancy hunting rifles

264

cradled in her hands. "What happened? Where were you, Preacher?"

The old mountain man swung down from his saddle. He didn't answer Helena's question but asked one of his own. "Where's Hank Wilkerson?"

"Dead," Helena said. She seemed to have assumed the role of spokesman for the group. In fact, she was the only one who didn't look completely shaken up and scared out of her mind, Preacher noted. That included the count.

"Hank was caught in the stampede?"

Helena shook her head. "No, he was dead before it started. He and the men he hired."

Preacher frowned. "What? How in tarnation did that happen?"

"I don't know," Helena replied with a shake of her head. "But when I saw the fire and went to look for Mr. Wilkerson, I found him on the outskirts of the camp, the last place I had seen him earlier in the evening. He had been stabbed. When I went to look for the other guards, they were the same way. Someone murdered them before the stampede started."

"Wait just a doggone minute!" Preacher exclaimed. "That don't make any sense. Hank and the rest of those boys knew what they were doin'. It'd take somebody mighty dangerous to sneak up on 'em and kill 'em without wakin' up the whole camp."

Helena regarded Preacher coolly. "Someone

like you, perhaps, Preacher? You didn't answer my question about where you were when the stampede started."

Anger welled up inside Preacher. "Hold on," he snapped. "You don't really think I had anything to do with killin' those ol' boys, do you?"

"Mr. Wilkerson told me you were famous across the frontier for slipping into the camps of the savages and killing them," Helena returned.

"Yeah, but Hank and me were pards from 'way back!" With an effort, Preacher got control of himself. Helena and the others were waiting for an explanation, so he said, "Earlier this evenin', I told Hank I'd spotted some riders trailin' us. I dropped back to see if I could find out who they were and what they wanted."

"Well?" Helena demanded. "Did you find them?"

Preacher shook his head. "I reckon they must've circled around us, got north of that buffalo herd, and started that fire to stampede the buffs. That's the only thing that makes any sense."

"Why would these mysterious men do that?"

"I don't know," Preacher admitted. "Only thing I can figure is that they wanted to kill one of us and didn't mind wipin' out ever'body else to do it."

"That's insane!" Jiggers Dunlop said. "No one would do a thing like that."

"You inherited your money, didn't you, Dunlop?" Milton Packard asked. "You never had to fight for it. I've known men who didn't care how many they hurt to get what they wanted."

"So have I," Preacher said. "Tell me what happened after you found Hank and the other fellas, Countess."

Helena shrugged. "I knew there was a buffalo herd out there, and I was afraid the fire would make them stampede. I woke everyone up as fast as I could, and we ran for this hill. It seemed like the only safe place."

"There's a good chance you saved everybody's life," Preacher told her. "What about the horses?"

"There was no time to do anything with them. We grabbed a few guns and supplies, that's all."

Preacher nodded. The horses had been picketed, but with thousands of panic-stricken buffalo barreling down on them, chances were at least some of the animals had pulled free and bolted. Any of them who stumbled and went down probably had been trampled, but Preacher thought there was a good chance some of the mounts had survived. He might be able to find them once the sun came up.

One thing was certain: the hunting trip was over. His responsibility was to get those greenhorns back to the train. He wanted to track down the men responsible for that disaster and settle the score for Hank, but it would have to wait.

"Is anybody hurt too bad?"

As it turned out, a few bumps and bruises, plus

some ankles twisted in hurrying up the rocky hill, were the only injuries among the survivors. They were lucky.

Curtis, one of Senator Olson's aides, came up to Preacher and asked, "Did you happen to see the senator anywhere?"

Preacher shook his head. "Nope. I figured he'd be up here with you folks."

"We . . . we lost track of him," Curtis admitted. "When the countess raised the alarm, Jennings and I looked for him, but we couldn't find him."

"He was probably off answerin' the call of nature," Preacher said. "Sorry, young fella, but if he was down there, he's dead now. Nothin' you can do about that."

"If . . . if that's true, we ought to try to recover the body."

"Won't be no body to recover. Not so's you could tell who it was, anyway."

Even in the dark, Preacher could tell how pale and shaken Curtis was. The young man sighed. "I suppose you're right. This is a tragedy, a real tragedy. Senator Olson was a great man."

"Uh-huh," Preacher said. He hadn't met too many politicians he would consider great men. But even so, Olson probably hadn't deserved being ground into the dirt by the hooves of thousands of buffalo.

Preacher turned back to Helena. "You did a good job takin' charge, ma'am."

"Someone had to," she said with a little toss of her head and a scornful glance toward her husband.

"You believe me now that I didn't have anything to do with this?"

Helena hesitated, then said, "Since we're going to be depending on you to get us back to civilization safely, I suppose I have to. But I intend to hang on to this rifle."

"Dang right you are," Preacher told her. "You're gonna be standin' guard part of the night, in case that bunch comes along to see if anybody got out of the way of that stampede."

He thought there was at least a chance of that, so he quickly found out how many guns and how much ammunition the group had, then picked out men—and the countess—to take turns standing guard. They had to at least *try* to keep themselves safe.

They had one advantage over Wilkerson: they *knew* someone wanted them dead. Hank hadn't known there was any imminent threat. Under the circumstances, even greenhorns like those were likely to be pretty alert.

Preacher intended to remain awake all night himself. He could sleep again once they got back to the train and were rolling away from the scene of that debacle. He wasn't as young as he used to be, and didn't have the reserves of strength and stamina that he had once possessed, but he knew he could handle whatever he needed to. There wasn't any choice in the matter.

Then, once he had sent those pilgrims on their way . . . he could go on a hunt of his own—the varmints who had started the stampede as his prey.

CHAPTER 25

The rest of the night passed quietly, and Preacher was thankful for that. Though he didn't sleep any, he was able to rest some. So was Horse. They were in better shape by morning.

The same couldn't be said of the survivors of the stampede. Their comfortable cots and bed-rolls had been destroyed, and they were forced to sleep on the rocky ground. As the sky lightened with the approach of dawn, members of the group began to get up and hobble around as they tried to work the kinks out of their sore muscles.

They had grabbed a couple bags of supplies as they fled. Preacher went through the bags and found some coffee, but there was no pot in which to boil it. They made do with stale biscuits and some canned tomatoes.

After the skimpy meal, he gathered the group around him. "I'm gonna go see if I can round up some horses. If I can, that'll make it easier for you folks to get back to the train. If not, you'll have to hoof it."

Several of the men groaned in dismay. Countess Markova, who was still carrying her rifle, looked at them scornfully. "Go ahead," she told Preacher. "I will stand watch while you are gone."

He gave her a nod and mounted up, then rode down the hill and started along the path of the stampede. In the morning light, the damage done by the buffalo was even more appalling. He paused at several of the bodies but couldn't identify them. There wasn't even enough left to bury.

He had gone only a mile or so from the site of the destroyed camp when he spotted a couple horses grazing on a hillside. They didn't bolt when he approached. He was able to rip rope harnesses for them and led them along behind Horse as he continued the search.

By the time a couple hours had passed, he had rounded up eight horses. That was better than he'd expected. Some of the pilgrims would have to ride double, but at least everybody could ride back to the railroad tracks. They would have to manage bareback, but maybe they wouldn't fall off too many times.

Preacher drove the little herd northward. The smell of ashes lingered in the air. The horses were a mite skittish, but he kept them under control.

Cheers drifted down from the hilltop where the survivors were gathered when he and the horses came into view. The pilgrims streamed down from the knoll, bringing their few belongings with them.

"The sooner we get started, the better," Preacher told them. "I want the most experienced riders to handle the reins I've rigged up. The rest of you, pick somebody and climb up behind 'em."

With no stirrups to help them mount, some of the people had trouble, but Preacher managed to get all of them on the horses after a while. When the group was ready to ride, he called out for them to follow him and waved them forward. At a walk, they started south toward the railroad.

After they settled down and got a little more comfortable, Preacher was able to pick up the pace a mite. He intended to make it back to the train before nightfall.

They followed the trail of the buffalo stampede. Preacher intended to gather any stray horses they encountered along the way, but he didn't see any. It was possible the eight animals he had rounded up earlier were the only equine survivors.

They had gone several miles when Preacher suddenly heard a shout. He reined in and looked ahead, spotting a figure running toward them, waving his arms over his head. "What in blazes?" Preacher muttered.

Jennings exclaimed, "That's the senator!"

Indeed it was. Senator Sherwood P. Olson was running desperately toward them, shouting as if he had just seen something he regarded as a miracle. Preacher thought that was probably what it amounted to.

Curtis and Jennings dismounted and hurried forward to meet Olson, who was red-faced, out of breath, and panting as he came up to them. He stopped and bent over to rest his hands on his knees while he tried to catch his breath. Curtis gripped his arm to steady him.

Olson wore trousers, a shirt, and a pair of boots. His mane of silver hair was in disarray.

"Senator, where in tarnation have you been?" Preacher asked.

"We all thought you were dead, Senator," Curtis added.

"I thought . . . I thought all of you were dead," Olson responded. "I fled when those buffalo stampeded last night, and I was afraid all of you had been caught in their path and trampled."

"How'd you manage to get away?" Preacher wanted to know.

Olson wasn't quite as out of breath and was able to straighten. He looked at Preacher as he replied, "I had left my tent to, ah, tend to some private business, when I saw the fire and heard the horrible sound of those creatures charging the camp. I yelled a warning and started to run." Olson looked uncomfortable. "I know I should have made sure that everyone was alerted to the danger, but I . . . I panicked. I admit that. I'm sorry."

273

"I don't see how anyone could help but panic in the face of such a disaster," Curtis said. "You have nothing to apologize for, Senator."

Preacher didn't quite agree, and suspected that Olson wasn't telling the whole truth. More than likely, the senator had run like the very devil was after him as soon as he realized the buffalo herd was stampeding, rather than pausing to call out a warning. If he really had shouted, nobody had heard it.

But Olson's bravery or cowardice wasn't really an issue. The senator was alive, which meant another of the horses would have to carry double.

"What happened then, Senator?" Jennings asked.

"Somehow—and I really don't know how, everything about last night is just a blur—I managed to get out of the path of the stampede. I thought you were probably all dead, so I knew I'd have to get back to the train on my own. I started walking south and continued as long as I could before I finally had to stop and rest. When the sun came up this morning, I began walking again. I had gotten this far when something made me look around, and I saw all of you and the horses. It was like a miracle. I had been delivered from almost certain death."

Preacher wouldn't have gone so far as to say *that,* either. It would have been a mighty long walk back to the train for the senator and his feet would have been pretty sore when he got there, not to mention he would have been hungry and thirsty, but chances were he would have survived the trek.

"You can ride with me, Senator," Curtis offered.

"Nope," Preacher said. "We want to even the weight out among the horses as much as we can. Senator, you ride with Mr. McCormick. Mr. Dunlop, you get up here behind me." Preacher hadn't taken a second rider on Horse, but the stallion was strong enough to handle the double load.

Curtis looked like he was going to protest, but Preacher's hard stare silenced him. McCormick gave Olson a hand climbing onto the horse ridden by the journalist, and the party set off again.

At midday, they stopped to rest the horses and eat. The meal was just as skimpy as their breakfast that morning. Several of the men complained bitterly about everything—the food, the loss of most of their belongings, the soreness in their muscles from sleeping on the ground, and having to ride without saddles.

Preacher would have expected such grousing from a pampered female like the countess, but Helena seemed to be bearing up well under the hardships. Despite her wanton nature, she seemed to have a steely core of resolve.

He was curious about something, and while the

275

group was stopped, he managed to catch a moment alone with her to ask quietly, "Countess, just what were you doin' out and about last night when you realized what was going to happen?"

Her eyes met his squarely. "That's a rather indelicate question, don't you think, Preacher?"

"Yes, ma'am, and I'm mighty sorry about that. But I'd still like to know. I been doin' some thinkin', and it occurs to me that Hank Wilkerson wouldn't have been too suspicious if somebody like you came up to him to talk to him durin' the night."

Her nostrils flared as she drew in a deep breath. "You are saying I could have gotten close enough to him to kill him, as well as the other guards?"

Preacher shrugged. "Like I said, I was just thinkin'."

"My own life was in danger last night," she pointed out. "And I'm the one who alerted the others to the stampede."

"I didn't say it made sense, but neither does anything else about this whole mess."

Helena continued to look intently at him for a moment before she finally nodded. "You are right. You deserve an answer. I was on my way back to my tent when I smelled smoke, saw the glow in the sky from the fire, and went to look for Mr. Wilkerson. I had been with one of the gentlemen."

"You mean you and him—"

"That's exactly what I mean. My husband is not what you would call a passionate man, except perhaps when it comes to vodka and shooting things." She shrugged. "So I look for passion elsewhere. Alexi sleeps like the dead."

"You care to tell me who the fella was?"

She hesitated, then said, "Mr. McCormick."

"The newspaperman?"

"That's right."

Preacher thought back over the past few days. He had seen McCormick in Helena's company on numerous occasions and had noticed them looking at each other, as well as talking and laughing. He hadn't thought much about it—Helena had been more than a mite flirtatious with several of the men—but what she told him had the ring of truth to it.

"Are you going to say anything to him?" she asked.

Preacher shook his head. "Don't see any need to right now. I got a hunch you ain't lyin' to me."

"Thank you for that much, anyway," Helena said rather stiffly. It didn't bother Preacher. If she wanted to get her nose out of joint about it, that was her lookout, not his.

The group moved on a short time later. Preacher knew he was pushing them hard, humans and horses alike, but he didn't want to spend another night on the prairie unless they had to.

After a while, Jiggers Dunlop let out a

frightened exclamation. "Look!" He pointed. "It's those buffalo again!"

Preacher had spotted the shaggy creatures several minutes earlier. They were spread out on both sides of a valley to the east, grazing peacefully.

"Take it easy," he told Dunlop as he reined in. "There ain't nothin' to worry about."

"But the wild beasts might charge us again!"

Preacher shook his head. "That ain't likely. They ran themselves out last night, then drifted over yonder into that good grass. They've forgotten all about what happened, and they'll likely stay right where they are for a few days unless somethin' comes along to disturb 'em again."

Helena patted the polished wooden stock of her rifle and said, "We never did get to shoot any of them."

Preacher frowned and shook his head at her. "And we ain't a-goin' to now, neither. Wouldn't be no point in it. We don't need the meat, and you folks can't carry off any trophies. We'll just leave 'em be."

Count Markova glared at the old mountain man. "If my wife wishes to shoot one of those beasts, she should be allowed to do so. I wouldn't mind killing one of them myself."

"Anybody who wants to stop and take potshots at them buffs, I ain't gonna stop you," Preacher said. "But I ain't gonna wait for you, neither. You can get back to the train your own selves."

Jasper McCormick said, "It might be best to continue on to the train."

"I agree," Senator Olson added. "My God, I'm ready for some sign of actual civilization again!"

The others muttered their agreement. Markova scowled at Preacher but didn't argue. The riders moved forward again, leaving the buffalo behind.

The sun was still above the western horizon when Preacher spotted the long, narrow line of railroad tracks ahead of them. He could see the telegraph poles extending along beside the steel rails as well. The locomotive, along with its train of freight cars, private passenger cars, and caboose, sat on the siding, waiting for them. Preacher's instincts had led them back unerringly.

The others began to notice the train. Some of them cried out for joy while others gave heartfelt thanks.

Preacher kept riding, a grim expression on his bearded face. Too many questions were left unanswered, he thought. Who were the mysterious varmints who had been trailing them, and why had they started the fire that caused the buffalo stampede? Why hadn't the would-be killers come after them again? Preacher had been keeping a close eye on their back trail all day, and he felt certain nobody was following them.

Those mysteries nagged at him, and he wasn't

going to believe he and his companions were out of danger until they had been solved.

The hunters were thrilled to be back at the railroad. Some of them urged their horses to a faster gait in their eagerness to get in the passenger cars and experience some luxuries again. Helena muttered, "Ah, to have a bath again!"

Preacher didn't get in any hurry. In fact, he approached the train so deliberately that Jiggers Dunlop got impatient.

"Can't you hurry up?" the shipping heir demanded.

"We'll get there," Preacher said.

Dunlop didn't want to wait. He slid off the horse and ran ahead.

Preacher rode up while the other members of the party were dismounting, slapping each other on the back, and congratulating themselves for surviving the ordeal they had just gone through. Preacher brought Horse to a stop but stayed in the saddle. It seemed like every nerve ending in his body was tingling, and that was enough to tell him something was wrong. Why hadn't Chester Gearhart, the senator's secretary, come out to greet them? For that matter, the conductor and the rest of the train crew should have put in an appearance, too.

The alarm bells in Preacher's brain rang louder as Gearhart suddenly emerged from the senator's private car, stumbling onto its rear platform.

Another man stepped out right behind him. The second man was a stranger, but whoever he was, he knew Preacher.

He pressed the barrel of a revolver against the back of Gearhart's head and called, "Don't move, Preacher, or I'll blow this little fella's brains out!"

CHAPTER 26

Gearhart was a small man with thick spectacles, and his eyes looked huge behind those lenses as they bulged with fear. The gunman had one hand on his collar and the other held the gun against his head.

Tall and middle-aged, with a lean face under his black Stetson, the gunman looked like he meant every word of the threat. Despite that, Preacher didn't follow orders and freeze. With decades of experience making up for what he lacked in sheer speed, he drew his right-hand Remington, eared back the hammer, and aimed it at Senator Sherwood P. Olson. The whole thing was done in the blink of an eye. Preacher saw the gunman's finger tighten on the trigger of his Colt, but he didn't fire.

"You shoot Gearhart," Preacher said, "and I'll kill your boss."

"Preacher!" Olson gasped. "What are you doing?"

"Finally startin' to make some sense outta this deal. I reckon those fellas who started the buffalo stampede got ahead of us and took over the train, and I know good and well they work for you, Senator."

Curtis started toward Preacher. "You've lost your mind, you old lunatic! The senator was almost killed in that stampede!"

"We've only got his word for that," Preacher pointed out. "I think it's more likely some o' those fellas who were trailin' us slipped into camp, killed Hank Wilkerson and the other guards, and took Olson out of there so he'd be safe when the stampede started."

Helena was listening carefully to Preacher, as were the others from the hunting party. She asked, "Why would the senator want all the rest of us killed?"

"I ain't sure about that, but I got a hunch he wasn't after all of us. Just me."

Olson glared darkly at Preacher. "Like Curtis said, you're insane," he barked. "Now put that gun down. I'm sure we can work all this out."

Slowly, Preacher shook his head. "There ain't nothin' to work out. You're part of that damned Indian Ring, ain't you, Senator?" He was guessing, but the idea that had popped into his head made sense. "You and your cronies are up to no good again, and you want me dead so I won't get mixed up in it. Only . . ."

Only that didn't fit together, Preacher realized. If Olson wanted him dead, there had been plenty of chances for him to accomplish that goal earlier, with a lot less trouble.

Another theory suggested itself. "You didn't know, did you, Senator?" The long-barreled Remington in Preacher's hand never wavered. "You came along on this huntin' trip just for the publicity in Mr. McCormick's newspaper. But somethin' came up while we've been out here, and the rest of the Ring sent those hombres on the train to get rid of me. Easiest way to do that would be to wipe out the whole bunch of us, but your pards didn't want you gettin' killed along with the rest of us. So they came in and got you, killin' poor Hank in the process, and then sent them buffalo chargin' down on the camp. Thing of it was, you didn't know I wasn't there. And most of the folks got lucky and got out of the way of the stampede in time.

"Then today, when they came back to check and make sure I was dead, bringin' you with 'em, they must've been surprised as all get-out to see me. So they sent you back to join us and spin that cock-and-bull yarn about how you got away. By then you knew the Ring wants me dead, so your job was to make sure we came on to the railroad while the others rode ahead and took over the train."

283

Preacher paused and took a deep breath. "Phew! That's more'n I talked in some whole months, up in the mountains durin' the Shinin' Times."

As he had spun out the theory, he had watched Olson, and knew by the fear and surprise in the politician's eyes that he had guessed correctly.

Olson glared at him again. "You're a fool, Preacher. My men would have made it look like a holdup and just killed you. Now all of you are going to have to die." Olson glanced at the man holding the gun on Gearhart. "What do you think, Bannister? Can we make it look like Indians slaughtered the lot of them?"

"I reckon we can do that, Senator," the gunman drawled.

All the other members of the expedition were staring at Olson in amazement, including his two aides. Obviously they had known nothing about Olson's treachery and his connection to the Indian Ring.

"I think you're forgettin' something," Preacher said. "I've still got my gun pointed at the senator here."

Bannister shook his head. "That's not really a problem, Preacher. You see, the fella who gave us our orders, the fella who's paying us, said we ought to keep Olson safe *if we could* . . . but the most important thing is that you wind up dead."

The senator's jaw dropped. "You . . . you can't be serious! You work for my associates!"

"And they're not all that worried about you staying alive," Bannister said.

Preacher glanced along the train as Olson turned pale with fear. All the senator's arrogance and confidence had deserted him in the blink of an eye. Preacher saw several rifle barrels sticking out of windows in the passenger cars. Most of them were aimed at him, but the members of the hunting party were close to the line of fire. When the shooting started—it was no longer a matter of *if*—some of them might get hurt.

But the Indian Ring's hired assassins meant to kill them anyway, so they might as well go down fighting.

Preacher wasn't the only one thinking that way. Countess Helena Markova suddenly jerked her rifle to her shoulder, shouted, "Chester, get down!" and pulled the trigger.

Bannister hadn't expected that from a woman. He hesitated for a split second before pulling the trigger, giving a desperate Chester Gearhart time to dive off the platform. Bannister's bullet went over his head.

At the same instant, Bannister's head jerked back as the slug from Helena's rifle left a red-rimmed hole in his forehead as it bored through his brain and exploded out the back of his skull in a grisly spray of blood and gray matter. Bannister's knees unhinged and dropped him to the platform. He was dead before he got there.

Preacher yelled, "Everybody scatter!" and threw himself out of the saddle.

His bones were getting too old for this, he thought.

He slapped Horse on the rump as he fell and sent the stallion lunging away from the train. Preacher landed with a jolt, rolled, and came up aching from head to foot. The pain didn't stop him or even slow him down as he dashed toward the train, triggering both Remingtons at the windows where rifles showed.

It was Olson's bad luck to be too close to him. The hired killers sprayed lead at Preacher, and the senator was in the way of some of the slugs. He cried out in pain as the bullets struck him and made him jerk back and forth in a macabre dance. Crimson flowers blossomed on his shirt as blood gushed from the wounds.

Preacher saw that from the corner of his eye and considered it good riddance. If he'd had time, he would have told Olson not to look so surprised —he had it coming.

Instead, Preacher bounded to the platform of one of the cars and kicked the door open as bullets whined around him. The assassins who had been crouched at the windows whirled toward him. Gun thunder filled the car and powdersmoke rolled as both of Preacher's Remingtons roared out their deadly song.

Seeing that all of the gunmen in that car were

down and kicking out the last of their evil lives, Preacher jammed both revolvers in their holsters and grabbed one of the iron rungs bolted to the side of the car. He swarmed up the rungs and pulled himself on top of the car, stretching out so he couldn't be seen as easily from below. That gave him a chance to thumb fresh cartridges into the Remingtons.

Too old for this, too old for this. The refrain beat in his brain. But too old or not, he had to deal with it. He came up in a crouch, holding both guns, and started along the top of the car. Glancing down on the south side, he saw the horses the killers had ridden. He and the others hadn't seen the animals as they rode up. On the north side lay several bodies. Olson, of course, but also Jennings —one of his aides—and Count Markova. From the looks of the bodies, both men were dead.

Preacher would feel sorry for them later. He had to concentrate on saving his own hide, and those of the others from the hunting party. It looked like they had scattered and were hiding somewhere.

Preacher headed for the caboose. It was the most likely place for the train crew to be held prisoner. If he could set them free, it would help even up the odds. The conductor, the engineer, the fireman, and the brakemen were all tough hombres.

Guns roared behind him. He felt a bullet rip past his head. He threw himself down, twisting as he fell so he was facing toward the front of the train again. Several of the hired killers were on top of the next car, shooting at him.

Stretched out on his belly, Preacher returned their fire as bullets chewed splinters from the top of the car around him. One of the gunmen clutched his belly, screamed, and toppled off the train, but his two companions kept throwing lead at Preacher.

Another man suddenly threw up his arms and pitched off the train as a rifle cracked. Preacher turned his head and saw that Helena had gotten in the fight again. Unfortunately, her fancy rifle was a single-shot, and she had to reload. The remaining gunman hesitated, unsure whether to try to kill her or continue firing at Preacher.

That was a foolish mistake. Preacher planted a couple .44 rounds in the man's chest that knocked him over backward. The heels of his boots drummed on the car roof as he died.

Preacher scrambled to his feet, yelled, "Get under cover!" to Helena, and turned toward the caboose again.

"Preacher, no!" she shouted back. "The rest of them are headed for the engine! I saw them!"

Biting back a curse, Preacher swung around again. He ran toward the engine, hoping Helena would have sense enough to lie low now that she had warned him.

Somehow, he didn't think so.

Bullets slammed through the air at him from

the cab of the locomotive as he reached the coal tender. He had to fling himself down on the coal to avoid the shots. He was pinned down, at least as far as going forward was concerned.

"Preacher! Preacher!"

The soft-voiced call came from below him. He scuttled backward and saw Helena looking up at him. She had climbed onto the coupling between the tender and the freight car next in line. She had discarded her rifle and had a six-gun that she picked up somewhere in her hand.

"I'll go along the ledge on the side of the tender and distract them," she said. "That will give you a chance to go over the top to the cab."

"You'll get your dang-fool self killed," Preacher protested.

Helena tossed those blond curls defiantly. "They want to kill all of us anyway. What does it matter?"

Looking at her like that, gun in hand, face smudged with powdersmoke, Preacher grinned at her. "Countess, if I was forty years younger . . . hell, even thirty! . . . you'd be in trouble."

"Some things are just not meant to be, I suppose."

"Reckon not." Preacher took a deep breath. "All right. Just get close enough to distract 'em. I'll do the rest."

Helena nodded and began to slip along the narrow walkway on the side of the coal tender.

Preacher waited, his nerves drawing taut as he did so. He probably shouldn't have said that to the countess, he told himself. Her husband had just been killed, after all. Helena might not even know that yet.

A moment later, shots rang out as she moved far enough forward to lean out and open fire on the men in the cab. Preacher heard the high-pitched whine of bullets ricocheting off iron and bouncing around. He leaped to his feet and charged recklessly over the pile of coal, hoping he wouldn't lose his footing and fall. At his age, he might break a hip.

The four gunmen were trying to get a shot at Helena, but they saw him coming and jerked their Colts upward at him. Preacher's Remingtons roared and spouted flame as he showered lead down on them like an avenging angel. The bullets drove the men back against the front of the cab. One by one, they collapsed as Preacher's bullets tore through them. The fight was over in a matter of heartbeats.

"Countess, are you all right?" Preacher called to her.

"I'm fine. What about you?"

"I'll be mighty sore come mornin', but right now I got no complaints."

Preacher holstered his guns, climbed down into the cab, and started reloading as he stood next to the pile of bullet-riddled corpses.

Helena climbed around the end of the tender and swung into the cab to join him. "Such savagery. You're like a Cossack in my country, Preacher."

"Don't know nothin' about no Cossacks," he said as he snapped one of the Remingtons closed. "I just don't cotton to it when varmints try to kill me or other innocent folks." He paused. "Speakin' of which . . . I'm sorry, but it looked like the count was hit when the ball started."

Helena heaved a sigh. "I know. And I am sorry, too. Even though our marriage was not good, Alexi was not really a bad man. I'm sure I will shed tears for him . . . later."

Preacher nodded. "We better go see who else was hurt, and how bad."

They found the other members of the hunting party hiding in the caboose. Packard and Skillern had gotten hold of guns and almost shot Preacher when he came in, before they realized who he was.

"We were going to put up a fight," Packard growled.

Jennings, Markova, and Senator Olson were the only fatalities besides the hired killers, all eight of whom had been wiped out by Preacher and Helena. Jiggers Dunlop and Jasper McCormick had both suffered minor wounds. McCormick was too excited to feel much pain.

"What a story this will make," he kept saying. "What a story!"

291

Preacher didn't care about that. He wanted to know why the Indian Ring was so interested in having him killed.

When he said something about that, Chester Gearhart spoke up. "I might be able to shed some light on that, sir," the senator's secretary said. "As you know, the train crew set up telegraphic communication here at the siding in case Washington needed to get in touch with the senator."

Preacher nodded. "You're sayin' he got a wire from back east?"

"No, sir. *You* got a wire . . . from Colorado."

Gearhart held out a telegraph flimsy. Frowning in surprise, Preacher took it.

"What is it?" Helena asked. "What does it say?"

"It's from a friend. More like family, really," the old mountain man said. "Fella name of Smoke Jensen. He says his adopted brother Matt is in some sort of trouble down in Nevada, at a place called Halltown. Smoke wants me to meet him there as quick as I can."

"If the railroad goes anywhere near there, you can be there in no time at all," Packard said. "Skillern and Dunlop and I all have some influence with this line, and after everything you've done, we'll see that you get what you need."

Preacher nodded. "I'm obliged for that."

"But how does that so-called Indian Ring tie in with it?" McCormick asked.

"Don't know, but Smoke and Matt and I crossed trails with 'em before, and I ain't surprised they want us dead. They must've found out somehow that Matt sent for us to help him, and they're tryin' to stop us from gettin' there."

"Then this other friend of yours," Helena said, "this man called Smoke . . . he could be in danger, too?"

"Yeah," Preacher said as a grim smile slowly curved his mouth. "But if the Ring's sendin' gun-wolves after Smoke, they better send more than they did after me . . . elsewise it ain't gonna be nowhere near fair for those varmints!"

BOOK FOUR

CHAPTER 27

Nevada

Smoke stepped down from the train that had rolled into the Southern Pacific depot in Reno a minute or so earlier. It had been a whirlwind trip from Big Rock after sending the telegram to Preacher in care of the newspaper-sponsored hunting expedition. Smoke had caught the first train to Denver, taking the 'Paloose with him in a freight car that had been converted to animal stalls. From there he had traveled as quickly as possible through Cheyenne, Laramie, Rawlins, Salt Lake City, and on across the Humboldt Basin to Reno. It was the closest he could get to Halltown. A spur line was being built from there to the settlement, but it wasn't completed yet.

Preacher's group was somewhere north of Cheyenne, on the Union Pacific line that ran in that direction. He and Smoke were supposed to leave word for each other at the Reno depot when they arrived, so as soon as Smoke had seen to having the 'Paloose and his gear unloaded, he walked over to the stationmaster's office and knocked on the door. A voice called for him to come in.

The black-suited, balding man in the office looked up from a paper-littered desk. "Can I help you?"

"My name is Jensen," Smoke said. "A friend of mine is supposed to be arriving in Reno at any time, and we agreed to leave word for each other. He's an old mountain man who goes by the name of Preacher."

The stationmaster frowned and shook his head. "I haven't talked to anybody like that. You might ask the ticket clerks, or even the telegrapher."

Smoke nodded. "I'll do that, but I reckon it's more likely he would have talked to you, since you're in charge."

"Well, I'll keep an eye out for him." The stationmaster shrugged. "Can't promise anything, though." He looked down at his paperwork for a second, signaling to Smoke that the conversation was over, then he glanced up again with his eyebrows lifting. "Jensen," he repeated. "Not Smoke Jensen?"

It was Smoke's turn to shrug. "That's what they call me."

The stationmaster stood up and came quickly around the desk to extend his hand. "I've heard a lot about you. It's a pleasure to meet you, sir."

"Likewise," Smoke said as he gripped the man's hand. Both his pa and Preacher had taught him to be polite to folks, unless and until they demonstrated they deserved to be treated otherwise.

"What brings you to Reno? Not trouble, I hope."

Smoke decided it might be worth talking to the stationmaster for a few minutes. "I'm actually headed for a settlement called Halltown. I looked it up on the map in the Denver depot, and I saw that it's north of here a ways."

"You mean Helltown?"

Smoke frowned. "No, I don't think that's the name of the place."

The stationmaster chuckled. "Sorry. You're right, of course, it's Halltown. But I've heard some folks have started using that other name for it."

Somehow, Smoke wasn't surprised Matt had wound up in trouble in a place that had been dubbed Helltown.

"There's a spur line being built up in that direction, isn't there?"

The stationmaster's jovial attitude turned serious. "That's right. Cyrus Longacre is putting it in."

"What's he like?"

"I couldn't really say," the stationmaster replied with a shake of his head.

"You've never met him?"

"Oh, I've met him. He's on good terms with my bosses at the Southern Pacific."

Smoke thought he knew what the man meant. The stationmaster didn't like Cyrus Longacre, but he wasn't going to speak up against him. It might get him in trouble with his own employer.

But the stationmaster surprised Smoke by adding, "I don't care much for some of the men who work for Mr. Longacre. They seem to me like nothing more than hired guns."

The history of the railroads being built across the frontier was littered with hired guns, Smoke thought. More than one small-scale war had broken out between rival companies as they strove to be the first to lay down the steel rails into lucrative areas. Smoke had even taken part in some of those dust-ups.

He wasn't shocked to hear Longacre had employed gunslingers to help him push his spur line through. From the sound of disapproval in the stationmaster's voice, the situation was worse than usual.

"Something going on up there I should know about if I'm headed in that direction?" Smoke asked bluntly.

The stationmaster hesitated. "It's not my place to spread rumors. . . ."

"We're just a couple fellas talking," Smoke assured him. "And I don't plan to be spreading around anything I hear inside this office."

"Well . . . there's talk there might be trouble between Mr. Longacre and some Paiute Indians who live on the other side of Halltown. I've heard there might even be another Paiute war if things keep going the way they are."

The mention of the Indians rang an alarm bell

in Smoke's mind. He already thought Matt's summons might have something to do with the reborn Indian Ring. What he was hearing from the stationmaster added weight to that theory.

"Do you know what the problem is between Longacre and the Paiutes?"

The stationmaster shook his head. "I honestly don't, but even if I did, I've probably said too much already. Like I told you, Mr. Jensen, it's not my place."

Smoke could tell he wasn't going to get any more information out of the man. He nodded. "Thanks anyway. If you happen to see the old-timer I was asking about, you'll tell him I was here and I've gone on to Halltown?"

"I sure will," the stationmaster replied with an emphatic nod. "I'd be glad to do that."

"So long, then." Smoke shook hands with the man again and turned to leave the office.

As he stepped back into the depot lobby, his eyes quickly scanned the room. It was a matter of habit, the sort of caution that had kept him alive in a world full of enemies. He spotted the men who started toward him, two from his right and another pair from his left.

Smoke instantly pegged them for what they were—hired guns. One of the men to his right wore buckskins while the other was dressed in range clothes. The men on his left were another saddle tramp and a gent in a derby and flashy tweed suit. They all had hard faces and eyes that looked like chips of agate. Smoke felt them looking at him and knew they were there to kill him.

Unfortunately, quite a few innocent people were moving in and out of the depot at the moment. Smoke would worry about them, but the hard-cases wouldn't. They'd probably gun down anybody who got in their way and never even blink, as long as they killed him, too. That was what they had been paid for.

Though Smoke knew he was guessing, Cyrus Longacre's name sprang into his mind again.

The door of the stationmaster's office opened again behind him. The man stepped into the doorway and called, "Mr. Jensen—"

The man in the buckskins on Smoke's right slapped leather.

"Get down!" Smoke shouted as his hand streaked toward the Colt on his right hip. "Every-body down!"

The man in the buckskins was pretty fast, but not in the same league as Smoke Jensen. Smoke's gun roared first. The bullet punched into the would-be killer's chest and rocked him back a step. He had cleared leather, but his revolver was still pointed at the floor when his finger clenched spasmodically on the trigger and sent a slug into the polished hardwood planks.

All across the lobby, women screamed, men

yelled curses and questions, and everybody started scurrying for cover or throwing themselves behind the benches in the waiting area.

Smoke was already partially turned to his right. His second shot blasted at the same instant the man in range clothes pulled trigger, so the two reports sounded like one. Smoke felt as much as heard the slug smack through the air next to his ear.

His shot was more accurate. It ripped into the gunman's neck, causing blood to geyser from severed arteries. The shower of gore added to the screams from the terrified bystanders.

The man in buckskins was on his knees, still trying to lift his gun. Smoke snapped off another shot that drilled cleanly into the center of the man's forehead and flipped him backward.

Only a couple of heartbeats had passed since Smoke reached for his gun, but he knew that trapped in a crossfire, it was already too late for him to down the other two men before they could draw a bead on him. He whirled toward them, and threw himself forward in a sliding dive. Bullets whipped through the air where his body had been a split second earlier. The shots echoed back from the depot's high ceiling, booming like thunder.

From where he lay on his belly, Smoke triggered again. Traveling at an upward angle, the bullet struck the man in the derby just under his right eye, bored through his brain, and blew out the top of his head, causing the derby to flip in the air. The hat and its dead owner hit the floor about the same time.

That left just one gunman. Having seen how Smoke had killed his partners in little more than the blink of an eye, the man flung one last shot at his intended target and turned to run. Smoke surged to his feet and ran after him. He wanted to question that hombre and find out who had hired him . . . although Smoke already had a pretty good idea who that was.

Somehow the Indian Ring had found out that Matt had summoned him and Preacher, Smoke thought. Still smarting over what had happened the year before in Wyoming, those conspirators didn't want to deal with all three of them again. Knowing he would probably pass through Reno on his way to Halltown, the Ring had sent gunmen there to watch for him and ambush him as soon as he showed up. It made sense, though he didn't yet know the motivation behind the whole thing.

Nobody tried to stop the fleeing gunman. The people in the train station were only interested in getting out of the way of any flying lead. Smoke bounded past them. The hired gun twisted and snapped a shot at him, but it went high. He triggered a shot as the man ducked through the doorway. Missing by a narrow margin, the bullet struck the doorjamb, showering splinters over the gunman.

Smoke's .44 was empty. He holstered it and pulled the gun from the cross-draw rig on his left hip. He heard shouting, a gunshot, and what sounded like a scream of pain from a horse outside. As he raced through the doorway and out of the depot, he spotted a knot of people in the street. One man had hold of a horse's reins, trying to control the animal as it reared and plunged, its eyes rolling wildly.

Smoke looked for the man he was chasing but didn't see him anywhere. The gunman hadn't had time to get out of sight. That left the crowd near the spooked horse. The men stepped aside nervously as Smoke approached them, gun in hand.

"Don't shoot, mister," one of them said. "If you were after that fella, you don't have to worry about him anymore. He ain't gettin' away."

That was true. The gunman was stretched out on the street with a puddle of blood around his head, soaking into the dirt. The middle of his face had a grotesque, pushed-in look.

"That horse kicked him in the head, didn't it?" Smoke asked.

The bystander who had spoken up nodded his head. "Yeah. That fella came runnin' out of the train station and tried to steal the first horse he came to. The owner tried to stop him, and the fella took a shot at him. But he nicked the horse, and the varmint went plumb crazy. Reared up and planted a hoof right in the middle of the fella's face." The man telling the story shook his head. "That was sure some bad luck."

Bad luck indeed, Smoke thought. He couldn't force the gunman to reveal who had hired him. But it was a lot better than being dead himself.

A burly individual with a lawman's badge pinned to his vest lumbered up holding a shotgun. "What in blue blazes is goin' on here?" he demanded, pointing the Greener in Smoke's general direction. "You better holster that hogleg, mister, before I get nervous."

"I wouldn't want that, Marshal," Smoke said, having read the designation on the badge. He slipped the Colt back into leather. "I can tell you what this is all about."

"Good," the marshal said with a curt nod, "because I got a feelin' it's gonna be a mighty interestin' story."

CHAPTER 28

The marshal was quick to accept Smoke's story that the men had tried to kill him because they wanted to be known as the hombres who killed Smoke Jensen. It was one of the drawbacks of owning a reputation as one of the fastest guns in the West.

He didn't explain his theory about the Indian Ring trying to prevent him from reaching Halltown—or Helltown, as the stationmaster had called it. The Ring had a history of paying off corrupt lawmen to do their bidding. Smoke didn't know who he could trust in Reno, so it was better not to trust anybody.

The marshal seemed happy to see him ride out of town. Monte Carson was the only lawman who really liked having Smoke around. Most other star packers he encountered considered him a magnet for trouble. There was some truth to that idea.

He headed north, following the route of the spur line Cyrus Longacre was building, but Smoke soon veered off to the west into a range of hills. If Longacre and the Indian Ring were behind the attempt on his life in Reno, it stood to reason they might have more hired killers watching for him. He planned to stay out of sight as much as possible as he proceeded toward Halltown.

He knew he wouldn't reach the settlement by nightfall, but if nothing further happened to delay him, he ought to be there by noon the next day. He kept the 'Paloose moving at a steady, ground-eating pace as he rode through the hills, occasionally catching a glimpse of the railroad tracks in the distance.

Just before dark he stopped and made camp at the foot of a hogback ridge. He didn't build a fire, but made a skimpy meal from the supplies he'd picked up in Reno. It would have been nice to boil some coffee, but Smoke knew he'd be all right without it. He had made many a cold camp back in his wandering days, when he was still going by the name Buck West and was considered an outlaw. Before he met Sally . . .

Thinking about her as he sat with his back propped against a rock made her image appear in his mind, and as usual it was so vivid he felt like he could reach out and stroke his fingers along the smooth skin of her cheek, let his hand stray through the silky strands of her dark hair, lean toward her and taste the warm sweetness of her mouth . . .

"Daydreamin' like a calf-eyed boy! I'll swan, Smoke, you're gettin' careless in your old age. If I was out for your hair, you'd be—"

"Putting a bullet through your scrawny old gizzard right about now, Preacher," Smoke said as he moved his hand enough to reveal the Colt he held alongside his leg. "Yeah, I was feeling a mite homesick, but I still knew you were there. Shoot, I smelled forty-year-old bear grease on those buckskins of yours five minutes ago."

Preacher chuckled as he stepped out of the shadows on the other side of the camp. "Well, I'm glad to know that bein' an old married man ain't made you totally soft."

Smoke stood up and holstered his gun, then stepped forward to greet the man who was as much like a father to him as his own pa, God rest

Emmett Jensen's soul. He clasped Preacher's outstretched hand, then they pulled each other into a fierce, back-pounding hug.

"I asked about you in Reno," Smoke said.

"Decided not to go through there. Smoke, I had some trouble over yonder in Wyomin'. The Injun Ring sent some varmints after me, and the only reason I can figure why they'd do that is to keep me from gettin' to Matt."

Smoke nodded. "They had gunnies waiting for me in Reno. They probably would have tried to cut you down too, if you had shown up there."

"I ain't a bit surprised. Dead?"

"Yeah."

"I don't know why I even asked. Did you get a chance to ask any questions 'fore they all crossed the divide?"

"No, things didn't work out that way," Smoke replied without going into details. "There's no doubt in my mind who hired them, though."

"Mine, neither. You got any idea what sort of scrape Matt's got hisself into this time?"

"Nope. All I know is that I got a wire from him telling me to rattle my hocks to a place called Halltown." Smoke grunted. "Helltown, I'm told some folks call it."

"Helltown," Preacher repeated. "Yeah, that sounds like a place where Matt would wind up."

"How did you know where to look for me?"

Preacher made an expansive gesture. "I figured

you'd start for this Helltown place after you came through Reno. I knowed you'd stay off the beaten path, and this seemed like a likely path for you to follow. So when I got here yesterday, I just sort of squatted to wait for you. Found me a high spot and kept an eye on the countryside. I seen you comin' this way before it got dark."

"You always did have eyes like an eagle."

"You want to head for the settlement tonight?"

Smoke thought about it, then shook his head. "No, I've never been to Halltown before, and I wouldn't want to miss it in the dark. We'll ride on in the morning. Ought to be there by the middle of the day. That's soon enough."

"You hope," Preacher said. "We don't know what sort of fix Matt's in."

"That's true, we don't. I'd hate to get there too late to help him." Smoke rubbed his jaw and frowned in thought. "Maybe we'd better keep moving for a while. We can stop later to get a little sleep and let the horses rest."

"Now you're talkin'." Preacher let out a low whistle, and his gray stallion clopped out of the shadows. "Me an' Horse are ready to go."

Smoke swung his saddle back onto the 'Paloose. "You said the Indian Ring sent killers after you, too?"

"Yep. Raised seven kinds o' hell with that huntin' party I went along on. Killed ol' Hank Wilkerson, the no-good skunks."

"I'm sorry to hear that. Are they all dead?"

"Yep."

Smoke gave a grim laugh as he mounted up. "I don't know why I even asked."

Late the next morning, Smoke and Preacher rode into Halltown. It appeared to be a bustling settlement, and it would grow and thrive once the railroad got there.

Smoke hadn't shaved, so his cheeks and jaw were covered by beard stubble. His hat was pulled low over his face. It wasn't much of a disguise. If the Indian Ring had killers looking for him and Preacher, they would be spotted. It was impossible to make Preacher look like anything other than what he was, an old mountain man.

As they entered the main street, Preacher grunted and said quietly, "You see what I see up yonder at the other end of town, Smoke?"

"It's a gallows," Smoke replied, his voice grim. "But there's nobody hanging from it."

"Yet."

A man stood on the death platform, testing the mechanism of the trapdoor. It looked like an execution was imminent.

Preacher went on, "You don't reckon that Matt—"

"I don't know." Smoke turned the 'Paloose toward a hitch rail in front of a general store. "Let's see if we can find out."

An air of excitement gripped the town. Hangings did that. But some people seemed to be anticipating the hanging, while others appeared to be upset about it. Luckily, no one was paying much attention to the two strangers in their midst.

Smoke and Preacher dismounted, tied their horses to the hitch rail, and went up the steps to the mercantile's porch. Saloons were usually the best place to find out what was going on in a town, but the Ring's hired guns would more likely be hanging out in a saloon. Somebody in the store ought to be able to tell them what all the hoopla was about.

The place wasn't doing much business at the moment. An attractive young woman with red hair was behind the counter in the rear of the store, talking to a middle-aged matron. When the older woman left, Smoke ambled toward the counter and gave the redhead a nod and a friendly smile.

The look she gave him in return was downright frosty. "If you're one of Mr. Longacre's new men, we'd just as soon not have your business," she snapped.

So she had taken him for a gunman, Smoke thought. Well, that didn't come as much of a surprise. "No, ma'am, my pard and I don't work for Longacre. Fact is, right now we don't work for anybody. We're sort of on the drift, I reckon you'd say."

The young woman's expression softened a little. "I see. Do you need supplies?"

"Well, maybe. Mostly, though, we'd sort of like to know what's going on here in town today. Is it a holiday we don't know about?"

The redhead sniffed, and Smoke saw tears shining in her eyes. "No, it's not a holiday." Her voice caught a little as she went on, "They're . . . they're getting ready to hang an innocent man." She glanced at the banjo clock on the wall. "Any minute now, in fact."

Smoke stiffened. He didn't have time to be discreet anymore. "This innocent man they're fixing to hang, his name wouldn't be Matt Jensen, would it?"

The young woman's beautiful green eyes opened wide in amazement. "How did you—" She looked from Smoke to Preacher, who had stopped to look at a glass-fronted display case full of penny candy, then back again. "Oh, my God. You're Smoke and Preacher!"

Smoke reached across the counter and grasped her arm. "You know Matt? He's the one they're going to hang?"

The redhead jerked her head in a nod. "Yes, at noon! They said he killed a woman, but he didn't do it, I know he didn't do it! It's all part of Cyrus Longacre's plan—"

Smoke had heard enough. They could find out all the details from Matt, once they got him out of that mess.

And they didn't have much time to do it. The hands on the wall clock stood at two minutes until twelve.

Smoke whirled away from the counter. "Preacher, come on! They're about to hang Matt!"

"Tarnation!" the old mountain man exploded. "I was afraid it was gonna be somethin' like that when we saw that dang gallows!"

They ran onto the porch and saw crowds of people swarming toward the gallows. Based on what the young woman had said, Matt had some friends in Halltown, but they seemed to be outnumbered. Smoke's gaze darted here and there, picking out men who appeared to be hardcases—probably more of Longacre's hired guns. A tingling sense of excitement and fear had settled over the town, like the electric crackle in the air before a terrible thunderstorm was about to break.

Shouts went up as a knot of men forced their way through the crowd toward the gallows. The group bristled with rifles, shotguns, and pistols.

In their midst, striding along with his back held straight and defiant, was a tall, fair-haired figure.

Matt!

"Grab the horses," Smoke told Preacher. "No time for anything fancy!"

"Damn right!" Preacher said. "Cut loose your wolf, boy, and let it howl!"

Time was up, Matt thought. Hope was gone. Smoke and Preacher weren't going to get there. Even if they rode in right then, it was too late. Longacre had at least two dozen men scattered along the street, not to mention Sheriff Walt Sanger and the corrupt lawman's deputies. Nobody could stop the hanging.

Nobody except Matt himself.

He looked through the crowd and saw Long-acre and Judd Talley waiting at the foot of the steps leading up to the gallows. Longacre had his thumbs hooked in his vest and wore a solemn expression, as if he were there to see justice done. Talley, his face swollen and bruised from the punches Matt had landed earlier, didn't bother with any pretense. His usual arrogant smirk stretched across his face, telling all the world he was going to enjoy what he was about to witness.

Matt drew in a deep breath as he and the guards surrounding him approached the gallows. He would go out fighting, make them shoot him, so at least he wouldn't have to endure the indignity of kicking out his life at the end of a rope. His biggest regret was that he wouldn't get to see Smoke and Preacher again.

A sound uncannily like the howl of a wolf cut through the hubbub of the street. Matt's eyes widened in surprise as people began to yell. His head jerked around and so did everyone else's. He saw two familiar figures on horseback galloping toward him as the crowd scrambled to get out of the way of the pounding hooves.

"Stop them!" Longacre yelled. "Kill Jensen!"

They hadn't bothered to tie his hands, planning to do that once he was on the gallows, Sanger had explained. That was a bad mistake. Matt's right hand shot out, grabbed the twin barrels of the sheriff's shotgun, and wrenched them upward as his left fist crashed into Sanger's face. Tearing the shotgun out of the stunned sheriff's grasp, Matt whirled to drive the butt of the weapon into the belly of a deputy. He shouldered another man aside and whipped the shotgun around so it pointed at Longacre and Talley. The remaining deputies leaped out of the way.

Talley had jerked his gun out but launched himself at Longacre and drove the railroad man out of the way as Matt pulled the triggers. The shotgun boomed and sent buckshot tearing into the gallows steps, but Longacre and Talley had rolled clear of the charges.

Chaos erupted in the street. Longacre's gunnies tried to draw beads on Smoke and Preacher, but they were moving too fast, their guns roaring. Some of the hired guns spun off their feet as lead ripped into them while others jumped for cover.

Smoke and Preacher closed in on the gallows.

Matt saw Talley's revolver swinging toward him and launched the empty shotgun like a missile. It crashed into Talley's chest and knocked him backward, causing his shot to go high.

"Matt!" Smoke yelled as he pouched his right-hand gun and reached down.

The next instant, Matt leaped up, reaching for Smoke's hand. They clasped wrists, and Matt swung up on the 'Paloose's back behind the saddle. Smoke sent the big horse racing past the gallows while Preacher brought up the rear, twisting from side to side, firing his Remingtons, and keeping up that nerve-shattering howl.

The three of them galloped out of Halltown while Cyrus Longacre practically danced in a fit of apoplectic rage, screaming, "Go after them! Go after them!"

Nobody seemed to be in too much of a hurry to do that until Judd Talley gathered a group of Longacre's gunhawks out of the confusion in the street and set off in pursuit.

By that time, the only sign that remained of Smoke, Matt, and Preacher was a dwindling haze of dust in the air.

CHAPTER 29

The 'Paloose was big enough and strong enough to carry double without much trouble, but the added weight cut down on the gallant animal's speed and stamina. After galloping for a couple miles, Preacher signaled to Smoke they should stop.

"Matt, change horses," the old mountain man suggested. "I don't weigh as much as Smoke does, so it'll even out better and this ol' stallion of mine can handle it."

"Good idea," Smoke agreed. As Matt slipped down from the 'Paloose and swung up behind Preacher, Smoke hipped around in the saddle and looked back toward the settlement. He saw a pillar of dust rising between them and Halltown. "Looks like Longacre's men are coming after us."

"What'd you expect?" Preacher asked. "He went to so much trouble to keep you and me from ever gettin' here, Smoke. He must want Matt dead mighty bad."

Matt said, "He wants all three of us dead now, I'll bet. Thanks for showing up and pulling me out of there. I was about to make a grab for a gun and go down slinging lead. They weren't going to hang me."

"What in blazes is this mess all about, any-way?" Preacher wanted to know.

Before Matt could answer, Smoke said, "We can talk about that later, if we're all still alive. Right now we'd better find a place to hole up, otherwise we're going to be trading bullets with Longacre's gunnies in a few minutes."

"I've got an idea where we can go," Matt said.

He gave them directions, and they set off again at a gallop.

Matt sent them toward the village of Chief Walking Hawk. "The Paiutes are at the center of this," he explained, raising his voice to be heard over the drumming hoofbeats. "Longacre wants their land. He needs to build a trestle over Big Bear Wash, but the treaty gives the Paiutes control over the best place to do so."

"Why doesn't he just buy a right-of-way from them?" Smoke asked. "If he's rich enough to build a spur line, he ought to be able to afford that."

"I reckon he could, but he doesn't think he should have to. He believes he has the right to just take what he wants, and the Indian Ring is backing him up."

Preacher grunted. "Of all the dang fool things! All this because the varmint's too full of hisself to pay for what he wants?"

"That's right." Matt nodded as he rode behind the old mountain man. "Loco, isn't it?"

"That's what happens when a man gets too full

of himself," Smoke said. "It's not a matter of money anymore. Longacre's mad because somebody dared to stand up to him, so he's got to crush them to teach everybody else a lesson."

Matt nodded again. "Yeah, and he's willing to do whatever it takes, too . . . even having his own mistress murdered."

Smoke glanced over at him in disbelief. Matt went on to explain about Virginia Barry's death and how Longacre and Talley had made it look like he was responsible.

"I figure his cronies back in Washington put some pressure on him to make getting rid of me look legal," Matt concluded. "That's the only reason for him to go to so much trouble."

"I think you're probably right," Smoke said. "The whole thing's gone too far now, though. Longacre won't worry about keeping up any pretense. He'll just have his men kill us on sight."

"If they find us," Preacher said. "How much farther's this Paiute village you talked about, boy?"

"There's Big Bear Wash up ahead. Follow it, and we'll be at the village in another few minutes."

Smoke glanced at their back trail again. Judging by the cloud of dust, their pursuers had closed in a little, but not enough to stop them from reaching the Paiute village. "You know we'll be bringing down trouble on the heads of those folks."

"They've already got trouble," Matt pointed out. "I don't think Longacre's men will attack the village. He's brought in more gunnies to reinforce Talley and the rest of that bunch, but there still aren't enough of them to take on the whole tribe. At least that's what I'm hoping."

Smoke figured Matt was right. It was really their only chance.

They turned Horse and the 'Paloose northward along the edge of the wash, crossed over when Matt pointed out a spot where the banks had caved in enough to allow passage, and rode on to the Paiute village.

As Matt had predicted, a few minutes later they came in sight of the conical wooden lodges clustered among some scrubby trees along the bank of a small creek that flowed into the wash, where the water was swallowed up by the sandy ground. It wasn't a very appealing place, Smoke thought . . . typical of the land the government was willing to cede to the Indians by treaty. But no matter how good or bad it was, it belonged to the Paiutes, and Cyrus Longacre had no right to come in and take it.

Judging by the number of lodges, approximately five hundred people lived there, and that meant at least a hundred warriors. The Paiutes were peaceful now, but in the past they had put up quite a struggle at various times against the whites encroaching on their territory. Smoke knew a couple dozen gunmen wouldn't likely attack the village.

But it would only be a matter of time before Longacre came up with some other way to strike at his enemies, in particular Smoke, Matt, and Preacher.

The village dogs set up a commotion as the riders approached. Men gathered at the edge of the village, some holding rifles, others armed with bows and arrows.

A big man with graying hair and a dignified demeanor stepped out in front of the others. "Is that Walking Hawk?" Smoke asked Matt.

Matt nodded. "Yeah. He ought to remember me. I came out here and talked to him a couple times."

Smoke and Preacher brought their mounts to a halt when they were still about twenty feet from the group of warriors. Tension filled the air, and it didn't ease when Matt slid down from Horse and walked forward, his hand upraised with the palm out.

"Chief Walking Hawk," he greeted the chief. "It's good to see you again."

Walking Hawk nodded gravely. "And you, Matt Jensen. Who are these men?"

"My family," Matt replied. "Smoke Jensen . . . and Preacher."

The surprise that showed on Walking Hawk's face gave a lie to the idea that Indians never expressed emotion. Some of the warriors recognized the name, too, judging by the muttering among them.

"Looks like they've heard of you, Preacher," Smoke said in a low voice to the old mountain man.

"Yeah, but that ain't always a good thing," Preacher said. "I'm on good terms with the Paiutes, though, as far as I recollect."

Walking Horse nodded toward Matt's companions. "Ghost Killer?"

"That's right," Matt told him.

"I have heard of Smoke Jensen as well. All of you are welcome in our village."

"Thank you, Chief. But I have to warn you . . . Longacre's men are after us. They may pursue us all the way here, or they may turn back when they realize where we've gone."

Walking Hawk turned to look at his warriors. Several of them brandished their rifles, and a couple let out strident yips.

"Let them come," Walking Hawk said as he turned back to Matt. "They will wish they had turned back."

Matt couldn't help but grin. "Thanks, Chief. I was hoping you'd feel that way."

"There is more trouble?"

"I'm afraid so."

"Come," Walking Hawk invited. "We will talk."

They ate, too, sitting cross-legged in the village's largest lodge. Smoke, Matt, and Preacher enjoyed

323

the bowls of stew one of Walking Hawk's wives brought them. They knew certain things had to be done, a protocol as strict as any in societies considered more civilized. Preacher had always thought civilization was highly overrated. He was more at home in a place like that than almost anywhere else.

While they were eating, one of Walking Hawk's warriors came into the lodge and spoke quickly to the chief in their own tongue. Walking Hawk replied, then turned to the visitors as the warrior went out. "I sent my men to watch the trail along the wash. They saw the men from the settlement following your tracks."

"Longacre's gun crew," Smoke said.

Walking Hawk nodded. "When those men realized where your trail led, they stopped and talked among themselves for a while, then turned and rode back toward the town. They did not want to risk the wrath of the Paiutes."

"Just like I thought would happen," Matt said. "Thanks again for taking us in, Chief. You probably saved our lives."

"For now," Smoke added. "Longacre won't stand still for this. He'll figure out a way to come after us."

"Perhaps you should go, while his men are not looking for you," Walking Hawk suggested. "If you ride away from here and do not come back, you would be safe."

Preacher snorted. "And let that varmint Long-acre get away with what he's tryin' to do and what he almost did to Matt? No offense, Chief, but there ain't no way in Hades that's happenin'."

Walking Hawk smiled faintly. "Your answer does not surprise me, Ghost Killer. Will you slip into the camp of the enemy and cut all their throats while they sleep?"

"Well . . . I reckon I could, mind you, but I ain't sure that's the best way to go."

Smoke said, "In the eyes of the law, we're fugitives now. Matt will be wanted for murder, and Preacher and me for rescuing him from that hanging. Even if we got away, we'd be wanted men. I've lived that sort of life, and I don't want to go back to it. I've got a wife to love and a ranch to run."

"Then what do we do?" asked Matt.

Smoke had been thinking about that. "We need to prove that the charge against you is bogus, Matt. If we can establish Longacre framed you for killing that girl, then I reckon that would clear Preacher and me for helping you, too."

"How can we do that? Those people who testified at the trial were telling the truth about seeing Virginia arguing with me. The only one who actually lied was . . ." Matt drew in a deep breath. "Wait a minute. That hotel clerk in the Sierra House lied. He said he heard Virginia scream *after* I went upstairs. That's not possible, because she was already dead. The clerk lied, and Longacre figured that was the final nail in my coffin. But if we could get hold of him and find a real lawman, then make the clerk tell the truth . . ."

Smoke nodded. "If he would admit that Longacre forced him to lie at the trial, or paid him off to do so, it would go a long way toward clearing your name, Matt."

"That wouldn't prove you didn't kill the gal, Matt," Preacher pointed out.

"No, but it's a start," Matt said. "Maybe the clerk saw Talley go upstairs while Virginia was still alive. I'm convinced he's the one who really killed her."

Smoke nodded. "Like Matt said, it's a start. We'll knock Longacre's house of cards down one card at a time if we have to. But I've got a hunch if we pull out one of them, the whole thing's liable to collapse."

"How're we gonna get our hands on that clerk?" Preacher asked. "It ain't gonna be so easy. If we show our faces in town, all hell's bound to break loose."

"That's right, and we don't have much time, either," Smoke said. "You know Longacre a lot better than we do, Matt. How long is he going to wait before he makes his next move?"

"Not long at all," Matt replied with a shake of his head. "It wouldn't surprise me if he's already up to something else rotten."

● ● ●

Cyrus Longacre brought his fist down hard on the table beside him in the sitting room of his suite. "I want them found and killed, all three of them, by God!" He glared at Walt Sanger. "Do you understand me, Sheriff?"

The lawman looked more miserable and hangdog than ever. "Yeah, sure, Mr. Longacre, but I, uh, I only got a few deputies—"

"Deputize Judd and his men," Longacre snapped as he nodded toward Talley, who stood to one side with his massive arms crossed over his slab-muscled chest and a scowl on his handsome face. "In fact, I don't care if you take your deputies or any of the townsmen with you. My men will be enough . . . although they've certainly failed spectacularly at most jobs I've given them recently," he added in a scathing tone.

"We won't let you down, boss," Talley said. "I want Jensen and his friends dead more than I've ever wanted anything else."

"See to it, then. Take the sheriff along so it'll be legal."

Talley smiled. "Nobody's going to question the killing of three fugitives."

"Blast it, I can't afford to have any stain of suspicion now! Not with the army coming in any time now."

"The . . . the army?" Sanger quavered.

"That's right. There's a troop of cavalry on the

way here right now. As soon as they arrive Hall-town will be placed under martial law due to the Paiute uprising and the rampant lawlessness gripping the area."

Sanger frowned. "What Paiute uprising?"

"The one that has the townspeople living in terror of an attack."

"Nobody's said nothin' to me about—"

"They will. They'll tell the soldiers how afraid they are. And the ranchers on the other side of Big Bear Wash will confirm the Indians have been stealing their stock and ambushing their cowboys."

Sanger shook his head. "Walkin' Hawk and his people haven't done anything like that."

"Good Lord!" Longacre exploded as his face darkened with anger. "Do you people *want* the railroad to come in here and make all your lives better, or not?"

"Well, sure, but—"

Longacre hit the table again, striking it with his open hand in a sharp slap. "Then it's time for this farce to end. To save the town and the ranchers, the cavalry will wipe out the Paiutes. I'll build my bridge, and everything will be fine. I just don't want to take a chance on Jensen and his friends talking to the authorities."

"But if they're holed up with the Injuns, there ain't no way to get 'em out," Sanger protested. "Not until the soldiers get here, anyway, and then you run the risk of them gettin' to the officer in charge of the troop."

"You're not telling me anything I don't already know, you addlepated old fool." Longacre swung toward Talley. "Judd?"

"Leave it to me, boss," the gunman said with a smile. "I know just how to get Jensen and his friends out where we can get rid of them once and for all."

CHAPTER 30

After the excitement of Matt Jensen's rescue from the foot of the gallows had died down, things went back to normal in Halltown. As normal as they were those days, anyway. The unsettled atmosphere of the town remained. The feeling that violence might break out at any minute still hung over the town.

Colin Ferguson sighed as he lowered himself into the chair behind the desk in his office in the hotel. His bad leg ached from weariness. He had spent the afternoon going around town try-ing to stir up some support for opposing Cyrus Longacre's reign of terror. His efforts had ended in abysmal failure.

Some of the people he talked to were honestly baffled as to why Longacre's actions were all that bad. The railroad represented progress and profit for the town, and it would be better if it could be extended through the lush cattle range between there and the mountains. What did it matter if the Paiutes were driven off their land . . . or even killed? They were just savages, after all, and rumors were already plentiful that they were planning to attack the town. It was just a matter of time before the Paiutes went on a bloodthirsty rampage.

Only a small minority of Halltown's citizens felt that way. Most of the others were just scared of Judd Talley and the rest of Longacre's hired guns. Give Longacre what he wanted, they argued. That would be best for the town, and more important, nobody else would get hurt. Most of them also genuinely believed Matt Jensen had killed that girl and deserved to hang. All the evidence had been against him, after all.

Ferguson could understand why they felt that way. If he and Maureen hadn't gotten to know Matt as well as they had, he might have thought the young man was guilty, too. Nobody wanted to risk their own lives and maybe the lives of their families by standing up to Longacre over a no-good killer.

Ferguson opened a drawer in his desk and took out a bottle and a glass. He uncorked the bottle and poured a couple fingers of fine Irish whiskey into the glass. The liquor wouldn't help the situation that plagued Halltown, but it might ease the ache in his leg a little. It might also allow him to forget for a moment that he and his niece were probably the only friends Matt Jensen had left in Halltown.

With a horde of ruthless killers after them, it was only a matter of time before Matt and his friends were brought to bay. Longacre wouldn't take chances again. Ferguson was sure Longacre had given Judd Talley firm orders to kill their prey on sight.

Ferguson was about to lift the glass to his mouth when the office door opened. He looked up and saw Maureen standing there. "What is it, girl?" he asked. "Why aren't you at the store?"

When he noticed how pale Maureen's face was and saw the fear in her green eyes, he knew something was terribly wrong. He started up from his chair.

Maureen stumbled a little as she was pushed into the room. Judd Talley's huge form loomed behind her, making her look almost like a child. The gun in his hand came up and pointed at Ferguson.

"Don't try anything, old man," Talley warned. "I don't want to shoot you, but I will if I have to."

"Wh-what are you doing?" Ferguson sputtered. "If this is some sort of holdup—"

"You're not even close," Talley said. "The only thing I want is you and your niece. You're coming with me."

"Coming with you? But why?"

Talley grinned. "You and Maureen are the only friends Jensen's got left in town." He unknowingly echoed the very thought that had gone through Ferguson's brain only moments earlier. "I figure you'll make the best bait for the trap."

"The hotel clerk's name is Joseph Spivey, if I remember right from the trial," Matt told Smoke and Preacher. "I don't know where he lives, but I'm sure Mr. Ferguson can tell you. He knows just about everybody in Halltown. Once it gets dark, if you can make it to the hotel without anybody seeing you, Preacher, you can slip in the back door and talk to Mr. Ferguson."

The old mountain man snorted. "Remember who you're talkin' to, boy."

Walking Hawk nodded solemnly. "No one sees Ghost Killer if Ghost Killer does not want to be seen."

"Dang right," Preacher said.

Smoke said, "If we can get our hands on Spivey, we can take him to Carson City and go all the way to the governor if we have to, to get somebody in authority to listen to us. I'm sure we can count on the governor of Colorado to put in a word for us if need be."

"Sounds like a good plan," Matt said, "as long as Longacre doesn't come up with something else in the meantime. He's bound to be frustrated enough now that I wouldn't put much of anything past him."

"From the sound of it, there wasn't much he wouldn't do to start with." Smoke shook his head. "Having a woman killed just to frame you, Matt . . . A bullet in the head's too good for a snake like that."

The other three men in Chief Walking Hawk's lodge nodded in solemn agreement.

As he came abreast of the Sierra House, Captain Edward McKee raised his hand in a signal for the troops following him to halt. McKee turned his head and said to his noncom, "Have the men dismount, Sergeant, but stand ready to ride again."

"Yes, sir," Sergeant Haney said. He turned to the troop and bellowed, *Disss-mount!*"

McKee took his gauntlets off as he went into the hotel. He held them in one hand and slapped them in the palm of the other. A clerk behind the desk stared at him. McKee approached the man and was about to ask for Mr. Cyrus Longacre, when a voice hailed him from the stairs.

"Captain?" The man reached the bottom of the stairs and came toward McKee with an outstretched hand. "I'm Cyrus Longacre. I believe you were supposed to meet me here."

"Yes, sir, that's correct." McKee grasped the railroad man's hand and gave it a brief shake. H much preferred exchanging salutes, but yo couldn't do that when you were dealing with civilians. For that matter, he preferred not dealing with civilians at all, but he was a soldier. He followed orders, and his were to report to Longacre, assess the situation, and render all due aid to the man in putting down an uprising of the local Indian tribe.

"You arrived a little sooner than I expected," Longacre commented.

"My orders were to proceed here without delay," McKee explained. "My men can cover a lot of ground in a hurry when need be."

"Well, I certainly appreciate that. Come up to my suite and have a drink with me," Longacre invited.

McKee hesitated, but after the long ride he and his men had just made, a drink sounded very appealing.

"I have some excellent cigars as well," Longacre added.

That made up the captain's mind. "Lead on, sir," McKee said.

A few minutes later, with his hat off, McKee was comfortably ensconced in an armchair in the sitting room of Longacre's suite. He had a glass of brandy in one hand and a fine Cuban cigar in the other.

"To the U.S. cavalry," Longacre said as he raised his own glass. "The finest fighting force in the world."

"I'll drink to that." McKee tossed back the brandy and enjoyed the warm feeling it kindled in his belly. That was what he needed. "So, tell me about these Indians who are causing trouble."

For the next half hour, McKee listened as Longacre recited a litany of complaints about the Paiutes. According to the railroad man, the savages had attacked his surveying parties, attacked the men he sent out to negotiate a right-of-way agreement with Chief Walking Hawk, rustled cattle from the ranchers on the other side of Big Bear Wash, threatened the cowboys who tried to recover those stolen cattle, and promised to make war on Halltown itself, leaving the settlement's citizens in a state of fear.

When Longacre was finished, McKee nodded. "The Bureau of Indian Affairs is supposed to send an agent out here as soon as possible, but that may be a couple months. Until then, my instructions are to pacify the Indians and move them off the land they currently hold, pending a review of their rights under the treaty they signed several years ago. Does that agree with your view of the situation, Mr. Longacre?"

"Very much so," Longacre said.

"These orders come directly from the War Department, you know," McKee commented. "From the office of the Secretary of War himself. That's rather unusual." McKee suspected there was some sort of connection between Longacre and the political bosses in Washington. He wouldn't have had enough influence to have the army sent in to help with what was actually a business problem.

Those sort of things were none of his business, McKee told himself. He had his orders.

"Well, I'm just glad you're here, Captain," Longacre said. "I know this ordeal will soon be over and I can get on with the job of building my railroad line."

"Yes, sir."

"When do you expect to have the Paiutes moved out?"

"We'll begin operations against them first thing tomorrow morning." McKee shrugged. "Who knows, they may cooperate."

"And if they don't?"

"We'll do whatever is necessary to compel them."

"I think they'll probably put up a fight," Longacre warned.

McKee smiled. "Then they'll pay the price for doing so."

Longacre returned the smile and reached for the brandy bottle. "Another drink?"

"Don't mind if I do," McKee said.

Preacher rode out at dusk. In the uncertain light, the old mountain man in his buckskins and the rangy gray stallion he rode were hard to see, especially since he knew how to take advantage of every bit of cover there was. Talley had likely left some of the hired guns to keep an eye on the Paiute village, but Preacher figured they wouldn't spot him. He might not be as young and slick as he once was, but he was still plenty slick enough to outsmart a bunch of cheap hardcases.

Like the phantom that had inspired his name among the Blackfeet, he slipped through the growing darkness until he neared Halltown. When he spotted the lights of the settlement, he dismounted and wrapped rags around Horse's hooves to muffle the sound of the animal's progress. It wasn't the first time Preacher had done such a thing, so Horse didn't spook at having his hooves wrapped.

Preacher led the stallion forward in almost complete silence. He stopped in a grove of trees not far from the edge of town and tied Horse's reins to one of the slender trunks. Patting the animal on the shoulder, Preacher murmured, "I'll be back for you, old fella."

Then he catfooted toward the back of the building closest to him.

Matt had told him how to find the hotel owned by Colin Ferguson. Preacher studied the town's layout as he approached, and plotted how he would get to where he needed to be, picking out the deepest patches of shadow and other cover along the course he would take. He moved slowly. Stealth was more important than speed.

When he reached the back of the building he knew was the hotel, he went to the rear door. It was unlocked, so he slipped inside with ease. He had to find Colin Ferguson's office.

No light showed under the office door when Preacher found it. He could hear people moving around in the hotel and wanted to get out of sight before somebody wandered along the corridor and spotted him. He muttered a curse, then tried the knob. It turned under his fingers. He opened the door just long enough to slip into the darkened office.

What now? Preacher was a man of action. He didn't cotton to standing around. Thinking maybe Ferguson had left something that would tell where he was, Preacher moved carefully. With one hand outstretched and the other resting on the butt of one of the Remingtons, he made his way across the room toward the spot where a desk should be sitting.

A moment later he bumped into what he was looking for, and he felt around to make sure it was a desk. When he was satisfied that it was, he fished a lucifer out of his pocket and used a thumbnail to snap the match into life. He'd just take a quick look around. . . .

As the match flared up and its glow washed over the desk, Preacher cursed again at what his eyes, squinted against the glare, saw there.

The desk was littered with papers, and standing out in bold relief on them were several drops of blood, scattered in a curving line across the desk. The chair behind the desk was overturned.

There had been a fight . . . which meant wherever Colin Ferguson was, he probably hadn't gone there of his own accord.

If he was even still alive.

CHAPTER 31

When a soft knock sounded on the door of his suite, Cyrus Longacre slipped his hand under his coat and closed his fingers around the butt of a small pistol in a shoulder holster. He went to the door and called, "Who is it?"

"Just me, boss."

Recognizing Judd Talley's voice, Longacre let go of the pistol and opened the door. The big gunman came into the room wearing his usual self-satisfied smirk.

"You took care of that matter we discussed earlier?" Longacre asked as he closed the door.

Talley took off his hat and tossed it casually on a side table as he nodded. "Yeah. Ferguson put up a little fight, but it didn't amount to much. We've got him and the girl stashed where nobody'll ever find them unless we want them to."

"Not that same shack your men used before, I hope," Longacre said sharply.

Talley shook his head. "No, Jensen knows about that one. They're in a cave up in the hills. I left eight good men guarding them. There won't be any slipups this time, boss."

"Good," Longacre said. "You've sent a rider to the Paiute village?"

"Yeah. He wasn't too crazy about the idea, but I told him he'd be safe enough as long as Jensen knows we've got Ferguson and his niece. I just hope you're right about Jensen and those other meddlers being with the redskins like you think."

"Where else could they hide out as easily, and still be relatively close to town?" With the certainty born of his natural arrogance, Longacre nodded. "They'll be there. I'd bet almost anything on it."

"Well, if they are, my man will deliver the message," Talley declared.

"I've been thinking. I have another job for you." Longacre took a cigar out of a vest pocket, bit off the end, and clamped the cylinder of rich tobacco between his teeth. "There's another weak link we need to take care of," he said around the Cubano. "Joseph Spivey."

"The hotel clerk?" Talley asked with a frown.

"That's right. He's the only one who testified at the trial who actually lied. If he were to change his testimony about when he heard Virginia scream, it would cast doubt on the whole case. I don't want to take a chance on him talking to any outside authorities, even though it's unlikely such a thing will ever happen."

"You want me to get rid of Spivey, just to make sure?" Talley asked the question casually, as if the idea of murdering the clerk didn't bother him a bit.

Longacre nodded again. "That's right. Don't do it here, in town, though. Take him somewhere out of the settlement and leave his body where it won't be found."

"I can do that," Talley said with a chuckle. "Where is he? Working downstairs at the desk?"

"No, I already checked on that. He's not working tonight. He has a little house on one of the side streets." Longacre told Talley how to find the clerk's place.

"All right, I'll go take care of it right now. No point in putting it off."

"None at all," Longacre agreed. "I'll feel better once it's done. Captain McKee seems like an agreeable man, the sort that won't cause any trouble for us, but I'd like to be sure there's no chance of him hearing anything he shouldn't."

Talley nodded, picked up his hat, and left the room.

Two gun-wolves he bossed were waiting for him in the lobby. He jerked his head at them, and they followed him outside.

"I've got a job for the two of you," he said. "That hotel clerk, Spivey, needs to be taken care of. Grab him, take him out of town somewhere, and make sure nobody finds him."

One of the men grinned. "Not unless it's a buzzard or a coyote, eh, Judd?"

Talley shook his head and repeated, "Nobody. I want him planted good and proper."

The hardcase who had spoken shrugged. "Sure. We understand."

"Do we do it now?" the other man asked.

"Yeah." Talley told the two killers where to find Spivey. "Remember, keep it quiet while you're here in town."

The men nodded and drifted off into the night on their mission of murder.

The varmints never looked back. No reason for them to. They thought they had the whole town buffaloed.

They never saw the lean, dark shape slipping through the shadows behind them.

Preacher had been counting on Colin Ferguson to tell him where to find the hotel clerk, Spivey. Obviously, judging by the blood he'd found in Ferguson's office, something bad had happened to the man. Preacher wanted to get to the bottom of that, but his job was to grab Spivey, the man who could start breaking up the murder frame around Matt.

Spivey clerked at the Sierra House. Under the circumstances, Preacher supposed that would be the best place to start looking for him.

Luck had brought him to the alley beside the hotel when the towering gunman and his two pards had stepped into the street. Preacher had seen the big man earlier, when he and Smoke had rescued Matt from the hanging. He knew from talking to Matt since, the man was Judd Talley, Longacre's segundo and probably the one who had really killed that girl.

Preacher could have picked them off then and there and been done with it, but before he could draw his guns, he heard Talley say something about Spivey. The old mountain man wasn't close enough to make out all the words, but unless there was some other Spivey in town, they were talking about the man Preacher wanted to find.

After a minute, Talley and the other two men split up. Talley started across the street toward one of the saloons, while the two gunnies walked off like they were setting out on some sort of mission. Preacher knew he had to play a hunch.

He followed them.

It was easy enough, since that possibility never occurred to them. The trail led to a shabby little house on the edge of town. No lights burned in the windows, but the two gunmen went to the door anyway. One of them pounded on it.

A moment later, Preacher saw a faint glow

343

inside the house. Somebody had lit a candle or a lamp. The door swung open, spilling out enough light to reveal the two hardened killers waiting on the porch. As he crouched nearby in the shadows, Preacher heard a gasp of surprise from the man who had opened the door. The man tried to slam it, but one of the intruders shoved it back.

"Are you Spivey?" he demanded.

"I . . . I . . . What do you want? I haven't done anything. Leave me alone—"

Lamplight reflected off cold steel as one of the men shoved a gun barrel up under the man's chin.

"Blast it, answer the question! Are you Spivey?"

"Yes, I—"

"You're comin' with us, then," the gunman growled.

He stepped back, still covering Spivey, while the other man reached for the terrified hotel clerk, who wore a nightshirt and peered at them through round spectacles.

Preacher's keen brain knew why Talley had sent those men to Spivey's house. Longacre had decided the hotel clerk needed to be shut up permanently, to make sure he could never reveal his part in the scheme to blame Virginia Barry's murder on Matt.

The old mountain man's arm lifted, went back, shot forward again. More steel flickered through the night. The razor-sharp blade of Preacher's

344

Bowie knife, thrown with such force, buried its entire eight inches in the back of the man trying to grab Spivey. The gunnie made a low, keening noise and lurched forward to collapse at Spivey's feet.

Preacher had kept moving when the knife left his hand. As the second gunman turned toward his fallen comrade in surprise, Preacher palmed out one of the Remingtons, reversed it quickly, and struck with all the strength of his whipcord frame behind the blow. The butt of the heavy revolver crashed against the gunman's head, the man's skull giving way under the impact. The gunman went down as heavily as his partner had.

The violence lasted barely longer than the blink of an eye. Spivey still stood in the doorway in his nightshirt, looking frightened and confused. Preacher flipped the Remington around again so he gripped the butt and said, "Joe Spivey? The clerk at the Sierra House?"

"Y-yes. Who—"

Preacher didn't let him go on. He rapped Spivey on the head, using the Remington's barrel, hitting him just hard enough to knock him out for a few minutes. Spivey collapsed next to the bodies of the two men who had intended to kidnap and kill him.

"You don't know it, son," Preacher muttered, "but I just done you a heck of a favor. And you're gonna pay it back."

He pouched the iron and bent to grasp the shirts of the dead men. One by one he dragged them into Spivey's house, then blew out the lamp the clerk had lit a few minutes earlier and closed the door. Reaching down, he got his arms around Spivey and lifted him, draping the unconscious form over his shoulder. It was a good thing Spivey was a skinny cuss, Preacher thought as he hoofed it out of town toward the trees where he had left Horse.

Smoke and Matt had stretched out on the buffalo robes in the lodge Chief Walking Hawk had provided for them, and although they had dozed off, both men slept lightly as a matter of habit. They woke up fully alert, as the village's dogs started raising a commotion. When they sat up, each man held a gun.

"You reckon Preacher's back already?" Matt asked.

"Possible, but it doesn't seem likely." Smoke sprang lithely to his feet. "Maybe we'd better have a look."

When he pushed aside the hide flap over the lodge's entrance and stepped out with Matt following closely behind him, Smoke saw several of the Paute warriors coming toward him. A few fires still burned in the village, casting a dim glow over the scene.

The warriors had a white man with them. A

couple of them held his arms and forced him along. Walking Hawk followed behind them. Smoke's eyes narrowed as he studied the stranger. He didn't recall ever seeing the man before, but the man's hard features and the low-slung holster on his hip—now empty since he had been disarmed by his captors—identified him as a gunman. Probably one of Longacre's men, Smoke thought.

Walking Hawk stepped around the prisoner and said to Smoke, "This man was captured by our sentries as he rode toward the village. He says he has a message for Matt Jensen and his friends."

Smoke moved closer to the man, who had stopped struggling against the warriors. "Better speak up and make it quick, amigo," Smoke advised. "I think my friends here would enjoy having a little sport with you."

The implied threat of torture at the hands of the Paiutes made the man's jaw tighten, but he didn't give in to his fear. "I got a message for Matt Jensen."

Matt stepped up. "Talk."

"If you want to see that pretty redheaded Ferguson gal and her uncle again, you better come with me, all three of you."

Matt's gun came up level with the prisoner's face. He eared back the hammer. "What did you say?"

The man swallowed hard. "We got Ferguson

and the gal. You come with me, we'll turn 'em loose. If you don't . . ."

He didn't finish the threat, but Smoke and Matt both knew what he meant. The barrel of Matt's gun trembled a little as Matt struggled to control his anger.

"Blowing his brains out won't help us any, Matt," Smoke said quietly.

"They tried using Maureen as a hostage before, Smoke. She was terrified then. It's got to be even worse on her now, since they've got her uncle, too."

"Yeah, but we'll get them away from Longacre's men, don't worry," Smoke assured him.

After a moment, Matt slowly lowered his gun and stepped back. "What are we going to do?"

Smoke looked at the prisoner. "You know where they're being held, don't you?"

"You can't make me talk," the man replied stubbornly.

Smoke laughed. "You really believe that, friend? Take a look around."

The hardcase glanced from side to side at the pitiless faces of the Paiutes who surrounded him. "You can't kill me," he blustered. "If I don't come back by morning, and if you're not with me, Ferguson and the girl will die. You can count on that."

"Nobody's going to kill you," Smoke said.

"You'll just *wish* you were dead," Matt added.

Chief Walking Hawk nodded in solemn agreement.

The gunman stared back at them defiantly, and after another moment, Smoke shrugged. "All right, Chief."

Walking Hawk made a curt gesture to his men. They started to drag the prisoner away, and his resolve broke. Cracked right in two, in fact. "Wait! Wait, for God's sake! I'll tell you where they're being held."

"Figured you might," Smoke drawled.

"But you can't kill me," the man continued. "You'll need me to get in there. Otherwise they'll just kill the prisoners."

"Don't worry, you're coming with us," Matt told him. "And if anything happens to Maureen and Mr. Ferguson, I can promise you one thing, mister . . . You'll be the next one to die."

An hour or so later, Preacher arrived back at the Paiute village with a pale and frightened Joseph Spivey. He pushed the hotel clerk into the lodge where Smoke and Matt were staying. They had rekindled the fire in the center of the lodge since it looked like they wouldn't be getting much sleep the rest of the night. As soon as Spivey saw Matt in the flickering light from the flames, his eyes got wider and more panic-stricken.

"Please, Mr. Jensen, don't kill me," he babbled. "I had to lie at the trial, I just had to. Talley would have . . . He threatened to do terrible things if I didn't—"

Matt lifted a hand to stop him. "Take it easy, Spivey. I know Longacre and Talley forced you to lie about what happened. What we want you to do is tell the truth to the authorities."

"What authorities?" Spivey asked. "Sheriff Sanger is too afraid of Longacre and Talley to do anything against them."

Smoke said, "As soon as we take care of another little chore, we're going to head for Carson City, Spivey, and you're coming with us. If we can reach the governor, he can start getting to the bottom of this mess."

"I don't know. I don't know." Spivey looked like he wanted to be sick. "Talley will kill me if I talk—"

Preacher leaned closer to the clerk and said with a grin, "Who do think is more loco, son? Talley . . . or me? You better think hard about your answer."

Spivey lifted his hands and ran his fingers through his lank, tangled hair. "Oh, God. Maybe . . . maybe if I told the captain of that cavalry troop, he could have the soldiers protect me from Longacre's men."

Smoke took a quick step closer to Spivey. "What cavalry troop?" he asked sharply.

"They rode in late this afternoon," Spivey said. "I don't know how many soldiers. A lot, though. A hundred or more."

Smoke, Matt, and Preacher glanced at each other. Matt said, "You reckon Longacre got his partners in the Ring to have those troopers sent in?"

Smoke nodded. "I'd say it's pretty likely. It wouldn't surprise me a bit if the Ring's influence stretches all the way to the War Department."

"Dadgum it!" Preacher said. "You mean we got to fight soldiers, too, and not just Longacre's gunnies?"

Smoke rubbed his chin as he thought. "Maybe not. The Indian Ring may be responsible for sending those troops here, but that doesn't mean their commanding officer is taking orders from Longacre's friends. If we could get to him and talk to him without Longacre being around, we might be able to convince him we're telling the truth."

"I can still do a lot of things," Preacher said, "but sneakin' into an army camp and carryin' off the fella in charge probably ain't one of 'em. When I was younger, maybe . . ."

Spivey said, "You won't be able to get to Captain McKee. Now that I think about it, when I was eating supper in the hotel dining room before I went home, I heard rumors that the cavalry is riding out here in the morning to move these savages off this land."

"Blast it!" Matt said. "This just keeps getting worse. Longacre's got us blocked at every turn, especially as long as he has Maureen and her uncle as hostages."

"Wait a dadblamed minute," Preacher said. "I ain't heard about that part of it."

Quickly, Smoke and Matt filled him in on what they had learned from the man who delivered Longacre's message. "There's only one way to ride up to that cave where Maureen and her uncle are being held," Smoke concluded. "If all three of us, along with Longacre's man, don't show up there tomorrow morning, the prisoners will be killed."

"But you ain't gonna let that happen," Preacher said. "You got some plan, Smoke, I know you do."

"Maybe"—Smoke nodded—"but from the sound of it, the cavalry's liable to attack Walking Hawk's people about the same time we're trying to rescue Maureen and Mr. Ferguson."

"We can't be in two places at the same time," Matt said.

Smoke thought about it for a moment. "We'll see about that."

CHAPTER 32

As the sun rose the next morning, four men rode along Big Bear Wash where it twisted into the hills. Smoke and Matt flanked Longacre's gunman, whose name, they had discovered, was Grady Malone. The fourth figure, who brought up the rear, rode the rangy gray stallion called Horse and wore buckskins, along with a broad-brimmed felt hat adorned with an eagle feather that was pulled down to shield his features.

The face under that hat was the coppery, hawk-like visage of one of Walking Hawk's warriors, a man named Pine Tree.

He was dressed like Preacher and rode Preacher's horse, and Smoke and Matt hoped that, from a distance, it would convince Longacre's hired killers that the old mountain man was with them.

Actually, Preacher was back at the Paiute village. It was his job to keep Spivey safe, stall the cavalry, and prevent a battle from starting before Smoke and Matt could rescue Maureen and Ferguson and return with them to the village.

"That's all you want me to do?" Preacher had asked caustically when Smoke laid out the plan the night before. "Why don't you ask me if I can flap my dang arms and fly to the moon, too?"

"If anybody could do that, I figure it would be you, Preacher," Smoke had said with a smile.

Now he glanced over at Malone, who held the reins fairly naturally. Anybody watching them wouldn't be able to tell the gunman's feet were tied together under the horse's belly. The pistol that rode in Malone's holster was an old, rusty cap-and-ball revolver that hadn't worked for years. One of the old men had taken it off a dead soldier after a Paiute skirmish with the army two decades earlier. Malone's gun, a well-cared-for Colt .44, was tucked behind Matt's belt, since his holster was somewhere in Sanger's office back in Halltown.

"Use your head and you just might come out of this alive," Smoke told the gunman.

Malone's face wore a bleak look. "I don't think so. Once the three of you are dead, Talley will kill me for telling you where we're going."

"You were supposed to bring us here anyway," Matt pointed out. "What's the difference if you told us?"

"You wouldn't know about the riflemen hidden on both sides of the gap that leads to the cave."

"You think we wouldn't have guessed as soon as we saw the layout?" Smoke asked. "This isn't the first trap we've ridden into on purpose."

Malone's voice was surly as he replied, "Yeah, well, Talley'll kill me anyway, just out of sheer meanness if for no other reason. I just know it."

"You may be right," Matt said. "After all, Talley cut that poor girl's throat without a second thought, didn't he?"

Malone's eyes flicked toward Matt, but he quickly looked down again and muttered, "I don't know nothin' about that."

Smoke nodded toward the hills ahead of them. "That's the gap you were talking about?"

Malone lifted his head to check the terrain. "Yeah, that's it. The cave's in the base of the ridge just past it, on the left."

Smoke studied the rugged landscape they were approaching. Two ridges angled toward each other to form a rough *V* with a small opening at the base where they didn't quite come together. The gap was about twelve feet wide and fifty feet long, with steep sides that rose maybe thirty feet before dropping back a little and then climbing still higher. The setbacks on both sides of the gap were littered with boulders and smaller rocks, providing cover for the riflemen who were hidden there, three on each side according to Malone. They were supposed to let Malone and the others ride into the gap, then open fire when Malone suddenly spurred ahead.

Smoke glanced up. Longacre's men would be watching their intended victims approach, not looking above them.

At least, that's what Smoke and Matt were counting on.

They were only a couple hundred yards from the gap. The sun was up, flooding the landscape with reddish-gold light. It was going to be a beautiful day—for those who survived the next few minutes.

Malone suddenly said, "For God's sake, why didn't you just ride away after you stopped the hanging in Helltown? You were free and clear of all this. Why didn't you just keep going instead of staying to fight Longacre?"

"Because somebody's got to stop folks like him who think they can just take anything because they want it," Matt said.

"But he's bringing in the railroad! That's a good thing."

"Not if he tramples on people's rights to do it," Smoke said.

"You're loco," Malone insisted. "All of you. You can't fight somebody who's got all the money and power Longacre has. Not for very long, anyway. He'll crush you."

Smoke ignored the gunman's ranting. "Here's the gap. Don't even think about calling out a warning, Malone. You'll die a split second after you do."

Malone fell silent except for muttering some frightened curses as the four men rode between the ridges.

Smoke and Matt looked calm, but they felt tension grip them as they waited for the ball to start.

They didn't have to wait long. The crash of gunshots suddenly filled the air.

The shots weren't aimed at them, though, and they didn't come from the boulders where Longacre's men were hidden. The bullets rained down from higher on the ridges, where some of Walking Hawk's warriors had scaled those almost perpendicular slopes during the night and slowly, silently worked their way into position to ambush the ambushers.

Smoke heard cries of pain and surprise from Longacre's men as he dug his heels into the 'Paloose's flanks and sent the horse lunging forward. "Let's go!" he called to Matt and Pine Tree. Their only hope of saving Maureen and Ferguson was to take their captors by surprise and reach the cave before the gunmen could kill the prisoners.

Puffs of smoke jetted from the rifles of the Paiutes on top of the ridges. Under attack, Longacre's men tried to fight back. They forgot about the men in the gap and turned to fire up at the Indians. Smoke spotted one of Longacre's bushwhackers who stepped out from behind the boulder where he had been hidden and sprayed lead toward the top of the ridge as fast as he could work his Winchester's lever. One of the Paiutes was hit and silently toppled off his perch, clutching his belly where the bullet had ripped into him. He plummeted into the gap below.

Smoke lifted his Colt and snapped a shot at the man who had just killed the Indian. The bushwhacker spun around and dropped his rifle as the slug from Smoke's gun punched into him. He plunged off the ledge, but he didn't die silently. He let out a short-lived scream that ended abruptly as he crashed into the rocky floor of the gap.

Smoke, Matt, and Pine Tree galloped past both bodies. Smoke was sorry one of Walking Hawk's warriors had been killed . . . but unless they were lucky, he wouldn't be the only Paiute to die that day.

Malone had whirled his mount and fled as soon as the shooting started. Smoke hated to let him go, but there hadn't been any other choice. If he had tied a lead rope to Malone's horse, Longacre's bushwhackers would have noticed it and might have realized something wasn't going according to plan. Malone would probably head straight for Halltown to warn Longacre and Talley. That couldn't be helped. Smoke and Matt would have to move fast enough that it wouldn't matter.

As they stormed out of the gap, Smoke caught sight of the cave up ahead. It was under the huge slab of rock that formed the ridge on the left, about a hundred feet away. Several of Longacre's men had come running out when the shooting began. Smoke figured it was their job to finish off any survivors who made it through the ambush in the gap.

They could see the ambush hadn't gone as planned. The rifles in their hands came up and started to spout flame, but the three riders were moving fast and had already closed part of the gap. Smoke drew his second gun and guided the 'Paloose with his knees as he opened fire with both Colts. Matt's gun was roaring, too, and the whipcrack of Pine Tree's rifle also blended with the thunder of galloping hoofbeats.

They hoped Maureen and Ferguson were tied up deep enough in the cave that they would be out of the line of fire, but Smoke and Matt both knew the prisoners might already be dead. It was a grim possibility they weren't going to acknowledge as long as they didn't have to.

Longacre's hired killers crumpled under the deadly hail of lead that scythed through them. In a matter of heartbeats, only one man was left on his feet. The others were either dead or kicking out their lives on the ground.

The lone man whirled and dived back into the cave, heading toward a couple of struggling, trussed-up figures deep in the cave. Matt leaped out of the saddle and followed with the .44 in his hand.

"Stay back!" the gunman yelled over his shoulder. "Stay back or I'll—"

Matt left his feet in a diving tackle that caught the man around the legs and sent both crashing to the ground. The bone-jarring impact jolted the guns from their hands.

The gunman kicked free of Matt's grip, rolled over, and came up flailing punches at him. Matt ducked under the wild blows and sunk his left fist in the man's belly, causing the man to gasp and bend forward in perfect position for the short right cross that Matt smashed to his jaw. The perfectly timed punch sent the man sprawling on the floor of the cave again.

Unfortunately, he landed next to the gun that had gone skittering out of his hand a moment earlier. He snatched it off the ground, rolled again, and brought the weapon up. Flame spouted from its muzzle as he fired at Matt.

Matt had already spotted his .44 and threw himself toward it, feeling the wind-rip of the hired killer's bullet as it whipped past his ear. He scooped up the .44, fitting the grip in his palm with an easy familiarity and his finger went to the trigger with pure, swift instinct. The gun roared and bucked in his hand. The bullet drove into the gunman's chest and rocked him back. The man's eyes bulged from the pain and the realization he was about to die. He struggled to get off another shot, but the gun slipped from suddenly nerveless fingers. His head dropped back, and with a grotesque rattle his last breath escaped from his body.

Matt scrambled to his feet and ran to Maureen and Ferguson. "Are you all right?" he asked as he dropped to his knees next to them. Ferguson had an ugly, scabbed-over gash on his forehead, a souvenir of the pistol-whipping he had suffered the night before when Judd Talley kidnapped him from the hotel, but Maureen appeared to be unharmed.

"Uncle Colin's hurt, but I'm fine," she said.

"That little scratch is nothing to worry about," Ferguson insisted. "My head's too hard for a gun barrel to do much damage to it."

Matt tried to untie them, but Smoke appeared and used his knife to cut their bonds. "Pine Tree's making sure, but it looks like all of Longacre's men are dead."

"Pine Tree?" Ferguson repeated.

"One of Walking Hawk's warriors," Smoke explained. "He pretended to be Preacher."

"The old mountain man?" Maureen asked.

"We'll explain the whole thing later," Matt said. "Right now, we need to get back to the Paiute village. The cavalry's on their way out there this morning, and things could get bad."

"If Longacre has anything to say about it, they *will* get bad," Ferguson said. "He'd like nothing more than to have the soldiers come in and do his dirty work for him by wiping out those Indians."

"Yeah, I've been thinking about that." Smoke straightened to his feet and sheathed his knife. "I reckon there's a good chance Longacre will try to hedge his bets."

"How's he going to do that?" Matt asked.

"I don't know," Smoke said, "but whatever it is, I reckon it's up to us to stop it."

CHAPTER 33

The horses of Longacre's men were picketed nearby. Pine Tree selected a couple for Maureen and Ferguson, and Matt helped them mount up. The group rode out through the gap, where they were joined by the Paiute warriors who had thwarted the ambush. The man who had been shot off the top of the ridge was the only fatality, and his body was draped over the back of his pony.

The corpses of Longacre's men were left where they had fallen. If the scavengers got to them before somebody could collect them for burial, Smoke and Matt weren't going to lose any sleep over it.

They headed for Walking Hawk's village, but they hadn't gone very far when Matt pointed to their left. "Look over there."

Smoke had already spotted the odd, dark shape on the ground a couple hundred yards away. Although he didn't like the idea of delaying their return to the Paiute village, he wanted to see what it was. "Let's check it out."

As they rode closer, Smoke realized it wasn't one shape, but two: a horse, and a man pinned underneath it.

"Oh, my God, help me!" the man called when

he heard the approaching hoofbeats. "Somebody help me!"

Smoke swung down from his saddle. The trapped man was Grady Malone. The fallen horse rolled its fear-crazed eyes at Smoke and tried to get up, but one of its front legs was badly broken. When the horse moved, Malone screamed.

Smoke hunkered on his heels next to Malone and stroked the horse's quivering flank, speaking to it in a soft, calming tone. The horse's head dropped back to the ground as it settled down

"You look like you're in a bad fix, Malone," Smoke said.

"Stupid horse . . . stepped in a damn prairie dog hole," Malone panted. "Fell on me . . . I couldn't jump clear . . . because my feet were tied."

"That's a shame," Smoke said coolly. "Anybody who signs on to work for a man like Longacre has to figure he might come to a bad end. From the looks of it, you're pretty busted up inside."

"Blasted horse . . . wallowed all over me . . . I couldn't get away from it . . . Get it off me, Jensen. My leg's broke, I know, but if you'll just get this horse off me—"

Malone broke off as a fit of coughing seized him. Bloody foam bubbled from his mouth. When Smoke saw that, he knew at least one broken rib had pierced a lung. Malone was drowning in his own blood, and from the curiously flattened look of his midsection, that wasn't all the damage the horse had done to him. Smoke was a little surprised the man had lasted so long.

"Moving the horse isn't going to do you any good," Smoke said bluntly. "You're dying, amigo. There's nothing we can do."

Malone let out a groan. "Damn . . . Longacre," he managed to say. "Damn . . . Talley." He gave a bitter laugh. "But I knew it was gonna . . . be like this someday . . . like this . . . or worse. Like you said, Jensen . . . a man who lives by the gun . . ." More blood bubbled past the man's lips. "It'll catch up with you . . . someday, too."

"More than likely," Smoke agreed. He debated what to do next. Before they rode off, he would put a bullet in the horse's head to end its misery. Maybe he ought to do the same for Malone.

The dying gunman laughed again. "You're gonna be . . . too late. The soldiers are gonna . . . wipe out those dirty Paiutes."

Smoke frowned and leaned closer. "How do you know? The captain might listen to reason when Preacher talks to him."

"Longacre's not gonna . . . leave it to chance. Talley and some of the other boys . . . they're gonna bushwhack the troopers . . . so they'll think . . . the redskins did it. Even if the cavalry . . . loses the battle today . . . nobody can . . . stop the war. They'll just send . . . more soldiers . . . until all the Paiutes . . . are dead."

Smoke felt a chill go through him at Malone's

words. He knew the gunman was right. If Long-acre and Talley could provoke a fight between the army and the Paiutes, nobody would listen to reason. One way or another, the killing would continue until Walking Hawk and his people were wiped out.

And just like that, Cyrus Longacre would win.

Smoke stood up and drew his gun. A shot blasted out, hammering into the injured horse's head. The animal's suffering was over.

As Smoke turned away, he slid a fresh cartridge into the cylinder to replace the one he had just fired. "Come on," he told his companions. "There's no time to waste."

"Jensen!" Malone screeched behind him as Smoke swung up into the saddle. "Jensen, don't ride off . . . you can't . . . Jensen!"

The hoofbeats of the galloping horses drowned out the agonized pleas that faded into the distance behind them. Smoke didn't look back.

A man who lives by the gun, Malone had said. He didn't have to finish the thought.

Dies by the gun.

Only Malone hadn't, not exactly.

Close enough, Smoke thought.

It was the first set of new buckskins Preacher had had in a while. Felt pretty good, too, the old mountain man thought. The round-faced, middle-aged woman who had brought the clothes to him had been all smiles. Preacher was too old for any frolicking, but he still enjoyed flirting a mite, he thought as he smiled back at the Paiute woman. That put him in mind of Helena Markova. He wouldn't mind seeing her again, even though it was highly doubtful that would ever happen. Any woman who handled a shooting iron like that Russian gal was worth spending some time with.

He was sitting on an Indian pony next to Walking Hawk, a short distance back from the edge of the northwestern bank of Big Bear Wash where the main trail from Halltown crossed it. Off to the left was a long, low ridge in which the wash cut a chasm. The morning sun painted the sandstone of the ridge blood-red. Preacher hoped that wasn't an omen.

More than fifty Paiute warriors accompanied him and Walking Hawk. Some of the men had been left back at the village to guard it, and they were guarding Joseph Spivey as well. Walking Hawk had made sure they understood how important it was to keep the pale-faced hotel clerk alive.

The chief wanted the confrontation with the cavalry to take place away from the village, away from the women and children. Preacher would handle the talking, if it came down to it. The old mountain man still hoped that Smoke and Matt would get back from their little chore in time to take care of that.

From the looks of the dust rising into the air on the other side of the wash that wasn't going to happen.

The cavalry was coming.

Preacher spat, then wiped the back of his left hand across his mouth. "You and your men stay here, Chief, I'll talk to them soldier boys."

"I will come, too," Walking Hawk declared. "I will be beside you, Ghost Killer."

Preacher nodded. "Suit yourself."

Walking Hawk turned and called commands to his warriors in the Paiute tongue, then he and Preacher moved their horses up to the very edge of the wash. Preacher could see the soldiers at the base of that dust cloud. They came on at a steady trot.

The troopers were about fifty yards from the wash when their captain held up his hand and the sergeant bellowed, "Company . . . *halt!*"

The soldiers brought their mounts to a stop and formed a fairly regular line facing the Indians on the other side of the wash. Leaving the noncom with the men, the captain rode forward alone. The officer wasn't lacking for courage, Preacher thought. Though the captain was doing Cyrus Longacre's dirty work for him, he might not realize it. Preacher hoped he could talk some sense into the man.

Holding up a hand in greeting, Preacher called, "Howdy!" across the wash.

"You're a white man," the captain said, sounding a little surprised.

"That's right. They call me Preacher." The old mountain man waited a second to see if the officer recognized his name. When the man didn't give any sign of it, Preacher went on, "I'm a friend to the Paiutes and come here today to speak for them."

"There's no need for any discussion. I'm Captain Edward McKee, and my orders are to remove those hostiles from their current habitation and accompany them to a more suitable location pending a review of the terms of the treaty they've violated."

Preacher shook his head. "No offense, Cap'n, but somebody's done told you wrong. Walkin' Hawk and his people ain't hostiles, and they ain't done anything to violate the treaty."

McKee gave a contemptuous snort. "No? Then what would you call rustling cattle and attacking railroad surveyors, Mister . . . Preacher, was it?"

"They ain't done those things. It's the other way around. They're the ones who've been attacked, by Cyrus Longacre's hired guns."

"Mr. Longacre is a well-respected businessman," McKee shot back. "You open yourself up to trouble when you start making baseless accusations against him, sir."

"They ain't baseless, and I got proof!"

368

McKee's eyebrows went up. "Oh? What sort of proof?"

"Back at the Paiute village, there's a fella who can tell you just what a no-good skunk Longacre is. If you'll just come with me, Cap'n, you can talk to him and hear the truth for yourself."

"You mean you want me to come with you to the Paiute village?"

For a second Preacher began to hope that he was getting through to McKee. He nodded. "Yep, that's right."

"Where I can be taken prisoner and used as a hostage?" McKee shook his head. "I don't think so."

"Blast it, Cap'n!" Preacher struggled to control his anger and impatience. "You don't know it, but you're bein' used by that varmint Longacre—"

"That's enough!" McKee snapped. "Are those savages going to comply with my orders . . . or do I have to force them to comply?"

Walking Hawk and some of the other Paiutes understood enough English to know what the captain was saying. Preacher sensed a stirring in the ranks of warriors behind him. The troopers on the other side of the wash looked just as nervous and angry. The tension, the sense of impending violence, was so thick in the air Preacher could practically smell it. All it would take to set off a frenzy of killing would be a single shot from either side.

Smoke, Matt, and Pine Tree held a discussion as they and the others galloped toward Big Bear Wash, raising their voices to be heard over the pounding hoofbeats.

"Where could Talley and his men hide to ambush the cavalry?" Matt asked. "The area where the trail crosses the wash is pretty open."

"Bloody Ridge," Pine Tree said. "My people call it that because of the way it looks early in the morning."

Smoke said, "You've been around here more than I have, Matt. You remember the place?"

"Yeah, now that Pine Tree mentions it, I do. It's a couple hundred yards from the spot where Preacher's supposed to stall the troopers. That's within rifle range for a good shot."

"It doesn't matter how good they are," Smoke said. "If Talley and his men open fire when the Paiutes and the cavalry are facing each other across the wash, the sound of the shots is all it'll take. Somebody on one side or the other will panic and start shooting, too."

"Then how are we going to prevent that, even if we get there in time?" Matt asked. "If we open up on Talley and the rest of those gun-wolves, then our shots will cause the same result, won't they?"

Colin Ferguson and Maureen were riding behind the three men. Ferguson moved his horse up alongside Smoke's 'Paloose. "Let me ride ahead and warn the soldiers. I can tell them what's going on."

"One of us could do that," Matt said.

Smoke shook his head. "As far as those troops are concerned, we're fugitives from the law, Matt. The officer in charge of them would be more likely to believe Mr. Ferguson." He turned to Ferguson and nodded. "That's a good idea. Can you get there on your own while we circle around to come up on that ridge from behind?"

"Of course. I've spent most of my time in town, but I've done a bit of exploring in the country-side hereabouts. I won't get lost, I assure you."

"I'll go with him," Maureen said. "The soldiers will listen to me, too."

"We can hope," Smoke said. "Just be careful. If you run into any of Longacre's men, they'll probably try to stop you, even if they don't know exactly what's going on."

"Don't worry about us," Ferguson said. "Just get there in time to stop Talley from ambushing those soldiers!"

He and Maureen veered off from the others. Smoke and Matt led the way toward a low line of red along the horizon. Pine Tree pointed toward it. "Bloody Ridge."

"Let's hope it doesn't live up to its name," Smoke said.

371

CHAPTER 34

If Judd Talley and his men were hidden on top of the ridge, as Smoke suspected, all their attention would be on the scene playing out in front of them. That was his hope, anyway. If any of the hired killers happened to look back and see the dust kicked up by the horses approaching the place, the chances of heading off a massacre would shrink even more.

When he and his companions were several hundred yards away, Smoke waved them to a halt. "We'll go ahead on foot now." He swung down from the saddle. "Pine Tree, tell a couple of your men to watch the horses."

Pine Tree passed along the order as everyone dismounted, designating two of the warriors to take care of the group's mounts. They didn't look happy about missing out on the action, but did as they were told.

Smoke, Matt, and the others ran toward the ridge. "Use what cover you can," Smoke said. "We don't want them to see us coming. And when we get there, try to keep anybody from getting a shot off."

He drew his knife from its sheath, and the others followed his example. The battle was going to be at close range.

In silence, the men hurried toward the ridge, darting from rock to rock and bush to bush, crouching in little gullies, pausing behind scrubby pine trees. Smoke spotted a couple men holding half a dozen horses each. He pointed them out to Matt. The two of them stole forward while Pine Tree and the other Paiutes hung back for a moment.

One of the men happened to glance around when Smoke and Matt were still a dozen feet away, and he opened his mouth to shout a warning. Smoke flung the Bowie knife in his hand, and the weapon flew straight and true. The keen-edged blade sank in the hardcase's neck, making him stagger back as blood gushed out of the wound. That caught his companion's attention, of course, but as the man tried to whirl around, Matt was already on top of him. Matt's left arm went around the man's neck to choke off any cry while his right hand shoved his knife into the man's back. The hired killer spasmed as the blade sliced between his ribs and into his heart. Matt pulled the knife free and lowered the dying man to the ground. The other man had already collapsed, and Smoke was retrieving his knife from the corpse.

Smoke waved the Paiutes forward as the horses began to shift around nervously. Quite a bit of blood had been spilled, and they didn't like the smell of it.

The men crept up the slope as quickly and quietly as possible. The skittish horses might bolt at any second. If they did, the rataplan of hoofbeats would warn the men on top of the ridge that something was wrong.

As Matt neared the crest, he heard Judd Talley's voice telling the rest of the hired guns, "Remember, shoot into the troopers, not the redskins. They won't think about where the bullets are coming from, they'll just open fire on the Paiutes."

Matt reached the top and saw Talley and a dozen of Longacre's hired killers crouched behind rocks, aiming rifles at the cavalrymen down below. Talley heard the scrape of boot leather on stone, and whipped around, his eyes widening at the sight of Matt lunging toward him.

Matt thrust the knife ahead of him, intending to sink the blade into Talley's chest, but Talley used the rifle he held to ward off the blow. The Winchester's barrel cracked painfully across Matt's wrist and sent the knife spinning away, as he crashed into Talley.

The two of them bounced off the boulder Talley had been using for cover. Matt's momentum drove Talley back, and suddenly the ground fell out from under them. Both men tumbled down the steep slope of Bloody Ridge.

Smoke, Pine Tree, and the Paiutes fell on the rest of the gunmen, striking fast so the men didn't

374

have a chance to fire. A couple died instantly as knives plunged into their bodies or slashed across their throats, but the others put up a fight. They were hardened killers, and Smoke and his allies found themselves in desperate struggles.

Smoke closed his free hand around the barrel of the rifle his opponent tried to bring to bear on him and wrenched it upward. He stabbed his knife at the man's throat, but the man caught his wrist and turned the thrust so it cut across his shoulder instead. The man's knee came up sharply as he fell back against a rock. The blow was aimed at Smoke's groin. Smoke twisted his hips at the last instant, saving himself from the crippling impact and taking the gunman's knee on his thigh instead. It was enough to knock Smoke off balance, and both of them went down, grappling with each other. The gunman lost his hold on the rifle, and it went clattering down the rocky slope.

Smoke brought his knee up, got his foot in his opponent's stomach, and heaved the man up and over his head. The man cried out in alarm for a second before he crashed down on the ground. He rolled over and clawed at the revolver on his hip. Before the gun could clear leather, Smoke landed on top of the man and drove the knife into his belly. Smoke ripped the blade from side to side, feeling the hot gush of blood over his hand.

All along the top of the ridge, similar life-and-death struggles played out. The man Pine Tree had tackled knocked the knife from his hand, but the Paiute warrior got the fingers of one hand locked around the man's throat while with the other he grabbed the gun the man had drawn. The Colt's hammer went back and then fell, but Pine Tree had already slid his hand along the cylinder so the hammer landed on the web between his thumb and index finger. That was a painful way of keeping the gun from going off, but it worked. Pine Tree maintained his grip on both gun and throat, bearing down until the gunman's face turned purple and his tongue protruded as his eyes glazed over in death.

And while all this was going on, the stand-off below continued, with the soldiers and warriors facing each other across Big Bear Wash having no idea what was going on, knowing only that they were ready to kill their enemies.

The sudden drumming of hoofbeats in the distance shattered the tense silence and made Preacher lift his head in surprise. Across the wash, the sergeant called, "Riders comin', Cap'n!"

McKee wheeled his mount around. "More savages, Sergeant?"

"I don't think so," the burly noncom replied. "They look like white folks to me."

That was true, Preacher realized. As the pair of riders galloped closer, it was impossible to miss the long red hair streaming out behind one of them. "Cap'n McKee!" the old mountain man called. "That looks like Maureen Ferguson and her uncle from Halltown. You better listen to what they have to say."

"Don't presume to give me orders," McKee snapped. But he went on, "Sergeant, escort those civilians to me. The rest of you . . . hold your fire unless I command you to shoot."

That was progress, Preacher thought. McKee was at least curious enough to want to know what was going on there. Preacher hoped the newcomers could explain.

The ranks of troopers parted to let the sergeant through as he rode out to meet Maureen and Ferguson. Preacher could see both newcomers well enough to be sure that's who they were. The sergeant brought them to the edge of the wash on the soldiers' side. Their horses were lathered and exhausted from a hard run, and the two riders looked pretty worn out as well. Ferguson had dried blood on his forehead from some sort of injury.

His voice was strong, though. "Captain, you're in command of these troops?"

"That's right," McKee said. "I'm Captain Edward McKee, and I'll ask the questions here, sir. Who are you, and what are you doing here?"

"Colin Ferguson's my name. I own one of the hotels and a general store in Halltown. This is my niece Maureen. We're here to stop you from making a terrible mistake, Captain. It's Cyrus Longacre who's to blame for all the trouble here, not Walking Hawk and his people."

McKee grimaced. "Not another crazy story about Mr. Longacre. I'm surprised a successful businessman would believe such a thing."

"Would you believe that Longacre sent his hired killers out here to ambush you and your men so you'd start a war with the Paiutes?"

"That's insane!" McKee snapped.

"Is it?" Maureen demanded. She pointed. "Then look up there on Bloody Ridge!"

Just as all eyes swung in that direction, two struggling figures appeared at the ridge's crest and plunged over the edge into a wild, out-of-control tumble down the slope.

The fact that the ridge wasn't a sheer drop saved Matt's life, but it was steep enough that he couldn't catch himself as he and Talley slammed into and bounced off rocks. They didn't come to a stop until they reached the bottom, some forty feet below where they had fallen.

Matt had lost his gun on the way down, but so had Talley. They were on even terms, other than the fact that Talley was several inches taller and probably forty pounds heavier. Both of them, shaken up by the fall, struggled to their feet about the same time. Talley shook his head like a bull to clear out the cobwebs, and then, still like a bull, he bellowed in rage and charged.

Rage of his own filled Matt. He met Talley's attack with a hard right punch that landed solidly on Talley's jaw. At the same time, one of Talley's big fists crashed into Matt's chest and knocked him back gasping for breath. For a second Matt feared the brutal blow had stopped his heart.

But the hammer of his pulse pounded inside his head, and he swung his fists in time to it, standing toe to toe with Talley and slugging, right, left, right, left. Talley dealt out as much punishment as he absorbed. Matt found himself forced to give ground. Talley was too big, too strong, and maddeningly fast. If he had any weak spots, Matt hadn't found them.

He was too busy to tell how the rest of the fight was going. The cavalry and the Paiutes could have been blazing away at each other across the wash, and Matt wouldn't have known it. He blocked one of Talley's punches but couldn't get out of the way of another. He weaved to the side and took the blow on his shoulder.

It landed with less force than the punches had earlier, Matt realized. Talley was tiring. His face was red, and he was struggling to draw breath. He had the size, but not the wind.

That realization gave Matt the effort he needed to redouble his efforts. He bored in, cutting and slicing Talley's face with short, sharp blows. Talley's swings became wilder, taking on a sense

379

of desperate flailing. Matt caught him in the throat with a punch, making Talley stagger back as catching his breath became even harder for him. Taking advantage of the opportunity, Matt peppered Talley's face with more blows.

He got too close. Talley roared and flung his arms around Matt, catching him in a bear hug. Matt felt his feet lifted off the ground. Now he was the one who couldn't breathe.

As Talley stumbled around, trying to crush his opponent, Matt got a foot behind one of Talley's knees and yanked. Talley's leg buckled and he went over backward with Matt on top of him. As they crashed to the ground, Talley's grip was knocked loose. Matt dug a knee into Talley's belly as hard as he could and levered himself up into a kneeling position. He brought a fist down into Talley's face in a savage punch that made the back of Talley's head hit the ground. Again and again, alternating fists, Matt pummeled the big man, pounding his face into a swollen, bloody mess. Talley wasn't fighting back anymore. He couldn't.

Somebody grabbed Matt from behind and dragged him off. Matt tried to twist around and strike out at the new enemy, but he heard Smoke's voice in his ear. "It's over, Matt! It's over!"

Matt heard hoofbeats then, and looked around through bleary eyes to see the cavalry captain riding up, along with Colin and Maureen Ferguson. Preacher was with them, too.

"That's enough," the captain called out.

Smoke let go of Matt. "More than enough, Captain." He pointed at Talley's senseless form. "You must have seen this man with Longacre in Halltown. He's Judd Talley, the boss of the hired guns who work for Longacre. He and a dozen of Longacre's men were up on that ridge, ready to ambush you and start an Indian war, so Longacre could get rid of the Paiutes."

The officer frowned. "That's insane."

Smoke took him by surprise by saying, "You're right. Longacre's so arrogant and full of himself, I reckon you could call him loco. He'd rather spill a lot of innocent blood to get what he wants, all to make a point that no one dare stand up to him."

"I . . . I don't believe that."

Matt's chest was heaving from the exertions of his fight with Talley. He managed to catch his breath enough to say, "Longacre had a young woman killed . . just to frame me for her murder. That's how crazy he is, Captain."

"And we can prove it," Preacher put in. "All you got to do is talk to the witness Longacre and Talley forced to lie at the boy's trial."

The officer looked around at all of them and shook his head. "This is all too confusing," he declared. "We're going back to Halltown, all of us, and I'm going to get some answers, by God!"

"You mean your troops, too?" Preacher asked.

The captain hesitated for a second, but he

nodded. "Yes. I'm not going to be responsible for starting an Indian war if someone has lied to me."

"Well, that's the first sensible thing you've said," Preacher snapped.

Smoke smiled wearily. Leave it to Preacher to speak the plain truth. Luckily, the captain didn't look too offended.

With a nod toward Talley, Smoke said, "You'd better take him and any of Longacre's men who are still alive back to town with you. Preacher, you fetch Spivey and meet us there."

The old mountain man nodded and wheeled his horse.

The captain frowned. "Just who are you to be giving orders here?"

"Name's Smoke Jensen. If you want to get in touch with Washington and ask about me, go right ahead. I've done a few favors for the War Department in my time, and some other folks back there, too."

"Don't worry, we're going to get this all sorted out. If you and your friends have been lying to me, Jensen, you'll pay the price. I'll see to that."

Smoke, Matt, the Fergusons, and Captain McKee rode ahead of the main body of soldiers as they approached Halltown. Several troopers accompanied them to act as guards over Talley and the three hired killers who had survived the battle on Bloody Ridge. Quite a commotion erupted in the settlement as the group rode in.

Cyrus Longacre heard the shouts, and stepped onto the porch of the Sierra House, backed by the rest of his gunmen. His teeth tightened on the cigar between them when he saw the bloody, battered, semiconscious form of Judd Talley surrounded by cavalrymen. Longacre's eyes glittered with hate as he looked at Matt.

Matt saw that as he reined to a halt in front of the hotel along with the others. He smiled grimly at Longacre.

The railroad man appeared to recover his wits. He took the cigar out of his mouth and said, "Well, well, Captain McKee, I see that you've captured a couple fugitives. That man"—he leveled a finger at Matt—"is a murderer! He killed an innocent young woman. Brutally slaughtered her. He was supposed to hang yesterday. I suppose we can have a hanging today, though, eh?"

"There's not going to be any hanging," McKee snapped.

"Oh? Matt Jensen was found guilty in a court of law and legally sentenced to death."

"By a judge you bought and paid for!" Ferguson said. "You'll not get away with it this time, Longacre."

Longacre shook his head and smiled tolerantly. "Really, Captain. Surely you can see these people are all lying. Why, a reputable witness testified at the trial that he heard the victim scream right after Jensen went up to her room."

Smoke looked back along the street. "What witness would that be, Longacre?" He jerked a thumb over his shoulder. "That one?"

Longacre turned his head, and his jaw tightened visibly as he saw Preacher and Joseph Spivey riding into Halltown.

Matt saw Roscoe Goldsmith in the crowd forming in front of the hotel. He called the lawyer over, bent down in the saddle, and spoke a few quick words to him. Goldsmith seemed a little more sober than usual. He nodded to Matt, then stepped toward McKee and raised a hand. "Captain, a word?"

"Who are you?" McKee asked impatiently.

"Roscoe Goldsmith, attorney-at-law, representing Mr. Matt Jensen. If I might be allowed to ask a few questions . . ."

"This isn't a court of law, blast it. Although I'm severely tempted to place this town under martial law. Where's the sheriff?"

Walt Sanger had come up to the edge of the crowd, Matt noted, but when McKee asked that, the lawman turned his back and quickly scurried away, ducking out of sight down an alley. Matt suspected they wouldn't see hide nor hair of Sanger again until it was all over.

Goldsmith ignored McKee's question and

turned toward Judd Talley as Preacher and Spivey rode up. "Mr. Talley," Goldsmith said sharply. "Mr. Talley!"

The big gunman slowly lifted his head, blinked his eyes several times, and looked around. Goldsmith pointed at Spivey and said in a loud voice, "The clerk has just testified that he saw *you* go up to Virginia Barry's room a short time before Mr. Jensen ever reached the hotel. He heard Miss Barry scream while *you* were up there, Mr. Talley, before Mr. Jensen even arrived! What do you have to say to that?"

"That . . . that's a lie," Talley mumbled through swollen lips.

"But he says he heard it," Goldsmith insisted.

"He couldn't have! She never . . . she never made a sound. She never even saw it comin'—"

Talley stopped short as he realized what he had just done. From the porch of the hotel, an obviously desperate Longacre exclaimed, "My God, Judd! You mean that you—"

"You told me to!" Talley screamed at him. "It was all your idea! You'll hang, too, you—"

On the porch, Longacre dropped his cigar, took a quick step back, and ordered the hired gunmen around them, "Kill them all!"

It was a desperate move, but Smoke knew what Longacre was thinking. The sergeant and the rest of the soldiers hadn't reached the settlement yet. If Longacre's men could kill Smoke, Matt,

Preacher, and Captain McKee, along with Spivey, Longacre could take over again. With his hired guns running things, the citizens would be too afraid to tell anybody the truth about what had happened in "Helltown."

And that's truly what it would be from then on. A dictatorship ruled by Cyrus Longacre.

There was one more thing Longacre needed to do to secure that outcome. As he ducked through the hotel door, he yanked a pistol from under his coat, jerked it up, and fired. Judd Talley's head rocked back as the slug smashed between his eyes, killing him. He would never testify in court that Longacre had ordered him to kill Virginia Barry.

As the shot rang out, Longacre's other men clawed at their guns, following orders to the last.

Both of Smoke's Colts were already in his hands, and Matt held the .44 he had recovered at Bloody Ridge. Preacher whipped out his Remingtons with blinding speed. The guns of those three men, those men who were as close as brothers or a father and his sons could ever be, roared out in a smashing wave of thunder. Bullets pounded into Longacre's men, ripped through their bodies, smashed windows in the hotel behind them. They got a few shots off, mostly into the planks of the boardwalk at their feet, as powdersmoke rolled and guns sang a song of death.

Captain McKee, seeing how he had been used by Longacre, unlimbered his revolver and joined in the fight, slamming a couple shots into one of the hired killers who was trying to draw a bead on him. Elsewhere in the street, people were yelling and scrambling to get out of the way of any wild shots. Roscoe Goldsmith reached up, grabbed Maureen, and dragged her off her horse to get her out of the line of fire as much as possible. Colin Ferguson joined them as they ran for cover in a nearby alley.

One by one, Longacre's men crumpled. But Longacre himself had disappeared into the hotel. As the last of the hired gunns went spinning off his feet, blood spouting from his wounds, Matt leaped off his horse and bounded into the building.

Anybody who had been in the lobby when the shooting started had lit a shuck. Matt ran up the stairs, taking them two and three at a time. As he reached the second floor landing, he spotted Longacre emerging from the suite at the end of the hall. He had a valise in his left hand and still gripped the pistol he had used to kill Talley in his right. He snapped the gun up and fired.

Matt felt the heat of the bullet as it sizzled past his ear. The .44 in his hand blasted a split second after Longacre's shot. The railroad man reeled back, dropping the valise. It came open, spilling cash across the floor. Longacre's gun sagged, but he tried to lift it again. Matt fired a second shot that punched into Longacre's chest and knocked him back through the doorway.

Matt approached cautiously. He could see Longacre lying in the sitting room, not moving. When he reached the doorway, he saw that the pistol had fallen on the floor. He kicked the gun away and stood over Longacre, who stared up at him through pain-wracked eyes. Blood from the wounds in his chest turned his expensive shirt-front into a sodden crimson mess. Longacre gasped one last time, then his eyes glazed over in death.

It was just about the same spot where he had found Virginia's body, Matt thought. Longacre's blood had spilled in the same place.

"Matt?" Smoke asked from behind him. "Matt, are you all right?"

Matt lowered the .44 to his side and turned away from Longacre's body. "Yeah," he answered. "You said it was over before, Smoke, but it really wasn't." Matt glanced back at the corpse as he stepped out of the suite. "Now it is."

"You can rest assured I'll make a full report of what happened here and who was really to blame," Captain McKee said. "But if everything you've told me is true, Mr. Jensen . . . I can't promise you what will happen to that report." The officer's mouth twisted in a grimace. "Things that are uncomfortable or embarrassing for certain parties tend to get lost in Washington."

"I understand," Smoke said as he nodded.

"But the truth can only be hidden for so long. Eventually, people figure out how to recognize a varmint for who he really is."

"I hope you're right." McKee put his hat on and held out his hand. "Good luck to you, Mr. Jensen." He smiled faintly as he and Smoke shook hands. "Having seen you and your, ah, friends in action, I don't suppose you really need that much luck. Just plenty of ammunition."

Smoke went out on the porch of the Ferguson Hotel to watch the cavalry ride away. Matt and Preacher came out of the building to join him.

"What's gonna happen to that railroad line now, you reckon?" Preacher asked.

Smoke shrugged. "Somebody else will take over and finish building it. Longacre's heirs, whoever they are, will probably sell the whole shooting match to the Southern Pacific."

Preacher scratched at his beard. "I was thinkin' I might hang around here for a while. Me and that lawyer fella been talkin' about how we want to make sure Walkin' Hawk and his people get a square deal when the railroad comes on through, which is bound to happen sooner or later."

"Bound to," Smoke agreed. "As long as it's done the right way next time."

"We'll see to that," Preacher said.

Smoke turned to Matt. "How about you?"

"I haven't decided what I'm going to do next," Matt replied with a shake of his head.

Preacher chuckled. "Reckon some of that will be up to the redheaded gal who's comin' across the street."

Maureen Ferguson and her uncle were coming toward them. Colin Ferguson had his cane again, and the local doctor had cleaned and bandaged the cut on his forehead.

As they stepped onto the porch, Ferguson said, "I was hoping you'd still be here, Matt. We have something for you."

"What's that?"

Maureen held out her hand. A sheriff's badge lay in the palm of it.

"We found that in Walt Sanger's office, but there's no sign of Walt," Ferguson went on. "It appears he's resigned his position and moved on to greener pastures, leaving Halltown in need of a sheriff."

"You want *me* to be take over as sheriff?" Matt asked.

"The whole town does," Maureen said. "As soon as you rode in, Helltown started becoming Halltown again."

"Well, I appreciate the offer, but . . . but . . ." Matt looked over at Smoke and Preacher.

"Don't look at us," Preacher said. "You got to make up your own mind, boy."

Smoke nodded. "Preacher's right."

"Well . . . maybe for a little while." Matt quickly added, "I'm not taking the job permanent-like, though. Just until you can find somebody better suited to it." He gave Smoke and Preacher a hard stare. "And I could sure use a couple deputies while I'm at it."

"Preacher's already said he's staying here for a while," Smoke pointed out. "Not me, though. I'm headed for Colorado as soon as that 'Paloose of mine rests up a bit. I've got a ranch to get back to"—he grinned—"and a pretty wife."

"I can understand why a man would want to get back to his wife," Maureen said as she looked at Matt. It was all Smoke could do not to laugh when he saw the flicker of panic in the younger man's eyes. Matt was going to have his hands full keeping the peace in Halltown . . . among other things.

Though Smoke would be headed back to Sugarloaf as soon as he could, he knew he would be seeing Matt and Preacher again. The Indian Ring was still out there, still powerful, and still up to no good. The way he, Matt, and Preacher got around, sooner or later they were bound to run up against some other scheme hatched by that crooked bunch.

When that day came, whichever of them was in trouble would put out the call, as Matt had done, and the others would come a-runnin'. Gunsmoke bound them together more strongly than blood.

And family always answered the call.

Center Point Publishing
600 Brooks Road ● PO Box 1
Thorndike ME 04986-0001 USA

(207) 568-3717

US & Canada:
1 800 929-9108
www.centerpointlargeprint.com